"No! I forbid it!"

She whirled to face hir  herself up to her full heigh but exploding from her. "_ _ _ _ _ _ _ _ _ _ _ _ _

She poked her forefinger into his chest as she sputtered the words. "No, sir, you do not. You cannot sway me, and I will not be denied. I do and say what I will, and you cannot stop me. You do not have the right to—mmh!" The last sound was a squeak of surprise as his lips pressed against hers, cutting off her words.

The kiss was hard, at first, punishing. His lips were firm against hers, the rasp of his chin rough against her own smooth skin. He tasted of the brandy he had drunk, laced with tea, and the sweet icing on the biscuit he had eaten with it. His cologne wrapped itself around her— exotic flowers, silk and cotton, the scents of places far, far away. His hands rested on her shoulders, warming her skin. Of their own volition, her hands touched his chest, her fingers pressed against the watery cool of his waistcoat, the hard warmth of his body below it. She could feel his heart beating, faster and louder than she would have dreamed possible.

The kiss softened until his lips caressed hers. His hands moved round to her back, drawing her closer to him. Her own arms moved up, encircling his neck, her fingers threading between the short hairs at the back of his head.

Viscount in Hiding

by

Caitlyn Callery

This is a work of fiction. Names, characters, places, and incidents are either the product of the author's imagination or are used fictitiously, and any resemblance to actual persons living or dead, business establishments, events, or locales, is entirely coincidental.

Viscount in Hiding

The Wild Rose Press, Inc.
PO Box 708
Adams Basin, NY 14410-0708
Visit us at www.thewildrosepress.com

Publishing History
First Edition, 2023
Trade Paperback ISBN 978-1-5092-4878-0
Digital ISBN 978-1-5092-4879-7

Published in the United States of America

Dedication

To John and Jo Large,
the best parents I could ever have had

Chapter One

January 1818

For the fiftieth time in as many minutes, Josh Summersby wondered at his folly. He could have been in a hotel in Dover now, legs stretched before a cozy fire and a glass of brandy at his fingertips. Instead, he travelled a badly made road surrounded by bare trees that glittered with ice, while the gray sky seemed low enough to touch. Josh wished it would snow. At least snow would warm the air.

His eyes watered and the tips of his ears burned cold. His fingers and toes had long since lost all feeling.

All this, for what?

There was no guarantee that his welcome would be any warmer than the cursed Sussex winter. For aught he knew, his father would order him thrown out of the house. He might even have Josh horsewhipped for daring to show his face. If the letter in his pocket had come from anyone but Hicks, Josh would probably have ignored it and stayed in India. But the valet knew the old man better than any other living person, and was loyal to his master to the death. If Hicks said the viscount needed Josh home as soon as he could arrive, Josh had to believe it was true.

The panicked tone of the letter had made him leave Madras immediately, paying extra to secure a berth on the fastest ship he could find. Even so, the journey had taken four months. Adding in the time the letter had taken to reach him, Josh calculated it was at least eight months since Hicks had sent it. If things truly had been as urgent as the valet suggested, it may well be too late already.

Nevertheless, upon reaching England, Josh had stopped only long enough to secure rooms and have his luggage delivered to them before riding as fast as the icy roads allowed, across Kent and into Sussex, praying with every mile that his journey was not wasted.

He rounded a bend and saw the village of Rotherton ahead. That meant he was only six miles from Frantham. If he pushed on, he could probably reach the manor house by dark.

Or, he could break his journey, stretch his legs, eat something, and allow himself to thaw. Surely, an hour's delay could not hurt.

Rotherton had hardly changed in the fourteen years he'd been gone. A larger village than Frantham, it boasted a High Street with a surprisingly wide range of shops. There was a dressmaker's and a milliner's, an apothecary and a bakery and a good-sized forge. The Assembly Rooms were at one end of the street, ionic columns standing proud and grand, like a dowager watching over a family of whom she slightly disapproved. In fact, the only reason it was known as a village and not a town was that it didn't hold a market.

The road through Rotherton was muddy and wet, the ice broken and churned into a thick soup by dozens of cart wheels. A small warmth emanated from the buildings on either side, their walls giving welcome shelter from the wind that had howled, unchecked, in the open countryside.

Halfway along the High Street, Josh rode into the cobbled yard of the Golden Goose Inn and dismounted. His knees stiffened and he grunted at the pain, then stood taller and straighter, trying to stretch his back. Contact with the ground after so long made his feet sting.

"Take your horse for you?" A boy of about twelve stepped forward, one hand outstretched to take the reins. He was dressed in thin rags and looked as if a decent meal would not go amiss, but his eyes were bright and his smile eager. Josh nodded and gave him a threepenny bit. The lad's eyes grew large and round at the sight of the coin, and his smile broadened. "I'll see he gets the best of everything," he promised.

"Don't give him oats," Josh replied. "I'll not be here above an hour." The boy saluted and led the horse away.

Another youth came out of the stable as the boy went in. He was older than the stable boy, and bigger, with broad shoulders and a barrel chest he pushed out proudly, a square face with narrow eyes and fleshy lips. His dirty blond hair was uncombed.

Without warning or provocation, he clipped the stable boy's ear. The boy ducked and glared at the bully, but he said nothing, just carried on until he and the horse disappeared from sight. The bully laughed and sauntered toward the inn.

"You leave young Caleb alone, Abe Sutton," growled an elderly ostler. The bully made an obscene gesture, then pushed open the inn door and went inside. The ostler muttered darkly.

Josh entered the inn, looking forward to settling in the private parlor with a hot meal. When he lived in Frantham, the Goose had had a fine reputation for good food. He prayed that had not changed over the years.

"Be with you in a moment, sir," said the landlord. He came out from behind the long counter, wiped his hands on the less-than-pristine apron tied around his thick waist, and smiled obsequiously at a small party who stood a few feet away from Josh. "This way, Mr. Bell, Mrs. Bell."

The middle-aged couple followed him, but the younger woman with them stayed where she was. She was the kind of woman who turned heads and stayed in the memory, although no one would ever have called her beautiful. Her mouth was wide, with the ends of her lips turned up in a perpetual grin. Together with her retroussé nose, it gave her an air of mischief. Blonde curls showed beneath her bonnet, and her winter-pinked cheeks made her blue eyes shine an ultramarine. She looked enough like Mrs. Bell to be her daughter.

The young lady tipped her head slightly to one side and looked at Josh, coyly, then lowered her eyes. When she looked up again, her gaze was fixed elsewhere. Josh grinned at the blatant flirting. The minx had probably practiced that move for hours in front of her looking glass, trying to make it as sultry as possible. He judged her to be about eighteen, almost ready to embark on her first Season. The saucy miss had best be careful. If she used tactics like that in the drawing rooms of Mayfair, she would likely get more than she bargained for. For a moment, he felt the pang of regret that it would not be him she fluttered her lashes at in future, but then he tamped it down. He was here to speak with his father, nothing more. Having discovered the reason for Hicks's letter, Josh would be on the first ship back to India. He could not be distracted by a mischievous minx, no matter how bright her eyes.

"Amelia!" Mrs. Bell's voice, clear, and to be obeyed instantly, brought him out of his reverie. The woman's frown revealed she had seen the exchange of looks between her daughter and Josh, and she heartily disapproved. It acted like a splash of cold water to his face. His lips tightened.

"A thousand pardons, miss," he said. "I did not mean to stand in your way." He stepped aside and the young lady walked past him. A delicate scent followed her, something floral, and very English. It made him think of soft summer days, when bright yellow buttercups dotted lush green meadows. For the first time in fourteen years, he admitted there was something he'd missed about his homeland.

He tipped his hat, first to the sweet-smelling young lady, then to her parents. Her mother raised her chin and looked as though a bad smell had lodged under her nose. Her father nodded a curt acknowledgement to Josh, then ushered his wife and daughter into the inn's only private parlor.

The landlord returned to the bar and smiled at Josh. "Now then, sir, what can I do for you?"

Ten minutes later, Josh sat in the quietest corner of the public bar, a tankard of ale and a plate of game pie on the table. The good food and warm room worked with the soft murmur of a dozen conversations, and a bone-deep weariness suddenly hit him. Just getting out of his seat was an effort. He knew, without a doubt, he could ride no farther this day. Frantham would have to wait for him until the morrow. And, mayhap, staying here overnight would allow him one more glimpse of the young lady with the mischievous face and the scent of summer.

He rolled his eyes at his own absurdity. He was filthy from his journey, his clothes plain and serviceable rather than fashionable. The shadow of a beard already itching at his chin could not hide the fact that his skin was permanently tanned by the Indian sun instead of the gentlemanly pallor the eligible bucks in Mayfair would sport. Miss Bell would not give him so much as a second glance. No young lady would, unless she was at her last hope.

On that sobering thought, he pushed the image of Miss Bell away and summoned the landlord. He ordered a room, then went out to the stables to give orders for the care of his horse and to collect his small valise, which was all he had brought with him.

It was almost dark now, the sky the gray of gunmetal, though tiny patches of lighter blue still poked through here and there. The whitewashed walls of the inn showed clearly, but the dark buildings in the yard were little more than silhouettes. The ostler shuffled past and lit a lantern, making a small circle of light that warmed the cobbles and colored the stable wall. Above that light, the sky seemed suddenly darker.

Josh went into the stable. The lanterns were already lit in here, making the place seem warm and safe and welcoming. The smell of hay mixed with horseflesh and manure in a way that was not altogether unpleasant. He looked around for the stable boy.

There was a rustle of straw, a man's harsh laugh, then a smacking noise, followed by a yelp and a thud. Josh frowned. If Abe Sutton had come back to bully the younger lad again, he would answer to him. It would do the bigger lad good to be on the receiving end for once.

He took a step forward, but a woman's squeal of

alarm stopped him dead in his tracks. The squeal was followed by another thud and more rustling of straw. Josh raced forward...

And found Miss Bell, lying on the ground in an otherwise empty stall, with Abe Sutton sitting astride her, pinning her down.

****

Amelia was in trouble. Again.

This time, she had the awful feeling she was not going to escape unscathed. It had seemed so easy when she made the plan: find Abe Sutton, make him agree to leave her sister alone, then take back the handkerchief he had stolen. Unfortunately, she had over-estimated her own abilities vastly, and underestimated Abe. Now she would pay the price.

When Amelia had promised Julia all would be well, she had firmly believed it. The hardest part of her quest, she'd thought, would be to discover Abe Sutton alone, so she could confront him without making the problem worse. The last thing her sister would want is for the stupid man's stupid friends to laugh and gossip about her. But nearly a week had gone by since Abe had snatched Julia's handkerchief, then refused to return it, threatening to tell the world Julia had given it to him as a token unless she gave him a kiss. In that week, there had been no sight of him at all. So, when Amelia looked out of the inn's parlor window and saw him going into the stable, she had seized her chance. Telling Mama she needed to visit the necessary, she'd run out of the back door and rushed over here.

"Abe Sutton, where is my sister's handkerchief?" she had demanded as she marched along the aisle toward him.

Abe grinned, showing off gaps where three of his teeth were missing. "You mean this one, Millie Bell?" He pulled the lace-edged handkerchief from the pocket of his loose-fitting breeches, held it to his nose, and gave an exaggerated sniff. "Ah, yes," he said. "Smells just like her."

"Give it back."

"She knows the price."

"Don't be ridiculous. Julia is not going to kiss you."

He wagged his finger. "Ah-ah. 'Twas only a kiss last Sunday. The price goes up with every day that passes."

"She's not going to pay any price to you." Amelia's temper rose, warming her cheeks and pushing all caution away.

"Then she won't get it back."

Amelia gritted her teeth and made an effort to keep her voice calm and even. She knew, from bitter experience, it did no good to yell at Abe when he was in this mood. "You've had your fun," she said. "Enough is as good as a feast. Give me the handkerchief and we can all remain friends." Although friend was not what she would likely call him once the handkerchief was safely back where it belonged.

"What if I don't want to be friends?" he asked.

You're going the right way to be sure that we're not. Aloud, she said, "Don't be silly. We have always been friends."

"Now I want more."

"Julia is not going to kiss you. Or…anything else. In fact, she's more likely to fetch the constable." As soon as she said it, Amelia realized her mistake and silently cursed her own stupidity.

Abe's grin widened, and his chest puffed out more

than usual, if that was possible. "I am the constable this year," he said. "Which puts you in a bit of a bind, because I won't arrest myself."

Amelia rushed him, trying to snatch the handkerchief. He expected the move and stepped back, hand high, out of her reach.

"Tell you what, Millie." He chuckled. " I won't make your sister pay me." He leered at Amelia. "You can do it instead."

"I will not!"

The words were hardly out of her mouth when he grabbed her. For a thickset man, he moved like lightning, and Amelia found herself trapped against him. His breath reeked of onions and ale, and his jerkin smelt strongly of his sweat, mingled with an odor of the horses he'd been working with all day. His eyes darkened, and he licked his thick lips as he contemplated the kiss—or more—that he thought he would take.

Amelia knew she couldn't escape by struggling. Abe was stronger, and he gripped her too tightly. He would let her squirm, to no avail, and enjoy every moment. If she was to best him, she must use her wits.

She made herself go slack in his arms. He stumbled under her dead weight, but quickly righted himself. Triumph lit his face as he cupped her bottom, pulling her hips closer to his. She felt the hardness of him and swallowed her disgust. So far, he was behaving exactly as expected.

The change in his hold freed her arms. Slowly, smoothly, she moved her hands up his chest, sliding her fingers over the rough wool of his jerkin. He swallowed. Amelia smiled, naughtily. He relaxed, and leaned forward to claim her lips.

At the last second, she bunched her fingers into a fist, swung with every ounce of her strength, and hit him hard on the side of his face.

Abe yelped in pain and surprise, and let go of Amelia. She hit him again and he fell backward, landing with a thud on the stone floor of one of the stalls, the heel of his hand covering his injured eye. The handkerchief fluttered down to rest beside him.

Her jaw tensed in grim satisfaction, Amelia retrieved her sister's handkerchief, then turned to leave. If she hurried, she could be back in the parlor before her parents noticed how long she had been gone. They would never know what had happened. And as long as Julia was more careful of her possessions in future…

The thought ended abruptly as Abe grabbed her ankle and pulled, hard. Amelia squealed and put out her hands to cushion the fall. Even through her leather gloves, the cold floor stung her palms. Motes of straw rose into the air, making her eyes feel gritty and filling her mouth with their sawdusty, animal-tainted taste.

She kicked out, but her skirts hampered her, and her boots could not find purchase in the straw. Abe flipped her onto her back and knelt across her stomach, pinning her in place.

"Get off me!" The words were squeezed by his weight upon her. She bucked, trying to dislodge him. It did not work. He merely gave her a leering grin. Amelia tried to move her arm. If she could just hit him once again…

Abe must have had the same thought, for he grabbed both her wrists and pushed them together above her head, holding them fast in one of his meaty hands. He licked his lips in eager anticipation.

Amelia swallowed and tasted hot bile in her throat as she realized there was no escape. She was not strong enough to fight off a brute like Abe Sutton.

She tensed her muscles against the onslaught.

Chapter Two

Abe grinned, leaned in closer, and licked his lips so they shone. Amelia's stomach churned. She screwed up her face and turned her head in a vain attempt to thwart him. Her hat dislodged, pulling at her hair. Her breaths were hard and short.

"I am certain the lady told you to get off her."

The voice was deep and cultured, and full of menace. Abe's eyes widened. He shifted slightly to look over his shoulder, allowing Amelia to see who had spoken. It was the stranger from the inn.

Amelia had thought the man tall when they stood side by side in the bar of the Golden Goose. Now, from the stable floor, he seemed colossal. His legs were long, the dust on his boots and spatters of mud on his breeches giving him a touch of flawed humanity that, somehow, made him more intimidating than perfection could have been. The brim of his hat shadowed his eyes in the dim stable, but the set of his jaw was unmistakably grim. He looked like an avenging angel, and Amelia would not have been surprised if he had used lightning to smite Abe for this outrage.

Or perhaps, she thought, her throat closing fearfully, it would be her he smote, for putting herself into this situation in the first place. Not for the first time in her life, Amelia cursed her impetuosity. Now the handsome stranger would think her a feather-headed wanton—

which she was, she admitted to herself, for why else would she have come here alone with no thought of her safety? And as if that were not enough, she knew Abe Sutton well enough to realize the two men might well come to blows over this. That would, inevitably, draw the attention of others, and Amelia would be ruined. She closed her eyes and fought the rising dread.

Abe said something to the stranger, an obscene word Amelia was not supposed to know. The stranger sniffed, clearly unimpressed. Amelia tried to squirm her way free, but Abe's grip held fast, and her movement did not unseat him, even a little.

"Release the lady."

Abe told the man to do something unpleasant, and Amelia gasped at the crudity.

The stranger's jaw tightened. "Now." His growl was not one Amelia would have dared to disobey. She prayed Abe also had sense enough to heed its warning.

He did not. "Or what?" he sneered.

Amelia should have known that would be the oaf's response. For as long as she could remember, Abe Sutton had considered himself king of the village. Bigger than most, and more than willing to swing his fists to back his words, he had put down all challengers until no one stood up to him anymore. It was how he had snagged the job of constable of the parish for the year; once Abe had made it known he wanted the position, nobody else had even tried for it. Now he would spend the next twelvemonth lording it over everyone, bullying people into doing what he wanted and, no doubt, lining his pockets at the same time. It was the way of things. All the local men knew it, and they did not cross Abe.

The stranger, however, did not know what all the

local men knew, and he did not seem ready to capitulate simply because Abe said he should. Amelia groaned, inwardly. This could not end well.

Then again, she reasoned, hope rising, the stranger was clearly a gentleman of quality. Surely even Abe Sutton would not think he could threaten a gentleman of quality.

Would he?

"Or what?" Abe asked the man again. He was tense, ready for a fight. Amelia despaired.

"You don't want to know the 'or what.' " The stranger's voice was quiet now, not much more than a whisper, and more terrifying than any shout could be.

Abe scrambled to his feet, his anger at the stranger's insolence far greater than his wish to torment Amelia. Freed from his weight, she breathed her relief and sat up. Julia's handkerchief again lay crumpled on the floor, forgotten by Abe, and Amelia snatched it up and stuffed it into her pocket. Then, carefully and slowly, trying not to divert Abe's attention and put herself back into the line of his fire, she got to her feet.

"Are you threatening me?" Abe asked. His eye was swelling from the blow Amelia had inflicted, and the skin around it was turning colorful, but it did not seem to give him pause when there was a fight to be had with a more worthy opponent.

"I don't make threats," the stranger answered Abe, who grinned, then winced and touched his eye.

Amelia sidled away. If they did come to blows, she needed to be in a position to escape.

"I make promises," continued the stranger.

The smile dropped from Abe's face. His good eye glittered, dangerously. "You know, you're in trouble already," he said. "So if you don't want to be hauled up before the beak…"

"On what charge?" The stranger gave a bemused smile. A dimple appeared on his cheek and Amelia scolded herself for noticing it. There were far more important things going on here. She moved another step away from Abe, who puffed out his chest, proudly.

"It's a serious offence to hit a constable." Then, in case there was a doubt, "I'm the constable."

The stranger nodded. "But I haven't hit you." His tone added, *yet.*

Abe touched his face, gingerly. The swelling had almost completely shut his eye now, which gave Amelia a certain pride. If she was going to be ruined here today, at least she would take Abe's reputation with her. He would never live down an injury inflicted by a mere woman.

At which point, she realized he did not intend to try. He had a perfect scapegoat in this man. A stranger in Rotherton, the man would have no friends to vouch for him. If the local constable accused him of assault and sported a black eye to prove the claim, he would be believed and the stranger convicted.

Amelia pursed her lips angrily. Abe clearly thought she would say nothing, unwilling to ruin her own reputation in a stranger's defense. To a point, he was right. She was not willing to be the subject of gossip and censure, nor did she wish for her sisters to have to face judgmental neighbors who would find them guilty by association. In her mind, she could already see the look of disappointment on Papa's face, and it broke her heart to think her actions might break his. No, she was not willing to face all of that.

But not being willing did not mean Amelia would not do it, and reluctant ruination was preferable to the only alternative course open to her: enduring the guilt and shame that would come of permitting an innocent man to be arrested simply because he had come to her aid.

So, hands on hips and defiance tensing her jaw, she stepped forward and faced Abe. "I gave you that black eye, Abraham Sutton, and if you dare try to blame anybody else for it I will proclaim the truth from the rooftops. Of course, I will also need to tell everybody that I did it in defense of my honor, and that the constable of this parish thinks he can attack defenseless ladies—"

"Defenseless?" Abe pointed to his eye. "You call this defenseless?"

"—which may make the magistrate think again about your suitability for the position," she continued, as if he had not spoken. "And for the rest of your life, everyone in Rotherton will know you were *bested by a female*." The last four words were spoken in a sing-song, taunting voice that made Abe's face darken and his good eye shine with fury. For a moment, Amelia worried that she had pushed him too far.

He glared at her, then at the stranger, who watched, impassively. Finally, Abe muttered a curse, snatched up his hat from the straw, and stormed out of the stable.

After he had gone, there was a moment of awkward silence. The stranger watched Abe leave, then turned back to Amelia. She felt his gaze on her like a physical force. It made her skin tingle, and she fought the urge to shiver. Nonplussed, she looked away from him and began to brush down her coat and skirt vigorously, ridding herself of the telltale straw and stable dust that clung to them. She would, undoubtedly, smell like the stable until she was able to return home and change her clothes, and that might make people speculate on what she had been doing, but a stray stalk clinging to her would let them know beyond doubt.

Amelia craned her neck to see over her shoulder, reaching back as far as her arm would go to brush between her shoulders.

"Allow me," said the stranger. He put his hand on her arm to turn her around. The warmth of him seeped through her clothes and into her skin. It was comforting and safe and terrifyingly dangerous at one and the same time.

He picked several pieces of straw from the back of her coat, and one from her hair, then brushed her down gently. Flutters filled her chest at his touch, and her stomach did a strange flip-flop. Amelia bit her lip to stop the whimper that threatened to escape. She wished he would stop and back away from her. She wished he would continue forever. She wished...

"There," he said, softly. "That should do it."

Amelia swallowed. "Thank..." Her voice was a mortifying squeak. She cleared her throat, and tried again, willing herself to sound more in control. "Thank you."

The stranger moved round to face her. This close, his eyes were no longer hidden in the shadow of his hat. Earlier, in the bar, she had thought them brown. Now, closer to, she could see they were an unusual hazel, not quite brown, not quite green either, and framed with impossibly long, dark lashes that matched his overlong hair. His skin was dark, too, as if he had spent more time in the sun than most. It made him look healthier, more masculine somehow, than the insipid gentlemen whose virtues Mama was always extolling. There was the slightest hint of an evening shadow about his firm jaw. He smelled of the stew he had eaten and the ale he had drunk, and something else, which Amelia guessed was his cologne. It smelled like nothing she had encountered before, like flowers wrapped in silk and dipped in a clear, cool stream. The scent wrapped around her, filling her senses and tempting her to lean nearer.

He seemed to move nearer to her, and her heart did a strange pit-a-pat. Was he going to kiss her? Was she going to let him? Surely, she could not! But then again...

"Your bonnet is crooked," he whispered in her ear, and broke the spell.

Amelia blinked and stepped back. Her face was hot, and shame weighed heavily upon her. Had she really just thrown herself at a man to whom she had not even been introduced? Perhaps she truly was as wanton as Abe's treatment of her might suggest.

Trying to cover her embarrassment, she turned away, reached up, and played with her hat, putting it in place as best she could without maid or mirror to aid her. "Thank you," she said. Her voice was unsteady, a mere croak. She cleared her throat, and said it again. "Thank you."

"Will you be safe now?"

"Yes," she answered, far too quickly. She swallowed, and willed her breathing to slow. "Yes," she repeated. "I—I think I must return to my family."

He nodded once, a curt, judgmental gesture. "If I may be so bold, Miss Bell, you would be wise in future, to be a little more careful when going about unaccompanied."

Amelia opened her mouth to give him a stinging retort, then closed it again. He was, of course, correct. She had been unpardonably careless. And if not for him...

But how dare he? Had he never made a mistake? Misjudged a situation? Probably not. Besides, as a man, he would not be judged so harshly for any fall from grace. *He* was free to do as he liked. It wasn't fair.

Angry, with him, with the world, she cast about for a means to retaliate, and seized on the one thing he'd done that she could reasonably take issue with. "We have not yet been introduced, sir. Yet you know my name, and use it without permission?"

"A thousand pardons." He gave a small but deferential bow. "I heard the landlord address you inside, and in the moment I forgot myself. Forgive me."

Shame washed over her at her churlishness. Amelia was the one who should utter apologies. She needed to leave, now, before she made things any worse. "Once again, I thank you," she said, and before he could answer, she turned and fled.

With relief, she returned to the parlor. Mama smiled at her. "Ah, there you are, my dear. We are almost ready to leave now. I trust you are, too?"

Amelia nodded. Mama continued speaking, her joyful prattle filling the air.

Papa said nothing, just watched Amelia, disappointment and suspicion on his face. She swallowed, and the guilt stuck in her throat.

He turned his head slightly, and she realized he had moved since she'd quit the room. Instead of sitting next to Mama, he now occupied the chair nearest the window, the one Amelia had used during their meal. Unlike the other chairs in the parlor, it afforded a perfect view of the stable.

Papa glared at her now, his meaning clear. Mama may not know where Amelia had really been, but he did. Amelia bit her lip and dreaded the talk he would doubtless insist upon when they reached home.

****

From the shadows at the entrance to the stable, Josh watched Miss Bell return to the inn. Her back was ramrod straight and her head held high, which made her bonnet, still slightly crooked, look ridiculous. Josh grinned but did not lower his guard until she was inside and any lingering threat posed by Abe Sutton or his ilk was spent.

He wondered at the young lady's audacity. On the one hand, he liked that she was no simpering miss who would wilt at the slightest problem. He admired her fire, the way she had stood up to the bully. At the same time, though, he feared for her. The chit had placed herself in a compromising situation the moment she had walked into the stable without so much as a maid to give her countenance. Her behavior would certainly have been frowned on in the time before he left England, and he did not think the rules of society could have changed so much in fourteen years. Could they?

Josh leaned against a post and pondered the question. He had last been here in the summer of 1804, so how could he know what was, and was not, acceptable behavior here? So much else had changed in the intervening years, how did he know manners and etiquette had stayed still?

When Josh left England, his father's rebukes stinging his ears and a bitter determination in his heart to show the old man he was capable of surviving without the Frantham connection, the world had been a very different place. Bonaparte had seemed unstoppable as he took Europe by storm, proclaiming himself Emperor and subjugating millions to his will. Now, he was soundly defeated and exiled and the continent was opening up, which must, in itself, engender a certain freedom.

England had changed, too. Fourteen years ago, George III sat upon the throne. Technically, he still did, although he was now unfit to rule and the Regent had taken power. From all Josh had heard, Prinny, as the satirists dubbed him, was a hedonist without par. With a ruler like that, who was to say what the rest of society were doing?

Besides, Josh himself had always found the dictates of society stifling. It was one of the reasons he had quarreled with his father. As a close confidant of the then Prime Minister, William Pitt, Viscount Frantham took protocol very seriously, and insisted on due deference at all times. Josh had chafed under an attitude he thought outdated and ludicrous, so he had ignored, and deliberately flouted, many of the rules, then and since. Which meant he'd be a hypocrite to judge Miss Bell for doing the same thing.

The lady had long since disappeared. Knowing she was safe, Josh walked back through the stables to see to his horse. It was in a small stall with straw bedding and fresh water, but no feed, as he had requested. The saddle and valise were still on the animal's back, ready for him to ride away.

The stable lad was nowhere to be seen, so Josh set about the work himself. He was more than capable; it wasn't the first time he had done such a job. Besides, by the time he had gone in search of the boy and given him his instructions, it could be done.

The thought occurred to him that the boy might be disappointed. If he remembered correctly, the landlord at the Golden Goose was something of a pinch-penny. Josh doubted he paid his stable staff well, and the lad probably relied on tips from customers to survive.

That was a situation Josh understood perfectly. Many times, in his early years in India, he had wondered where his next meal would come from. The kindness of strangers and the smallest of coins had been precious to him. Now he was as rich as Croesus, he was more than willing to pass that kindness on. He would do the work and tip the youngster anyway.

And did he not sound like a self-righteous prig! Shaking his head in dismay at himself, Josh took the saddle off the horse and rested it on the wall between this stall and the next and hung the bridle on a hook. He brushed the horse down and found feed for it, then picked up his valise and headed out of the stable. He was comfortably tired now, and looked forward to his chamber, where there'd be a warm fire, a glass of brandy, and perhaps even a bath to make him presentable before facing his father on the morrow. Fourteen years ago, Frantham had cut off his youngest son without a penny. The old man had fully expected Josh to fail miserably and return, chastened and willing to do as he was bid. It was a matter of pride to Josh that his father should now be able to see he had not only survived but thrived.

He came out into the yard as three well-dressed men rode in from the street. They dismounted, and both the stable boy and the elderly ostler approached to take care of the horses. At the same moment, the Bell family left the Golden Goose. Miss Bell glanced at Josh, colored prettily, and looked away. Josh's lips twitched. Lord, but she was lovely! He willed her to look his way just one more time. A smile from her would be a wonderful memory to dwell upon when he sat alone in his chamber this evening.

"Oh, Mr. Summersby!" called Mrs. Bell, joyfully. "How wonderful to see you."

Josh turned his startled attention to the older woman, frowning as he wondered how she knew his name. He would be most surprised if she had recognized him. The boy who left here in 1804 had been slight and soft, a scared child, barely even able to grow enough of a beard to make shaving worthwhile. The man he was now was much changed: bigger and broader, muscular from years of hard, physical work, and with the self-assurance that came from having made a success of his life.

Even if he had been instantly recognizable, though, Josh would not have expected Mrs. Bell to hail him. He did not know the family. He doubted they had even lived in the area fourteen years ago. So how could she possibly know him?

Watching her, he realized, with more than a little shock, that Mrs. Bell had not actually addressed him but one of the newly arrived gentlemen. The most elegant of the newcomers bowed to her and returned her greeting. Josh relaxed. It had been a coincidence of names, nothing more.

It was a strange coincidence, though. Summersby was hardly the most exclusive name in England, but it had never been common in these parts. Mayhap this was a distant cousin of his, although he knew of none such. The man shared Josh's height and coloring and, he supposed, in a certain light, there could be said to be a resemblance. Josh should go over and make himself known to the man and discover more.

A moment later, he froze in shock. Mrs. Bell bustled across the cobbled yard, her husband and daughter following her, less eagerly. As she reached the other Mr. Summersby, Mrs. Bell's face took on a solicitous expression, and she asked, "How is your poor father, sir? Such a pity to see a great man laid so low. But you must know, we pray for dear Viscount Frantham every day."

Chapter Three

Josh stood rooted to the spot and stared at the man Mrs. Bell had addressed. If he truly was the son of Viscount Frantham, he would be Josh's brother, and that was impossible. Josh did not have a brother.

He had had one. Humphrey had been the heir and Josh the spare, but Humphrey had died more than a year ago. Which would make this man, at best, illegitimate, and at worst, an imposter and a liar.

Josh curled his lip in a humorless grin. The man was certainly not his father's bastard. The viscount Josh knew had always been stiff-rumped with moral rectitude. He had frowned on the joyous laughter of first his wife, then his younger son, and his insistence on correct behavior and the following of rules bordered on the obsessional. He could no more have fathered a child outside wedlock—let alone acknowledge it and given it his name—than he could fly.

Which begged the question: Who was this Mr. Summersby?

Surreptitiously, Josh moved farther back into the shadows, where he was less likely to be remarked as he watched the little crowd on the cobbles. Mr. Summersby was unfailingly polite but distant, his demeanor contrasting sharply with the enthusiastic chatter of Mrs. Bell. His companions stood to one side, watching the exchange. They said nothing, but gave off an air of absolute boredom that bordered on rudeness. Their attitude seemed lost on Mrs. Bell, though, because she ignored them, concentrating her attentions exclusively on Mr. Summersby.

Mr. Bell's response to Summersby's presence was muted, so much so that Josh wondered if he actually disliked him. Miss Bell certainly seemed to do so. It was with a shaming satisfaction that Josh noted she was never more than coldly polite to the man.

He frowned, pondering why he should feel glad. Miss Bell was a chance-met stranger, someone he might never encounter again, especially if the meeting with his father did not go well on the morrow, so what did it matter to him that she liked, or disliked, anybody?

His musings were interrupted when Mrs. Bell mentioned India. The lady expressed a keen interest in all "dear Mr. Summersby" had seen, heard, and done in that country. "I have heard it is a fascinating place," she said, her smile widening until it must make her cheeks hurt. "One might almost say it was magical."

Josh's breath caught in his throat. The man had been in India?

Mr. Summersby nodded once. "Indeed it is, Mrs. Bell," he answered. "But after almost fourteen years there, I found I had had my fill. Enough, as the saying goes, is as good as a feast."

Had his fill? Josh could not believe that. India was a vast country that revealed new wonders daily. There was so much to see there, so much to learn. No man of imagination could have his fill of the place in a lifetime.

It also did not ring true that the man had been there for fourteen years. Summersby's face held the pallor of English winters, not Indian summers, and there was a softness about him that could never have survived the rigors of that country. Besides, he was too quintessentially *English*. India drew people in, whether they willed it or not. It melted them down to their very core, and then, if they survived the process, it rebuilt them in its own inimitable fashion. Even those who had tried to maintain the mores of English society were markedly different from their friends who had never left these shores. India stamped them all as clearly as an assayer stamped gold.

Summersby did not have that stamp. If he had ever been nearer to India than the East London docks, Josh was an elephant.

It took a few moments for the real extent of the situation to sink in. When it did, it took his breath. This man, Summersby, was not pretending to be Josh's brother at all. He was pretending to be Josh himself! Although how and why, and what possible gain there could be in the deception eluded Josh for now.

His first instinct was to go over and challenge the man, but he rejected that idea immediately. For one thing, there were three of them and, if things became ugly, Josh would likely not fare well. Pride in his family name and the wish to claim it from usurpers did not make him keen to have his nose broken. On top of which, at present, it would be a matter of his word against that of the false Mr. Summersby. Nobody here knew Josh, but they all thought they knew Summersby. Since Josh had already had a run-in with what passed for a constable in Rotherton, he was not eager to risk being disbelieved. It would be far more prudent to stay silent and wait to confront the imposter once he was in full possession of the facts.

Was this the reason Hicks had written to Josh, urging his return? If that were the case, surely it would mean Josh's father was aware of the deception, for the valet was too loyal to keep his suspicions to himself. And if he was aware of it, why had Father allowed it to continue? Why had he not thrown the man out, his angry denunciation ringing in Summersby's ears?

That led to an even darker thought. What if this deception actually had his father's blessing? More, what if it was his father's doing?

Fourteen years ago, when Josh had been sent down from Oxford, the viscount had had no compunction about ejecting him with only the clothes on his back and a stinging rebuke ringing through his head. The old man had raged until Josh had thought he would explode. He was still shouting that he would have no more to do with his "spare" son as Josh marched away.

Now, however, Humphrey, the intended heir, was dead and Josh was set to inherit. Would his father's disappointment in his irresponsible second son be so great that he would look for a substitute, a man he found more tolerable?

The idea left Josh feeling sick. There was a sharp pain in his heart, and he had to fight to stop himself massaging his chest to try to ease it. It took several seconds to pull his emotions back under control and return his attention to the conversation in the courtyard.

"But sir," Mrs. Bell was saying to Summersby, "you must have so many tales of the things you encountered there."

Yes, I daresay he must. Josh leaned his shoulders against the stable wall and folded his arms, keen to hear what the man would say.

Mr. Summersby gave a pained smile. "Not really," he said.

His companions were visibly irritated by Mrs. Bell's continued questions. So, it seemed, was Miss Bell, though her outward signs of this were limited to a tightening of her mouth and the shortest of eye rolls, while her father subtly attempted to move his wife on.

For a moment, Mrs. Bell looked disappointed at Summersby's reply. Then she pinned her smile back into place and changed the subject, briskly talking at the poor man once more. His friends made no move to relieve him. Mr. Bell tried, none too successfully, to hide his embarrassment at his wife's exuberance. Miss Bell looked away and found Josh.

He knew the moment she saw him in the gathering gloom. Her mouth softened, the ends of her lips curling up into that delectable perpetual smile. She straightened her shoulders a little. For his part, Josh stood up straight and unfolded his arms, then let them hang awkwardly at his sides, suddenly feeling he should occupy his hands and unsure how.

The sounds of the stable yard disappeared. The chatter of Mrs. Bell, the rhythmic ring of hooves on cobbles, the bark of a dog and the growled command for it to shut up, all were silenced as Josh stared at the lively beauty of Miss Bell. Around her, the people seemed to fade into the dusk, no longer part of the scene, until there was only Josh and her. The entire East India Company Army could have marched through the yard at that moment and he would not have known it.

He imagined them in a ballroom, the lights from a thousand candles making a halo of her bright blonde hair and dancing in her eyes, like the sun on the Bay of

Bengal at Visagapatam. The blush on her cheeks beckoned him closer, his breath shallowing as his heartbeat kicked. He wanted to take her in his arms and dance with her, something requiring close contact. A waltz. The thought made him smile. He wanted to feel her against him, warm and soft, her skin as soft as a rose petal beneath his fingers. He wanted...

She turned her head sharply, and the dream burst like a bubble. Josh took a sharp breath, once again in the yard of the inn, the darkness gathering about him. In the yellow light of the yard lamps, Mr. Bell nodded at the gentlemen and led his wife firmly away toward the street. His daughter followed. Josh watched her go. Behind the family, the three gentlemen shared a whispered joke and laughed, garnering his attention. His eyes narrowed as he watched them go into the inn.

There was an imposter at Frantham Manor. It was why Hicks had written to him—Josh was certain of that now. Suddenly, the prospect of a warm chamber and a bath did not seem so important as, teeth gritted in determination, he went back into the stable and re-saddled his horse.

****

Forewarned by what he had heard at the Golden Goose, Josh did not simply ride into the grounds of Frantham Manor, as he might have done before. Instead, he stopped a quarter of a mile down the road from the main entrance and tied his horse to the low branches of a tree, far enough from the road that it would be hidden from all but the most hawkeyed of passersby. Then, quietly, stealthily, he made his way onto the grounds.

Josh had often come and gone this way as a boy, when he'd needed to avoid the main gate and the inevitable thrashing should his mischief be discovered. Now he was glad of his misspent youth as he followed the almost invisible track, avoiding treacherous dips in the ground hidden by overgrown brambles and piles of rancid leaves. Small patches of frozen clay formed grotesque shapes along the pathway, and they threatened to upend him when he trod on them. Bare branches of elm and silver birch hung low, and he ducked to avoid their scratches, his breath steaming white in front of him.

He worked his way to the edge of the manicured lawns and stopped, still hidden by the trees. Cautiously, he looked around.

The house he had grown up in was a sprawling Tudor manor, gray stone walls and mullioned windows, some framed by thick ivy. The main door was black oak, studded with iron and pitted with scars that showed the violence of its past. Here, Summersbys had worked to keep their place of favor with the volatile Tudor monarchs and held out against siege by Cromwell, and they had never once lost possession. Josh grinned, wryly, remembering the family history that had been drilled into him from early childhood. Some things, it seemed, never left you.

Between Josh's present hiding place and the house were well-tended gardens: symmetrical lawns with statues, carefully placed to give balance. There was a small maze and an herb garden crisscrossed by perfectly straight, perfectly maintained paths of regularly raked gravel. As a child, Josh had kicked his way through those stones, enjoying the way they flew in all directions and left his sliding footmarks. Ever one for order, Father had scolded him and threatened to send him to bed with no supper if he ever did it again. Mama had been kinder, more understanding. It was to her Josh had made his promise not to disturb the paths again, and from then on he always walked on the grass. He wondered how his father would react if Josh discomposed his carefully ordered gravel now, and grinned at the wonderfully childish urge to do it.

The sound of feet on that gravel rattled in the still air. One person, walking at a slow, steady pace, making no effort to hide their approach. Josh remembered his father taking his evening constitutionals around the house, and hoped this was him now, for then Josh could come out of hiding and talk to him. He could discover immediately whether he was welcome, and have his questions answered without the humiliation of being ejected by the staff. If he was not wanted here, he could simply ride away and forget Frantham forever. He might spend a few weeks in London, enjoying the delights of the early Season or visiting clubs to renew ancient friendships, before sailing back to India and the life he had built there. Most of the vessels heading for that country would not set sail for another couple of months anyway; the weather in the Bay of Biscay was too hostile yet, and there was nothing to say he could not while away the waiting time in pleasurable pursuits.

Or perhaps he wouldn't go too far at all. He could make himself comfortable at the Golden Goose in Rotherton, far enough away that Father could do naught about his presence while he revisited his childhood haunts. And maybe, just maybe, he could make the acquaintance of a certain blue-eyed minx with a mischievous smile and a penchant for getting herself into scrapes. The thought made him smile. Perhaps he would see her at the Assembly Rooms. He might even get that dance with her after all. Although, he realized with a disappointed sigh, it was unlikely to be anything as intimate as a waltz. Still, a quadrille would serve to make her better acquaintance. And afterward, they could cool down with a cup of punch in a quiet corner of the room, public enough that all could see they were innocent, private enough for a flirtation...

The footsteps on the gravel grew louder, banishing his reverie. The walker turned the corner of the house. It was not his father taking the air. In fact, it was nobody Josh recognized, although that, in itself, was unsurprising. After fourteen years, there were bound to have been changes, some staff retired, others come to take their places. This was a youngish man, as tall as Josh, though a little stockier. He did not wear the Frantham livery, which surprised Josh. He could not imagine his father allowing any of his employees to go about looking like a common laborer, his powerful legs encased in loose breeches and thick stockings. Heavy clogs kicked up the gravel as he walked, and he wore a bulky coat of coarse wool, buttoned against the freezing air. His gloves were fingerless and his hat flopped, shapeless and ill-fitting, around his ears. But the thing that truly caught Josh's attention was the musket, held close to the man's chest, ready to be aimed and fired.

Josh frowned, wondering why Frantham would need openly armed staff patrolling the grounds. Was this because of whatever had upset Hicks enough to send the letter?

A twig snapped, making Josh start. He pulled back against the trunk of a tree, making himself as invisible as he could, as a silhouetted man stepped out of the woods twenty yards away. Josh stiffened, not even daring to breathe, every muscle and nerve tensed and alert.

The man on the gravel stopped his perambulations, planted his legs firmly in a defensive position and held his musket ready to fire.

"It's me," said the man from the woods. His voice was low, with a strong Sussex burr.

The man on the gravel relaxed his stance and pointed his musket downward. "What are you doing there?" His burr was less pronounced, more Kentish.

"Patrolling."

Gravel man guffawed.

"We was told to patrol the Frantham estate."

"Not all of it, bacon brain. He just means around the house."

Wood Man chuckled. "If you must know, I had to go and point Peter at the base of a tree." He stepped forward and the light from the sconces on the house walls illuminated him, allowing Josh to see him more clearly. Like Gravel Man, he was young, though he was much smaller, and wiry. He wore boots that met his breeches, and his coat hung open, carelessly casual. He also carried a gun.

Gravel Man laughed louder. "You honestly call your wotsit Peter?" he asked in response to Wood Man's last statement.

"It's a perfect name for it, seeing as how it can rise to the challenge three times a night."

"I don't believe that for a second." Gravel Man scratched his own crotch. "Anything else to report?"

Wood Man shook his head. "Quiet as a graveyard." He walked across the lawn toward his friend. Gravel Man muttered something, which made Wood Man laugh again, and then the two parted company and marched off along the path, each heading in a different direction around the house.

Why would Father need guards patrolling? Had someone threatened the manor? More worried than ever, Josh waited until the men disappeared, then moved round to the servant's entrance and slipped inside, carefully and quietly closing the door behind him.

The narrow passage was dark around the doorway, although light from the kitchen spilled out onto it farther up, along with chatter and laughter. There was a chill in this corridor that only ever existed in places where the floor and walls were made of plain stone. Josh hoped that would work in his favor: if the corridor was uncomfortable, servants were less likely to venture into it voluntarily, which meant they were less likely to discover him.

He could smell food being prepared in the kitchen, the delicious aromas of meat and potatoes, vegetables, and suet dumplings wafting out through the open door. Josh poked his head around the frame to take a quick look at the scene. The kitchen was well lit, with tallow candles and wood burning in a fireplace so big a man could stand up straight inside it. On the range, a pot boiled and steamed. A kitchen maid scoured another pot, while a second maid flirted with a young man, who grinned and encouraged her. A musket lay on the table beside him. Near the fire was a second armed man, and a butler. None of these servants were known to Josh, although he recognized Cook. She stood beside the range stirring the pot, her ample figure moving to and fro with the effort. He also recognized the last servant in the room, a man sitting at the table, drinking from a mug.

Hicks.

The valet looked much older than Josh had expected, even allowing for the passage of time. He was a small man, no more than five feet high, and slightly built, although he had always been well turned out, and that had not changed. Even in the steamy kitchen, his coat looked fresh and his hair, now an ash gray instead of the dark brown Josh remembered, was carefully in place. His face was deeply lined, and there were liver spots on the hands wrapped around his cup.

His shock at how Hicks had aged made Josh look for longer than he intended, and he only just pulled his head back out of sight as the butler turned to face the door. Josh pressed himself against the wall and waited, but there was no change in the conversation to indicate the man had seen him.

However, he was stuck. To go on into the house he must pass this open door, and the risk that someone would see him then was high. If he stayed where he was, it would only be a matter of time before someone saw him anyway. Going back outside was not an option he favored. He would then have to run the gauntlet of the patrolling guards as he looked for another way in.

Trying to decide what to do for the best, Josh peered around the door frame once more. This time, Hicks saw him. The valet tensed slightly, then looked away, covering his movement with a stretch and a yawn before he drained his cup and stood. "Time I was back on duty," he said.

One of the men snickered. "That old witch is with him. He don't need you." The flirty maid laughed.

Cook did not. She glared at the man. "Mrs. Hargreaves i'n't no witch," she said. "That woman is as good-hearted as they come. And if you bad mouth her again in my kitchen, I'll make sure your dinners are the worst you ever tasted. For a whole month." She turned her stare onto the maid, who stopped laughing and straightened her face.

The man answered back, which Josh thought brave. One thing he remembered about Cook was her inability to lose an argument. The woman did not ever accept defeat. She had boxed Josh's ears a few times, and he would not have been surprised to learn she had boxed the ears of everyone else in the household, too.

She and the servant now began a full-blown argument. While everybody else in the kitchen watched them, Hicks slipped out, closing the door tightly behind him. Even through the thick wooden door, Josh could still hear Cook berating the man. He winced in sympathy.

Hicks put his finger to his lips to indicate silence, then gestured Josh should follow him along the corridor and up a dark and narrow servant staircase. They climbed, then walked along another narrow passage. It followed the same path as the plushly carpeted, expensively appointed corridor on the other side of the wall. On that side, the family and honored guests would walk in comfort and light. Here, where they could not disturb anyone or spoil the view, servants moved from room to room like mice behind a massive wainscot.

Another flight of stairs and along another narrow corridor. Surely, Josh thought, amazed, the master suite was not this far from the kitchen? Good grief! By the time it reached him, Father's shaving water would be cold!

Halfway along the third passageway, Hicks stopped dead. Following close behind, Josh almost collided with him and had to put his hand against the cold wall to steady himself.

Hicks took a step back. "I beg your pardon, sir," he said. "But I believe nobody will hear us now." As an added precaution, he pitched his voice low anyway, so that he was almost whispering. "Firstly, may I tell you how happy I am to see you here? I have prayed every day that my letter reached you, and that you would respond by coming home."

"How could I not? The letter was disconcerting, to say the least. You made me fear for my father's well-being."

"You have every reason to do so," answered Hicks. "We have looked after him thus far, but—to be frank, sir, I do not know how much longer we can sustain our efforts. Come," and he turned away. "There's a door, just up here, which leads out onto the landing. It will be more comfortable for us, and easier to converse. I can tell you more as we walk." They went through the door into the main corridor, and Josh stopped, surprised. He had expected a carpeted hallway, with pictures hanging on the walls, and lamps lit at intervals along the way, welcoming people as they headed for their chambers.

Instead, the corridor had old stone walls, on which hung ancient tapestries, many of them fraying. The flagstone floor was uneven, a thin red runner laid along its middle the only nod to comfort. The corridor was dark and dreary, and very cold.

"This is not the way to the master suite," said Josh.

"Lord Frantham no longer occupies the master suite."

Josh stopped and stared at the valet, who merely gave a shrug that was part apology, part resignation.

"The man who is calling himself Mr. Summersby has moved in there," he explained.

"Before Father was dead?" Josh's eyes widened in disbelief.

Hicks hesitated before he replied. "If I am absolutely fair, I may say the—ah—the gentlemen did not expect Lord Frantham to be with us for long."

Josh nodded, once. "You had better tell me everything."

Hicks pushed open a door and ushered Josh into a room. Josh waited while Hicks lit a candle, which threw long, grotesquely shaped shadows in all directions. Thick curtains were drawn at the window, although they did not successfully keep out the chill of the evening. The four-poster bed which dominated the space looked ancient, its wood made of dark-stained oak. The curtains around it were serviceable but not of the first stare, and the blankets were clearly old. Beside the bed was a small nightstand, on top of which was a bowl and ewer. A wardrobe and a chest of drawers stood against one wall. A gentleman's grooming set was laid out very precisely on the top of the chest of drawers, and a small mirror had been placed above them. The hearth was cold, and the total lack of either firewood or coal suggested it was rarely lit, if ever.

"I do beg your pardon for the state of the room, sir," said Hicks. "I appreciate that it is cold in here. But then, I do not sleep here, so it doesn't matter. I merely need the room to change my clothes and see to my ablutions."

Josh raised an eyebrow. "This is your room?" Even in the half-light, he could see it was bigger and better than the room any other valet would expect to occupy.

"I insisted that I must be near my lord," explained

Hicks. "And when Lord Rotherton championed my cause…"

"Rotherton?" The Earl of Rotherton's estate bordered Frantham. Josh and David, the current earl, had played together as children.

"He shares my concerns, sir. He has taken to calling on my lord almost every day. I am certain that is the only reason your father is still alive. Although both Mrs. Hargreaves and I play our parts, the fact is, alone, we would be no real threat. But a peer of the realm, who is also a local magistrate—they did not dare harm him then."

Harm him? And who were "they"? Just what had Josh come home to?

Chapter Four

Hicks gestured that Josh should sit on the bed while he sat on the low stool beside it, his elbows resting on his knees as he carefully formulated his tale.

"It all began a year ago, with your brother's death. 'Twas a hard season, winter last year, snow up to the eaves of some of the cottages. Mr. Humphrey's chest was ever weak, but I don't need to tell you that, do I, sir?" He grinned, sheepishly.

Josh smiled, sadly.

Hicks' grin faded and he continued. "He had a cough, not a desperately worrying one, but it lingered. He went out anyway, and caught a chill." Hicks shook his head. "It was mercifully quick for him, but your father was never the same. Blamed himself, do you see? Said if he hadn't been so preoccupied in London, Mr. Humphrey wouldn't have had to take on so much here. Ridiculous, I know, sir, but, well, he was a grieving father."

"I read about it in the *Times*," Josh told him, a lump at his throat. By the time the paper had reached him it was more than four months old, and when he read the news, he grieved privately. He'd had to, as nobody in India knew anything of his connection to the family. He'd considered coming home then, but weeks went by, and more ships arrived, but no letter came from Papa, so Josh had thought he would not be welcome.

"Lord Frantham was away in London, working at the War Office. But as soon as he heard Mr. Humphrey was ill, he came home. Raced here, hell for leather, if you'll pardon the expression, sir. Made no difference. He was too late." Hicks stared sadly into the empty fire grate. "For days, he stayed in his room and wouldn't let anyone in. Not even me. Then, after about a week, he came out and tried to act as if nothing was different. Though you could see by the lines on his face and the stoop of his shoulders his grief weighed heavily. It was then that he instructed you be sent for," said Hicks, and he smiled, fondly. "He stomped around and grumbled about it, but then, that was ever his way, wasn't it, sir?"

His father had not wanted to send for him. Josh tried to feel anger at hearing that, but it didn't come. There was not even a slight irritation. Just an overwhelming sadness that he had so disappointed his sire that even fourteen years and the death of his heir could not overcome the older man's revulsion of him.

Hicks looked up at him, sympathetically. "He didn't mean it, sir, any of it. Surely, you know that? The truth is, despite all the show, he was very much looking forward to your return. He never thought you would stay away as long as you did, do you see?"

The lump in Josh's throat grew bigger. The backs of his eyes stung. "He told me never to darken his doorstep again," he pointed out.

"He… When he is angry, he says things, but he doesn't mean them." Hicks smiled ruefully. "I can't count the times I've been turned off. An hour later, he's ringing for me again. 'Twas the same for you. He thought you would come back after a month or two, when your money ran out."

"Crawling and with my tail between my legs, no doubt? Not my style, Hicks. He should have known that. Besides, I didn't have any money to run out. I left it all here. Didn't take a penny." He chuckled at Hicks' shocked expression. "Pride can make a man do many foolish things."

"'Tis a wonder you survived, sir."

Josh nodded agreement. Things could have turned out disastrously. He had spent those first nights hiding in barns, too cold to sleep. For breakfast, he'd eaten eggs stolen from henhouses. If he'd been caught, he would probably have been transported. But then his luck had turned, and he found himself on the road to Portsmouth at exactly the right moment. Coming across a sea captain being set upon by a gang, Josh had weighed in to help the man. In the fight, the captain broke his arm badly, which meant he needed someone on his ship who could read and write properly while it healed. So Josh's journey to India had begun.

"But we digress," said Hicks, pulling Josh back to the present. "The fact is, your father instructed Mr. Meriweather to write to you, asking you to come home. But then, poor Mr. Meriweather was killed by a horse and cart in Leadenhall Street. Ran him right down, so we were told. Went over him, horse hooves, cart wheels, the lot. The driver never even stopped to see if he could help. I ask you, sir, what is the world coming to, when a man of Mr. Meriweather's standing cannot cross a road safely?"

"I received no letter, from Papa's man of business or anyone else but you."

"I thought that might be the case." Hicks shook his head. "I never did like Mr. Meriweather's partner. Eyes too close together to be trustworthy."

"Meriweather's partner? What has he to say to anything?" This conversation was more circuitous than the routes Josh had travelled to avoid the Thuggee gangs who ambushed merchants in India.

"He took over your father's interests, do you see?" explained Hicks. "Mr. Teasel—Mr. Meriweather's partner—came here in May, bringing with him Mr. Summersby, Mr. Harcourt, and Mr. Sykes. They were, he said, newly arrived from India. Explained their short journey time by saying they had been coming home to England anyway, and they were only in Spain when they received the missive, but even so..."

"My father was fooled?" Josh could scarcely believe the old man would not know his own son, even after so many years.

"He was suspicious. As was I, and Grayson. You remember Grayson, sir? The butler?" Hicks shook his head, sadly. "Fell down the stairs in August. Broke his neck."

Josh narrowed his eyes. Perhaps his mind was more suspicious than it needed to be, but he found the idea of two trusted retainers dying in freak accidents in quick succession alarming.

"It was shortly after that when my lord spoke with the three gentlemen. I don't know exactly what was said, because they were in the library and I was not there, but we could hear the voices right along the corridor to the kitchens. What a set-to they were having! I never did hear the like, not even when you quarreled with him, and some of those times were, to say the least, memorable."

Josh grimaced with shame. He had not been the easiest of sons.

"And then, suddenly," continued Hicks, "Mr. Summersby came tearing into the kitchen as if old Nick himself was on his heels, shouting, 'Help! He's dead!' "

"My father?" Josh's blood ran cold.

Hicks nodded. "He had an apoplexy," he explained. "Just dropped like a stone, so they said. And who can wonder at it? All that anger, and shouting. It's no good to man nor beast."

"But…he's not dead?" Josh's voice was a whisper. His throat hurt, and his chest was heavy with the need to howl like a maddened wolf. All these years, wasted on useless anger and bitter pride. It could not be too late to set them right. It could not be.

"Oh, no, sir." Hicks looked horrified. "Lord Frantham isn't dead. Didn't I say that before?"

Josh slumped on the bed, and let out the breath he hadn't even realized he was holding. Of course Father wasn't dead. Had not Mrs. Bell enquired after his health at the Golden Goose? Thinking of the garrulous woman conjured up an image of her daughter, blonde curls peeking from a bonnet that was still slightly askew, while her mouth thinned in distaste at the imposter Summersby. No fool, her, he thought, and he liked her all the more. Once this mystery was solved and he had spoken to his father, Josh really must find a way to become better acquainted with her. If his father was as ill as Hicks had intimated, then Josh might have to stay for a while. He was sure that such a stay would be much more pleasant if Miss Bell were able to keep him company.

"No," said Hicks, shaking his head as if to emphasize his point. "My lord is not dead yet."

"I know," answered Josh, quietly. "Forgive me, I…"

He shrugged his shoulders.

Hicks gave a short and heavy sigh. "Mr. Summersby was a little previous in his pronouncement, do you see? My lord was, and is, very much alive. Although, we have Cook to thank in large part for that. Turns out her husband died of an apoplexy. The doctor who attended that unfortunate man told Cook all the things she could have done that might have saved him. Cook said she always thought it a cruel and unnecessary lesson, since the advice came too late to save her husband. But it came into its own for the master, and there's no doubt of that."

"So that's why you sent for me?"

Hicks pulled a face and rocked his hand from side to side in front of him, as if to say yes and no together. "In the weeks after my lord became ill," he said, "strange things began to happen."

"Such as?"

"All the staff were replaced, except for me and Cook. Me, because even in his weakened state, his lordship made it clear he would not see me go, and Cook because, well, there's nobody who can replace her, is there? You might remember, she's the best cook in the whole of Sussex."

Josh nodded. "I remember."

"Everyone else was turned off. Then Mr. Sykes insisted Mr. Summersby needed protecting—"

"From what?"

"I'm sure I don't know, sir. But he said it. And after that, the new men went around armed. That's when Lord Rotherton started visiting. 'Twas he who said to me that I should sleep near Lord Frantham's chamber. He said I was never to leave him alone, and he arranged for Mrs. Hargreaves to come each day to give me rest. Lord

Frantham seemed so frightened, do you see?"

"He would hate being helpless," Josh agreed. "Has his illness… Can he…?"

"Oh, 'twas not the apoplexy frightened him, sir. No, 'twas much more than that. Every time Mr. Sykes or Mr. Harcourt stepped into his chamber, my lord looked—I don't think I'm speaking out of turn here, sir, to say he was terrified. It was not so marked when the visitor was Mr. Summersby, but he was definitely afraid of the others. That's why I wrote to you, sir. And if you knew the trouble I went to in writing the letter and posting it without them being any the wiser…for I am sure that, had they known what I did, I might have fallen downstairs in the same freakish manner as Mr. Grayson!"

The valet's voice had grown shrill. He looked around, as if frightened of eavesdroppers.

Josh sniffed. Time to introduce a little matter-of-fact realism here. "At the risk of sounding crass, Hicks, if they wanted you dead, they would have done for you already."

Instead of looking relieved, the valet drew himself up to his full height and beamed. "They cannot," he said. "Lord Rotherton made sure of that. He's a clever one, if you ask me. Gives off that air of indolence and all his dandified manners, but he is sharp as a pin. Knew just what to do to guarantee my safety, he did. He said the butler's death was unsettling. One could not have servants dying in the execution of their jobs. Bad *ton*."

Josh raised an eyebrow. "Bad *ton*?"

"That's what he called it, sir."

That made Josh laugh. He could see Rotherton— Lord Rotherton, now—leaning against a fireplace, polishing his quizzing glass and making the comment as if it was carelessly thought, when in reality, every single word was weighed and balanced before being uttered.

"He said if there were any more 'accidents' he would be compelled to bring in investigators. Which he didn't want to do because it was such…"

"Damned hard work for him," Josh joined in to chorus the last words along with Hicks. He'd heard Rotherton utter them many times in their youth. A friendly warning that usually had the desired result of defusing a situation, so nobody got hurt and nobody needed to be arrested. But there was a huge difference between threatened fisticuffs at the summer fair and whatever was happening here.

"I am convinced his words are the only reason I am still alive," said Hicks. "And Mrs. Hargreaves is always met by her husband and at least two of her sons, so she's not placed in danger."

Rotherton had clearly thought of everything.

Josh took a minute to digest all he had learned. He agreed with Hicks and Rotherton. Something was very wrong. There had to be more at stake than simple robbery, because the imposter had gone to great lengths to take Josh's place as heir to the Frantham title and estate. True, it was a prosperous estate, well-husbanded by the present viscount, but it was not fabulously wealthy, and the spoils were not worth the effort and time invested by Messrs. Summersby, Sykes, and Harcourt. There were larger, grander, richer estates to plunder, and some of them would likely be easier to grab.

Perhaps Rotherton had formed a theory as to what was happening. As soon as he had finished here, Josh would go straight to the earl and see what he had to say.

Before that, though, another question nagged at him. "Why was my father removed from the master suite?"

Hicks bristled. "It was Mr. Sykes idea," he said. He all but spat the man's name. "He said 'the old man'— actually called my lord 'the old man'! Said he was like to die soon, and Mr. Summersby would not wish to have to sleep in the bed where his father died. So they removed him to another bed where, presumably, his death will not affect anyone's rest in the future." He took a deep breath to calm the anger that showed in every tensed muscle and the flush on his cheeks. "Mr. Joshua, if you could have seen him when he heard that." The valet's eyes filled. "Fair broke my heart."

It wasn't tears Josh wanted to shed over this indignity. Anger burned, hotter than the noon sun in Madras in May. Ruthlessly, he pushed it down. Now was not the time for acting on emotion. Doing that would make him careless, prone to error. If he was to help his father and thwart whatever nefarious plan the imposter had in mind, he would need to be cool and clear.

"So they removed him from his chamber," he said, "and put him here…" He looked around at the valet's room. "Damn it, Hicks, where are we? I don't believe I know this place."

"The west wing, sir."

The west wing? That part of the house had been shut off since before Josh was born. From his earliest childhood, he had been warned not to play there because it was unsafe, ready to fall down at any minute, and the roof leaked. And these people had put a sick, frail old man in there?

Hicks paced the floor, wringing his hands as he walked. "When I sent the letter to you, sir, 'twas my thought that you would ride up, expose the fraud, and send them packing. But now, I don't know. There are a lot of them, and I fear they may dispose of you. Well, they would have to do so, wouldn't they? They could hardly have you riding around Sussex being the heir, when they already have their own."

"It could prove a trifle inconvenient to them."

"Which is why I now believe it is better they do not know you have returned. Then, mayhap you and Lord Rotherton can discover what they are about and set things to rights."

There was some merit in the idea. If they did not know they were being watched, the villains would likely be less careful, easier to catch in the act of whatever it was they were doing.

"When you leave," continued Hicks, "you should not go through the staff entrance. Too many chances for someone to see you and raise the hue and cry."

"How else will I get out?"

Hicks smiled. "Being in the west wing does have its benefits, sir. I can show you a way to get in and out of here without detection." The valet clearly enjoyed the surprise on Josh's face, because his smile broadened. "This part of the manor was built when they had all that unpleasantness about Papists and Protestants, so they had an escape route built into it, just in case. It comes out in the family crypt, up on Frog Leg Hill. I'll show you."

Josh put up his hand to stop the eager man. "After I have seen my father?"

"Yes. Of course. But before I take you to him, I will send Mrs. Hargreaves home. Her family will be here for her by now, and I think it best she doesn't see you. The woman is not a gossip, but one never knows what she might let slip in all innocence. Women do like to talk, do you see?"

So do some men. Josh waited while Hicks went to prepare the way for him. Alone in the dark chamber, nervousness rose through him, churning his stomach and making his heart beat faster, and he cursed his stupidity for not asking Hicks exactly how his father was. That Papa was frail and unable to defend himself was clear, but what else? Were his wits gone, leaving a drooling shell of a man? Or was he mildly impaired, able to speak and think but physically weakened? Josh prayed for the latter, although he suspected a man as strong and vibrant as Father had been would not find either state tolerable.

Footsteps sounded in the corridor, brisk and light. Mrs. Hargreaves, he guessed. They faded and disappeared, and then Hicks was back, beckoning Josh to follow him.

The corridor's only light came through the windows. Outside, the clouds that had threatened the day had gone, leaving the night in all its finery. The almost full moon hung low and, around it, the soft black sky wore thousands of diamonds, as did the grass on Frantham's regimented lawns. Silhouetted statues and trees stood to attention. Josh felt a sharp pain in his side and realized how much he had missed this place.

The room Hicks led him into was cheerier than the valet's had been. A fire played in the grate, spreading warmth and light around. Several candles pushed back the shadows and gave the room color, and they smelled of beeswax, not the cheaper tallow the kitchen staff had been using. Josh supposed the imposter had not dared stint on the viscount's comforts in his room, not if the eagle-eyed Lord Rotherton were visiting regularly. The curtains, both the ones at the window and the ones around the bed, were thick and of good quality, and there was an abundance of blankets.

Strangely apprehensive, Josh approached the bed and saw his father for the first time in fourteen years. The sight shocked him, deeply.

Father was asleep, but his frailty was obvious. No longer the well-built man who had commanded his family with a fist of iron, now he was so slight his skin hung on him, his eyes sunken, his cheeks hollow and pale to the point of translucence. There were few strands of hair left on his head, but they stood proud, as if drawing attention to their continued survival when all others had succumbed. In sleep, his jaw was slack and his mouth open, and a line of spittle crawled over the corner of his lip, trying to work its way down his chin. Lovingly, Hicks wiped the spittle away.

Josh's sight blurred, and he was filled with an overwhelming urge to kiss the old man's fragile cheek. It took every ounce of his Englishness to stop him doing so. He took a deep breath, turned, and whispered, "I have to go."

Hicks nodded. "I'll show you the way," he said. "Then, if I may be so bold, you should visit Lord Rotherton. He can help you."

Josh nodded once, took a last look at his father, then all but ran from the room.

Chapter Five

Upon arriving home from the Golden Goose, Amelia's papa asked her mama to join him in his study. Mama looked as if she would argue, but his expression changed her mind and she followed him along the hall. Amelia handed her coat and bonnet to the waiting footman and stood by, expecting that she, too, would be summoned. When he closed the door leaving her outside, she breathed a sigh of relief. Perhaps he hadn't seen her after all. On that hopeful thought, she ran upstairs to see Julia.

Her younger sister was in the ladies' sitting room. Mama had chosen this room because it faced south and caught the sunlight. Today, it was warm and cozy, thanks to a large fire on which had been thrown some pine cones, if the pleasant aroma was to be believed. Julia sat, embroidering a delicate flower onto the corner of her new handkerchief. She looked up as Amelia entered.

"You look like the cat who got the cream," she said. "Why are you grinning like that?"

Amelia batted her eyelashes in a show of disingenuousness and put her hand over her heart. "Because, dear sister, I am a very clever woman, as intrepid and cunning as any hero you may care to name. Oh, and I happen to be the most wonderful of your sisters, as well."

"In fact," replied Julia, dryly, "your only flaw could

be said to be your overabundance of modesty."

Amelia shrugged. "One should not hide one's light under a bushel." She reached into her pocket, pulled out the rather crumpled and soiled handkerchief she had rescued from the stable, and waved it at her sister.

Julia's eyes widened and her jaw dropped. "He gave it to you?"

"In a manner of speaking." Amelia was reluctant to go into the details of her adventure, even with Julia, whom she trusted wholeheartedly. The fewer people who knew about it, the more quickly it could be forgotten. Although, even as she tried to push the whole sordid incident to the back of her mind, she couldn't help but picture the long legs and broad shoulders of her rescuer. He'd had the bearing of a gentleman, and a confidence that told her he could hold his own against the likes of Abe Sutton. She could still feel the soft warmth of his breath upon her cheek as he leaned in closer to her, his exotic, tantalizing scent teasing her. In that moment, Amelia had truly thought he was going to kiss her. More, she had wanted him to, had almost been able to feel his lips on hers.

And then he had destroyed the moment, and the dream. "Your bonnet is crooked," he'd said, before he raised his chin and, stiff-rumped as a preacher, scolded her.

She pursed her lips, in equal parts angry at the memory of his high-handedness and shamed that she had deserved his censure. And she was honest enough to wonder if it would have stung so much if he had not been so handsome, so very...manly, so very...

"Oh, thank you!" Julia's joyous cry brought Amelia back to the present with a start. Her sister shoved her embroidery aside and reached for the rescued handkerchief.

"Be more careful with it in the future," admonished Amelia, a little more sternly than she intended. The stranger was to blame for that piece of hypocrisy, too, she decided on a mental pout.

"What happened?" asked Julia. For a moment, Amelia thought she was asking about him. She opened her mouth to say she didn't know what Julia was talking about, nothing had happened, and she had almost completely forgotten him already. Thankfully, before she could say any such thing, Julia continued, "How did you get it? Surely Abe did not just give it up on your say-so."

Amelia smiled, too brightly, and waved her hand in a gesture she hoped conveyed nonchalance. "A lady has to have some secrets." And, she vowed, she would never tell a soul of the minutes spent in that stable with a man she did not know. Nor would she ever mention her wanton thoughts for, surely, they had been an aberration! She had never been so tempted before, and likely would never be again.

An aberration. Yes, that's what it had been. The gentleman had rescued her and, in her gratitude, she had imbued him with the super-human qualities of a Greek god. She made no doubt that, when viewed in the cold, calm light of an ordinary day, he would prove as disappointingly unexceptional as everyone else ever had.

Julia clutched the handkerchief to her chest and her eyes filled. "Thank you," she whispered. Then she pushed it safely into her pocket and became her usual, practical self. "Did you get my lace as well?"

And that, thought Amelia, was that. "Mama put it

into her reticule to keep it safe."

"Oh, bother. I hoped to get this—" Julia pointed at her embroidery, "—finished today."

"No matter," said Amanda on an exaggerated sigh. "She will bring it upstairs when she has finished talking with Papa." She flopped down into a chair near the fire and pointed her feet at the merry flames. "It grows quite cold out there once the sun begins to set," she said, then sat up straighter when someone scratched at the door.

"Begging your pardon, miss," said the maid who came in, "but Mr. Bell asks if you might join him and Mrs. Bell in his study."

This was it, then. Her moment of reckoning. She sighed and closed her eyes.

"Millie?" Julia's voice was filled with concern. "What's the matter? Why does Papa…"

Amelia jumped up and grinned. She intended her voice to be reassuringly bright and happy; instead it sounded desperately brittle. "'Tis nothing, I am sure."

"Is it to do with…?" Julia glanced at the side of her dress where her pocket was concealed.

"No, of course not. Better not keep him waiting," and Amelia almost ran from the room.

All the way downstairs, she wracked her brains for a good excuse for her behavior. Amelia did not relish telling a lie to her parents, but the alternative was to tell the truth and she would never do that to Julia. Bad enough that one of them would be in disgrace. It would not do for two of them to be there. Papa would expect it from Amelia—she was always in one scrape or another—but if he thought she had led the usually circumspect Julia astray, Amelia shuddered at what he might say to that. No, it would be better to keep the truth hidden and tell him some Banbury tale about hearing of a foal, or kittens to see. Yes. Kittens would do nicely. He knew she never could resist kittens.

He was waiting at the door for her, which wasn't usual. Normally, he would summon her, then sit behind his big, walnut desk, watching her with a stare that managed to convey both disappointment and exasperation. Standing in the hall, ready to usher her in, did not bode well. She swallowed, hard.

Papa waved her in and shut the door behind her with a decisive click. At the same moment, Mama leapt from her chair as if the seat had caught fire, her face mottled with fury. "How could you? How...?" Her lip trembled. "I never took you for a stupid gel, Amelia Jane Bell. How could you?"

"Mama..." began Amelia, but Papa stepped between them, and his fierce glare silenced her.

"Please sit, Letitia," he said to Mama. His voice was soft but brooked no argument. Mama set her chin to show her displeasure at the command, but she sat down. Then Papa turned to Amelia. He did not offer her a seat. Instead, she stood in the middle of his Aubusson rug, as she had done on so many other occasions over the years, her hands clasped demurely at her waist while she waited for him to tell her how dissatisfied he was with her behavior.

"I have informed your mother that you visited the stable," he said. His tone remained the same flat baritone, never wavering or showing any emotion. Amelia felt his disapprobation more keenly for the calm way he served it up.

Now was the time to deliver her excuse. Mentally apologizing for her untruthfulness, and promising God she would be as well-behaved as she possibly could be from now on, she began: "I had it from Caroline Walker that there were kittens…" It was not a lie, exactly, for her friend had told her about a litter of kittens born in the stable at the Golden Goose. However, that had been last August and the misdirection lay heavy on Amelia's stomach. If the truth had not been far worse, and involved Julia, Amelia would have confessed all.

"Do not insult my intelligence!" Papa hissed.

Amelia closed her mouth. Not kittens, then. Which meant she was truly in trouble, because if Papa was in no mood to accept her desire to visit baby animals, he would certainly not be in the mood to look kindly on the truth, even if she did feel free to relate it.

"You were not alone in the stable, Amelia," he accused.

She closed her eyes. He must have seen the stranger follow her inside. Would he believe their meeting unplanned and innocent? Of course he would! Not only was that part true, but Papa knew Amelia was no light-skirted dolly mop. Of all her misadventures—and there had been many, she had to confess—none had ever involved loose morals. She would not have Papa think such a thing!

And what of her rescuer? He had merely tried to play the gallant. He did not deserve to be forced into marrying her because she could not behave properly. Nor did she want a husband under such circumstances. When Amelia wed, she hoped it would be for love, or at least mutual attraction. And while she could not deny she had found him more than passably attractive, he had shown no sign of reciprocating. Indeed, if he had thought anything at all, it was that she was an annoying little schoolgirl who should know better. She could still feel the sting of his rebuke: *If I may be so bold, Miss Bell, you would be wise in future to be a little more careful when going about unaccompanied.*"

No. She would not marry him, no matter what Papa said.

Another thought occurred to her then. The stranger wouldn't offer for her anyway. He would simply tell Papa what had happened in the stable. The possibility of that was even more horrifying. Papa was angry enough when he believed she had been unchaperoned in company with a gentleman. If he learned she had really been alone with a lout like Abe Sutton, or that Julia was in any way involved… Amelia had to persuade Papa, and quickly, that all was well and he had no cause for concern.

Before she could say anything, however, her father continued his lecture, his voice taking on a hard edge she rarely heard him use. "Over the years," he said, "I have had to warn you more than once about your propensity for inappropriate behavior. It is by God's grace alone that you have reached eight-and-ten years of age without causing a catastrophe too terrible for repair. Far too often, I have pulled you from situations into which you have rushed headlong with not a thought for the consequences, especially when it comes to your reputation and the reputations of your sisters."

Mama sobbed, pulled her handkerchief from her reticule, and wiped the end of her nose. Amelia swallowed and lowered her eyes.

"I have always given you the benefit of the doubt," Papa went on. "Scolded you for your carelessness but believed in the purity of your intentions—SILENCE!"

He yelled the word as Amelia looked up at him and opened her mouth to speak. She closed it again, firmly.

"I have been lenient with you, time and again. Some might say lax. I have made allowances for your age and inexperience. You, however, have seen fit to interpret my kindness as weakness, and that I cannot allow."

Ashamed, Amelia fixed her gaze on the top of his expansive desk. The dark wood shone, a contrast to the matte green leather that covered the center. A blotter sat on the leather, along with an inkwell and pens, although no papers were in sight. Like his emotions, Papa rarely left his papers carelessly in view.

Now though, his emotions were all too clear.

He sat down in the captain's chair behind his desk, leaned forward, and steepled his fingers in front of his face. "Look at me, girl," he demanded.

Reluctantly, Amelia did so. His return stare chilled her to the bone.

A minute went by. Then he demanded, "What were you doing in the stable?"

Mama began to weep louder. Papa's eyes flickered to her, then back to Amelia. "I am waiting."

"I am sorry, Papa." It was not the answer he wanted, but it was the only one Amelia could give. She could not tell him the truth, even if he threatened her with the thrashing which, she supposed, she thoroughly deserved. She *had* been reckless with her reputation, and she *had* deceived her parents. But she could not tell Papa that without making things far, far worse. If he learned the truth, what Abe Sutton had done to Julia, what he had tried to do to her… If the shock did not kill Papa, he might well hang for what he did to Abe.

And under no circumstances whatsoever would she

bring trouble to the feet of the strange gentleman who had helped her. She clutched her hands in front of her waist and hoped against hope that he would have left the region before Papa had a chance to seek him out.

The thought of never seeing him again made her feel hollow inside. Which was ridiculous, she told herself, sternly. Why, she did not even know his name. It was absurd to imagine she could be bereft by his departure. For goodness' sake! She was acting like one of those hysterical females she and Julia had always scoffed over at the Assembly Rooms. She took a deep breath, pushed away all thoughts of the stranger, and concentrated on what Papa was saying.

"You're sorry." Papa's voice was dangerously quiet as he repeated her comment. "You are sorry. Is that all you have to say to the matter?" His lips thinned into a grim line and his eyes were chips of ice. "You have not only jeopardized your own good name," he continued, in the same low monotone, "but the names of your blameless sisters. You have broken your mother's heart and disappointed me. And all you can say is you're sorry?" He sat back in his chair and studied her, the way he might have studied some particularly nasty bug.

Amelia wanted to lower her own gaze, to look at anything but Papa. She did not dare.

Then he revealed his full hand. "Not only did I see you leave the stable in a state of disarray, I also saw the Sutton boy come out a few minutes before you did."

Mama cried a little louder. Papa clicked his tongue and rolled his eyes in annoyance at her.

Amelia closed her eyes in despair. She, who had always prided herself for her quick wit and ability to think on her feet, could not see how she could resolve this tangle.

"You were always a headstrong miss, Amelia," Papa went on. "As your parent, I must shoulder some of the blame for that. I am aware that I have indulged you and your sisters until you feel entitled to do exactly as you please, and the repercussions go hang. I should have reined you in—I SAID SILENCE! And I warn you, I shall not say it again."

Amelia's protest died on her lips.

"I have been remiss," he said, "and now I must hope it is not too late to rectify matters." He glanced over at Mama again. Amelia risked a look for herself. Mama sat, eyes closed, cheeks wet and the tip of her nose pink. She had crumpled her handkerchief inside a tightly held fist.

"There will be no Season for you this year," said Papa.

Mama flinched. Amelia turned sharply back to him. Surely, she had not heard him correctly.

"Don't look at me like that," he continued. "You cannot have thought I would allow you to go to London to bring yet more disgrace on the family name. It is bad enough that you run wild here in Rotherton, where people have always known you and, happily, have been inclined to excuse and tolerate you. The *beau monde* is not as forgiving."

Horror filled Amelia. He could not mean it. He would not do such a thing to her. He could not!

"You have nobody to blame but yourself," he told her. Another sob escaped Mama. Papa pursed his lips and glared at her. "Madam, it is no use you becoming a watering pot. My mind is made up. I will write to cancel the lease on the town house."

"No!" Amelia did not even realize she had said the

word aloud until he turned his attention back to her. She winced at the anger in his eyes.

"You should have thought of the consequences before you carried on a dalliance with that young man."

"But I didn't. Please, Papa…"

"I will not risk your behavior sullying the names of your sisters. Julia and Louisa deserve to arrive in town, in their turn, without people talking behind their hands and expecting them to fail."

"That will not happen, Papa, I promise…"

Papa held up his hand to stop the flow of her words. Amelia stared at him, her eyes pleading where her speech dare not.

"I have said all I intend to say," he said. "The subject is closed." He stood and walked to the tiny table in the corner, on which stood a decanter full of brandy, along with two rummers. He poured himself a drink and swallowed it, quickly. If Amelia had needed to ask how upset he truly was, that action made it plain. Papa always sipped his brandy, savoring it. To do otherwise now… There would be no point in speaking further with him this day.

Mama clearly believed it behooved her to try, though. "Amelia will not find a husband if she is not put in the way of eligible gentlemen," she said, her voice watery. She dabbed at her wet cheeks.

"Then you must put her in the way of such gentlemen here at home."

Such as whom? Amelia longed to shout the words at him, but she bit her tongue and tried to think of any gentlemen who lived in this area. Most were already married, betrothed, or expected to make offers soon.

An image of the man at the Golden Goose came into

her mind. He was a gentleman, well-mannered and courageous from what she had seen, and there was no question he was handsome. He appealed very much to the romantic side of Amelia's nature. But was he eligible? For aught she knew, the man was travelling to join his wife and six children. Besides, he was staying at the inn. By definition, he was not likely to remain there for more than a day, hardly long enough to interest him in a courtship. Mentally, she crossed him from her list.

Which left only three gentlemen whose proximity, unmarried state, and status in life made them even possible as candidates. Unfortunately, not one of them seemed, to Amelia, suitable.

Firstly, there was Mr. Burgess, the curate. He was socially her equal, but he was a man of such fastidiousness, such a *precise* character, Amelia made no doubt they would make each other miserable within a week. She would sooner die an old maid than marry such a man.

Then, there was Lord Rotherton. An earl, he was well respected in the area. He had wit and verve, and was very likeable. But, rumor had it, he had sworn to die a bachelor and said his life was far too well ordered to let a woman interfere with it. Which only left...

"There is Mr. Summersby," said Mama, and she turned to Papa, new hope shining in her eyes. "He is to be a viscount, and he is not the worst of catches."

Papa raised an eyebrow. Amelia didn't know if he was surprised at Mama's comment, or skeptical. She hoped he was unenthusiastic. Amelia certainly was. There was something about Mr. Summersby she could not like. She would sooner marry the curate!

"I watched him today," continued Mama, oblivious

to both Papa's skepticism and Amelia's horror. "He was most definitely looking at you with interest, Amelia. If we can put you in his way a little more, we may bring him up to scratch quite soon. Don't shake your head and gape like a fish, child. He is unexceptionable, a gentleman, and of good family." She nodded in agreement with herself. "Under the circumstances I feel he would do you nicely."

Amelia looked from Mama, who was pleased with herself for coming up with such a solution so quickly, to Papa, who looked nonplussed at the turn the conversation had taken.

Amelia's bottom lip trembled. "May I be excused?" She barely waited for Papa's nod before she all but ran from the room.

An hour later, she sat on the window seat in her bedchamber, staring out at the winter-bare garden. Her eyes were hot and swollen, her head ached fiercely, and her cheeks itched from her tears. She could not say which had upset her more, the cancellation of her Season or Mama's plans for Mr. Summersby. Both were disastrous.

Amelia had looked forward to going to London. She didn't necessarily dream of finding a husband in her first Season, although she knew she should. That someone would offer for her was, she had thought, a given. That she should make a good marriage had, up to this time, exercised Mama's mind much more than her own. Her own eagerness had been for other things entirely. She had longed for the parties and glittering balls she'd heard so much about, and dreamed of dining with aristocrats and other sophisticates, visiting the theatre, and promenading in Hyde Park in the fashionable hour.

All things that were now lost to her. Fresh tears started.

There was a small scratching on her chamber door, and then it opened slowly, tentatively.

"Amelia?" asked Julia, softly. Amelia sniffed. Julia ran across the room and folded her older sister into a firm embrace. "I am so sorry," she said. "I will go to Papa. If I explain to him…"

"No! You must not!"

"But if he knew the truth—"

"It would not help me. It would make things worse."

Julia shook her head. "I cannot let you fully take the blame."

"You can, and you will." Amelia knew she must convince her sister she was right, before the silly goose got herself into trouble. So she grinned too brightly and said, "Papa expects high spirits from me. Which means, when it comes to my behavior, his disapprobation does not last long. But if he suspected that my wildness had in some way infected you, his anger would be far deeper. I assure you, Julia, you cannot do anything but make this situation worse by confessing your part in it."

"But…your Season…"

Amelia shrugged. "The Season does not begin properly for a few weeks yet. Mayhap I can persuade Papa to change his mind. If I can show him I can be the model daughter…" Her mind turned the idea over, examining it from all angles. It might actually succeed. If she could show Papa that she had learned her lesson and could now be the obedient, well-behaved daughter he wanted her to be, he might agree to allow her a Season after all.

What did she have to lose by trying?

"I can behave like a proper lady," she mused. "I can be quiet and obedient to Mama and Papa."

Julia raised a skeptical eyebrow. "Obedient? You? And pigs fly in the air with their tails forward."

Amelia sniffed, disdainfully and determined to prove she could do it.

Chapter Six

Lord Rotherton bade Josh sit in a chair pulled close to the fireplace in his sitting room. Small flames played merrily over the logs and made the room smell pleasantly of pine. A lamp sat on a table beside the earl's own chair, a book beside it.

"Brandy?" he offered.

"I am sorry," said Josh, gesturing at the book. "I have disturbed your peace."

"Preserved it, rather." Rotherton smiled, ruefully. "I cannot imagine what possessed me to pick the wretched tome up. Mayhap I felt I needed to be punished for some great wrong I have done."

Josh laughed. "What the devil are you reading?"

Rotherton picked up the book and held it for Josh to take. "It's called *Mellincourt*, and it is written by one Thomas Love Peacock. Heaven knows, his first work was bad enough. But this one plumbs new depths. 'Tis supposed to be satire. It deserves to be sat upon."

"If you disliked the first so much, why bother with the second?"

"An excellent question." Rotherton walked over to the tantalus and poured two rummers of brandy. "My aunt sent it as a gift this Christmas. Next time I see her, she will, undoubtedly, ask if I have read it, and I have always found it difficult to lie to her." He handed one glass to Josh and took the other to his seat. He flicked up his coat tails, sat, and crossed one knee over the other. His pose was elegantly lazy, but Josh was not fooled. Rotherton's indolent air had always hidden a keen mind and a preparedness for action.

"Let us hope she doesn't ask if you enjoyed it, then."

"Hmm." Rotherton eyed the book with distaste, then smiled at Josh. "It is very good to see you again," he said. "Although your reappearance in the area is a surprise. I had heard you were in India."

"I was." Josh sipped the brandy. It was smooth and mellow, and much too high quality for the earl to have paid excise on it. "This is good. I have missed it."

Rotherton frowned. "They have brandy in India, surely?"

"Not like this." Josh took another sip. "I arrived in England yesterday," he said. "I reached Frantham four or five hours ago."

"To find much changed, I'll warrant."

"That's putting it mildly." He sipped his drink again, shook his head, and grinned ruefully. "Imagine my astonishment when I arrived, albeit clandestinely, at the manor and discovered I was already here."

Rotherton chuckled. "A truly shocking moment, I make no doubt."

Josh's smile faded. "I understand you've met him?"

"I have. He seems a pleasant enough fellow, if one speaks to him alone. But he travels everywhere in company with two friends. They are harder to like in themselves, and they seem to make a great change in his affability, too."

"Perhaps I am unreasonable," answered Josh, "but I find myself disposed to dislike Mr. Summersby, no matter how affable he may be. I don't believe I enjoy being impersonated."

Rotherton flicked an imaginary piece of lint from his pristine trousers. "He is very convincing. I've known you since we were both in short coats, yet I confess, he fooled me for a time."

Josh gave Rotherton a flat look.

"Hell, Josh, even your own father was not completely sure it was not you at first."

Josh raised his chin, defiantly. "I do not see we are that much alike."

"You've seen him then?"

"From a distance. Nothing about him reminded me one whit of the face I see in the mirror every day. Oh, I grant you, the man is as tall as me, and of a similar build. He has dark hair. But there, I would argue, the similarities end."

Rotherton nodded. "I see that now, when you sit across from me. Studied in close proximity, the differences between you are obvious. But remember, my friend, nobody in this neighborhood has set eyes on you in what? Fifteen years?"

"Fourteen."

"Half a lifetime, Josh. You were little more than a boy when you left. Now you're a full-grown man. People change drastically between one state and the other."

Josh grimaced. "Hicks knew me immediately."

Rotherton raised his rummer. "A toast to Hicks. He always did have a wonderful eye for detail."

The toast made Josh smile again, and reduced the tension that had filled the room. "I suspect you were not fooled long, either. What tipped you the wink?"

"What indeed?" Rotherton sat back and watched the firelight make his brandy gleam a dull orange. "He is good, Josh. As good as any actor treading the boards in Drury Lane. And, no matter what you may have to say to it, he does have the look of you. Do not scoff. It's not unknown to find people who resemble others. I understand the Prussians even have a word for it: *doppelganger*."

Josh sighed and rolled his eyes.

"However," continued Rotherton, "close though the resemblance may be, there is one small feature he overlooked and probably was never even aware of, if truth be known." He pointed to the small cleft in the center of his own chin. "The scar you have, here."

Involuntarily, Josh's hand went to his face and his fingers stroked the thin, white line in his skin. About half an inch long, and the width of a thread, it was the legacy of an afternoon spent with Rotherton, doing what they should not be doing while their tutors searched frantically for them. The skin had renewed itself many times in the years since, until Josh could barely feel the raised line where his beard always faltered.

"I gave you that scar when we were eight years old," said Rotherton. "You still bore it the last time I saw you, when we were, what? Eight-and-ten? I found it difficult to believe that, having stayed with you for ten years, it would have completely vanished by now."

"It's still here."

"And Mr. Summersby does not share it." Both men were silent for several seconds. Rotherton stared into the fire. Josh studied his brandy and wondered what would come next.

Finally, Rotherton downed the rest of his drink, put his glass beside the book on the table, and stood. He rested his foot on the edge of the hearth and his hand on the mantel, and watched the flames. "I fear for your father," he said, quietly.

"So do I." Josh put down his own glass and stood beside his friend. "Thank you for attending him these last few months. If Hicks is to be believed, your visits have probably saved his life."

"I cannot prove anything," said Rotherton, grimacing his frustration, "but I believe these are dangerous men. They play long and deep, but I have been unable to discover what, exactly, is their game."

Josh stared at the flames licking the pine wood in the hearth. "Once I discovered the duplicity, I wanted to march up to them and have it out with the imposter."

"I am glad you did not." Rotherton chewed at his bottom lip as he thought. "Josh, could you hold off revealing your identity? I understand it is a lot to ask, but I have my reasons."

Josh pursed his lips. "My father is trapped in that house, Rotherton, with what could well turn out to be a nest of venomous vipers."

"If I could have removed him, believe me, I would have done so. But I feared it was impossible without putting him at even greater risk. Instead, we resolved— Hicks, Mrs. Hargreaves, and myself—to ensure he was never left alone, while I endeavor to gather the evidence I need."

"Evidence of what?"

"I don't know." Rotherton picked up a poker and thrust it into the fire. The half-burned wood cracked, releasing red sparks which flew up the chimney to freedom. "I have been watching them for months now, Josh. But they are clever. There is, undoubtedly, something havey-cavey going on, but for the life of me,

I cannot discover it. Until I have an inkling, I am helpless. I cannot go charging in to one of the foremost houses in Sussex and accuse the heir to a viscount of nefarious deeds based on a feeling in my water."

"He is not the heir to a viscount."

"Before this evening, my only proof of that was my memory of a small, ancient scar. The rest of the neighborhood has accepted him. I could not raise my doubts on such flimsy evidence."

"You have stronger evidence now."

"Do I?" Rotherton turned to study Josh. "Why did you not confront the imposter today?"

Josh held Rotherton's stare for a few moments, then nodded, slowly, conceding that he, too, could not yet prove Mr. Summersby's perfidy. "What do we do?"

"We bide our time, hold our tongues, and watch." Rotherton patted Josh's shoulder. "To do otherwise might cause them to bolt."

An image of his father came to Josh's mind, old and frail, and in need of rescue. "Would that not be a good thing?" he asked. "If they are gone, they're gone."

"And we will never discover exactly what it is they plan to do. We also won't have the names of all involved." Rotherton met Josh's gaze, his own eyes pleading. "There is more to this confection than just Summersby, Sykes, and Harcourt. Over the past months, there have been a fair number of comings and goings and, although I have been unable to ascertain what they are about, I am sure there is something of great import in the wind. I need to find out what it is." He grinned, slyly. "What say you to helping me?"

Josh shook his head. "I have no experience of investigating crime. Especially when I don't even know what crime to look for." Rotherton raised an eyebrow, and Josh continued, "What could I do, anyway?"

"I have men watching the manor, but they must, of necessity, observe from a distance. They note the comings and goings, of course..." He grinned. "Which was why I was not particularly surprised when you called here this evening."

"Don't try to cozen me. Very little has ever taken you in surprise."

Rotherton laughed, then immediately sobered. "But to the point. My men cannot gain entrance to the house itself. And if they could, they would not know where to begin their search, or what to look for. They might see something as suspicious that a person who knows the house intimately would discard, and vice versa, wasting valuable time. You, however, know the house well."

Josh could not deny that.

"You would certainly be the best man for the job. The most likely to succeed. Not only will you see what is out of place, but should discovery be threatened, you know better than anyone else the best way to conceal yourself. You cannot tell me you have forgotten every hidden corner?"

Josh pondered Rotherton's words. It was true he was more than capable of carrying out this task, especially now Hicks had shown him a secret access that was a lot less likely to be discovered than the ways Josh had used in his childhood. Perhaps he could discover what the imposter and his cronies were about, put paid to their scheme, rescue Father, and take his own rightful place.

"One more thing," said Rotherton. "How to explain your presence here. We can hardly tell the world and his wife that you are Joshua Summersby, heir to Viscount

Frantham, when that gentleman is already sitting pretty, can we?"

"From the gleam in your eye, I surmise you have a solution." It was not a question. Josh was sure Rotherton had had all the details in place before he gave voice to the plan.

Nothing changes, thought Josh. As boys, it had always been Rotherton who led the pack. He thought up the wild schemes, built and developed them and made them whole, then dragged Josh, and others, into them. Although, to be fair, they hadn't needed much persuasion to follow him.

"Where are you staying?" asked Rotherton, cutting into Josh's nostalgia.

"At the Goose."

Rotherton shook his head. "No, you're not. You shall stay here. After all, I could hardly deny hospitality to my own cousin."

"Cousin?" Josh stared at him, one eyebrow raised.

"Second. Once removed."

"How very precise."

Rotherton waved a hand, dismissively. "One cannot be too careful. Too many people know I have but one first cousin, and you are not he."

"So, who am I, *dear cousin?*" Josh sat and crossed one knee over the other.

"You are Joshua Winter, the son of my father's late cousin, one Mr. Henry Winter of Lewes."

Josh nodded, sagely. "Your father had a very convenient cousin."

"Don't be difficult." Rotherton sighed. "It is best if we stay as close to the truth as we can. So, you are Mr. Joshua Winter, returning after several years in India. You might wish to be vague on how many years but you will be staying with me for a few weeks while you reacquaint yourself with English society. That story should allow you to move freely without attracting too much speculation."

Josh nodded. "In which case, Cousin, I will go to the inn, pay my shot, and collect my valise."

"And on the morrow," said Rotherton, "I will make you known to my neighbors, so we may cut off their curiosity before it begins to take root."

Chapter Seven

The next morning, Rotherton and Josh visited several of their neighbors. It was a very English winter's morning, the grass still white with unmelted frost, though it was now close to midday. A golden haze softened the outlines of bare-branched trees and rough stone walls. Cattle moved slowly through the field, their breath steaming, while sheep, thick with wool and fat with unborn lambs, wandered between them, chewing at the grass. Ice clung to the rutted mud in the road and made the shallow puddles solid. Josh realized with a start that he had missed this whole place more than he had known.

India had been good to him, and after his father had exiled him Josh had thought to stay there for the rest of his life. But just two days back in England and he knew he had been fooling himself. India was not home and never would be. This was home, and as he rode, he grew more and more determined nobody would take it from him ever again.

After taking tea at several of the finer households in the area, they eventually rode into Rotherton to visit Mr. and Mrs. Bell.

"Mrs. Bell is a very sociable woman," explained Rotherton, "and she has the ear of every gossip from here to Tunbridge Wells. Between her and Mrs. Maynard at Houseberry, I guarantee that, by this evening, nobody will be in any doubt that you are my cousin. Your reason for being in the neighborhood will not be questioned for an instant."

She also has a lovely daughter whose acquaintance I don't mind making. Josh said nothing aloud. Rotherton was far too perceptive to take any comment at face value, and he did not think Miss Bell would appreciate their encounter made known to any of her neighbors, even one as discreet as Lord Rotherton.

The Bells lived in an impressive house in the heart of the village. Set back from the road, it had a well-kept front garden, where dormant rose bushes sat in beautifully raked beds of dark soil. Marble steps led up from the garden path to a large, glossily painted front door.

They were shown into an opulent morning room. The walls were covered in cream and gold silk, and those colors were echoed in the upholstery on the sofas, easy chairs, and chaises longues scattered in studied abandon about the room. Small walnut tables were dotted around the floor, most of them covered in porcelain knick-knacks. A fire glowed in a large fireplace, its marble mantel covered with more knick-knacks, most of which seemed to be stylized shepherds and shepherdesses. Beside the fireplace was a coal scuttle designed to look like a cabinet, its intricately patterned wood beautifully polished, and a tantalus sat in the corner.

Mr. Bell entered, apologizing that his wife and daughters would be a few moments longer. He offered them drinks and they sat in the well-padded chairs. Mr. Bell studied Josh carefully for a moment, then said, "I have seen you somewhere before, sir."

Had the man seen Josh leave the stable after his daughter? For an instant, Josh froze. Would the man condemn him for his behavior? Eject him from the house? Or worse, seek to force him into a marriage?

Josh was not in the market for a wife. For one thing, he needed to concentrate all his efforts on the goings on at Frantham Manor and had no time to spend on other considerations. And even if the problems at home were not pressing, he would not think of taking an Englishwoman like Miss Bell to wife. Josh fully intended to return to India once the mystery at Frantham was resolved, and India was not an ideal climate for a softly bred young lady whose constitution and complexion knew nothing more harsh than the mild climate of southern England.

A picture of Miss Bell sprang into his mind: an attractive young woman with a mass of blonde curls and a mouth that smiled even when she was mired in adversity. He had the suspicion there was a great deal more to the lady than her pretty face, though. That she did not wilt in the face of danger, he already knew, and there was a lively intelligence in her eyes that suggested her company would never be dull. A few years in India, however, and she would be sallow and wan, bitter and resentful, desperate to return to England at the first opportunity. He had seen it so often in the ladies of Madras. They enjoyed their husbands' wealth and position, but they would have enjoyed it more from the drawing rooms of London. Many a man was pressured into returning to the old country when by himself he would have stayed. That would not happen to Josh. He took a deep breath and steeled himself to withstand the man's angry demands.

Mr. Bell, however, was not angry at all. "I remember now," he said, amiably. "You were in the Goose. We pipped you to the private parlor."

Josh relaxed a little. He shrugged his shoulders and tried to seem nonchalant. "It was of no matter. Better I ate in the public bar than your ladies did."

Mr. Bell nodded his agreement. Rotherton watched Josh with narrowed eyes.

To Josh's relief, the door opened and Mrs. Bell glided in, followed by not one but three young women. The gentlemen stood to welcome them.

"May I present my daughters," said Mr. Bell, proudly. "Amelia, Julia, and Louisa, this is Mr. Winter, Lord Rotherton's cousin." From the corner of his eye, Josh saw the two younger sisters curtsey prettily, but his attention was really on Amelia, and he saw the instant she recognized him. Her eyes widened just a fraction, then her face became blank and she too curtseyed before she sat beside her sisters on a sofa, smile pinned into place and hands demurely clasped in her lap.

Josh took his lead from her. If she would rather they acted as if they had never set eyes on each other before, so be it. He sat down and made polite conversation with all three young ladies.

Louisa was clearly the youngest. Josh guessed she was not yet sixteen years of age, with the chubbiness of childhood still in her pretty face. Her wheat blonde hair hung in ringlets over her shoulders and her clothes were more suited to the schoolroom than a fashionable drawing room. She had a propensity to giggle which she tried, in vain, to control, and she glanced at her mother several times, as if she were worried about committing some dreadful faux pas.

The middle daughter, Julia, was beautiful. Her face was classically shaped, with almond-shaped eyes the color of the clear blue shallows behind the coral reefs in the Indian islands, and hair the color of the golden sands on their shores. Josh foresaw a queue of eligible bachelors outside their home when that young lady had her Season.

However, to his way of thinking, the lovely Julia could not hold a candle to her older sister. True, Amelia Bell was not a classic beauty, and she would never be a diamond of the first water. Her nose tilted a little bit more than it should, and her mouth was too wide, the corners curved permanently into a delectable smile instead of forming the rosebud shape Society prized. Which just went to prove that Society did not know a rare treasure when it appeared amongst them.

He watched her as closely as he dared without drawing the attention of her parents. She did not look at him. Instead, she kept her head slightly bowed, her eyes lowered, and her conversation quiet. In fact, he noted with disappointment, she was a pattern card of the ladies to be found in any Mayfair drawing room. Of the woman who had been so indomitable in the stable, there was no sign.

Josh felt the disappointment keenly. The quiet little mice he had met during his one foray into London Society, and those he'd encountered at social events in India, had bored him. Most of them had more hair than wit, and they performed like trained monkeys, saying and doing only what their mothers had taught them.

Fourteen years ago, as the son of a viscount, Josh had had to dodge the London ladies and their scheming mamas. He was supposed to have been studying at university, but the promise of London's delights had been too much to resist, so he and his friends had sneaked out of Oxford and headed for the capital. Free of their leashes, they had run a little wilder than they had intended, losing most of their money to card sharps in the worst gaming hells before finding solace in the arms of willing—and educational—females.

Josh had only managed to attend a couple of respectable evenings of entertainment before his father found him and dragged him home. Secretly, Josh had been relieved, for that time in London had been more than enough to knock the gilt off the gingerbread for him. Left to his own devices, he would have learned from the experience and been a better man next time.

Instead, the week changed his life. He was berated, then disowned by an unforgiving father who, it seemed, cared more for his spotless reputation than for his youngest son. Now, with the benefit of hindsight, Josh realized Father had done him the greatest of favors. Had he not been forced to make his way in the world, he might have wasted his life, drifting aimlessly through London's drawing rooms until he found a debutante he could tolerate, and married her. That would have been a disaster. He would have been bored beyond reason within a week, and driven to drink inside a month.

In India, where he had been a nobody unworthy of their attentions, Josh was safe from the machinations of the eligible ladies. He had, however, watched them chase others. He'd seen the lengths some went to in order to ensnare their prey. It had made him wary; as his own fortune grew, he had done all he could to keep it quiet, living modestly, maintaining the outward impression that he was not a person of interest. It had worked, and he had survived where so many others had fallen.

It might have been different had his feelings become

engaged. Fortunately, the situation had never arisen. Not one of those young ladies, wilting in darkened rooms, sipping tea, and being cooled by wallahs barely old enough to hold the fans they wafted, had so much as given him pause.

Yesterday, though, Amelia Bell had seemed different. Her behavior had been regrettable, he could not deny that. But it had also been refreshing. Her courage and tenacity were beyond doubt, for he knew that, had he not happened along, the young lady would have fought tooth and nail for herself. She may not have had the strength to defeat a determined attacker, but Sutton would not have walked away scot free, either.

And then, her manner when she stood up to the bullying constable! The indomitable Miss Bell had been prepared to risk her good name and her reputation rather than allow Sutton to make life difficult for a chance-met stranger.

Today, though, her vivacity was conspicuous by its absence. Josh felt its loss keenly.

****

"That should do the trick," said Rotherton half an hour later, as they rode away from the Bell family's home. "Mr. Winter has well and truly come to stay."

"All untoward interest in him successfully averted," added Josh.

"Can't say I'm so certain of that. You are a new face in a very small social circle. People are bound to be curious. But they won't speculate on your identity, or jeopardize the investigation." He gave Josh a considered look. "I did not realize you had met the Bell family before."

"I hadn't. Our paths crossed when we were in the

same place at the same time, nothing more."

Rotherton nodded. "Miss Bell is a delight, do you not think?"

Yes, she is. "They all are," Josh said, carefully.

"But Miss Amelia was known to you already, I believe." Rotherton faced forward, as if he needed to concentrate on where he was going. Josh was not fooled. He knew the earl was marking every move he made, every expression on his face.

"We had never been introduced before today," Josh said, carefully keeping his answer truthful.

A long moment of silence. Then Rotherton grinned. "After nuncheon," he announced, "I intend to visit Frantham Manor. Are you ready to begin your search?"

Josh nodded. "I should like to see my father," he said. "I suppose it is not possible?"

Rotherton's face softened. "I do not think it a good idea at the moment, no."

"You believe he may give away my presence." It was not a question, but a reluctant acceptance of the truth. Papa's weakness meant he could no longer be relied upon to keep secrets.

"He may do," allowed Rotherton. "It is true he no longer seems to have full control of his faculties."

Josh winced, and felt a sharp pain in his chest to hear the truth so baldly spoken.

"But that is not my reason for saying no," continued Rotherton. "For the past year, I have been used to go to visit Frantham alone. I did not take Neville with me when he stayed last autumn, and he is my *first* cousin, and presumed heir. I fear it would raise questions if I suddenly insisted on bringing my more distant *second* cousin."

Josh sighed. "You're right, of course. You shall go to the front door and visit my father, alone. I will enter the house via the crypt and, God willing, remain hidden."

"You will need to show me this passageway from the crypt."

Josh looked his friend up and down, skeptically. "In those clothes?"

Rotherton glanced down at himself, then at Josh, mock offence in his eyes. "Are you saying I am a peacock, Joshua Sum… Winter?"

"If the tail feathers fit," chuckled Josh.

"I am beginning to remember why I disliked you, sir." Rotherton's nose went up a notch, which made Josh laugh all the more.

Chapter Eight

Amelia's father retreated to his study after Lord Rotherton and his cousin left. Julia dashed over to the morning room window and peered out at the disappearing visitors.

"Julia!" Mama was horrified. She glared at Amelia, as if this were somehow her fault. Amelia bit the inside of her lip to stop her anger, and said nothing.

"Mr. Winter is an exceedingly handsome gentleman, do you not think?" asked Julia. She turned and flashed a mischievous grin at Amelia. Amelia stared at her sister. Did the minx know more than she should? Had Amelia somehow given herself away? Or had Mr. Winter done something to betray her? Heat pricked her cheeks. Julia grinned, triumphantly.

Louisa giggled and ran to join Julia at the window.

"Goodness, child!" scolded Mama, and she moved forward to pull her errant daughters away. Thankfully, dealing with Julia and Louisa put her back to Amelia, which meant she did not see the telltale blush. Amelia took several deep breaths and willed a calm demeanor to return.

"What do you two know of handsome gentlemen?" continued Mama. "Come and sit down, and behave like the ladies you are supposed to be." She ushered her girls away.

"He sits his horse well," remarked Julia, with one

last glance over her shoulder.

Was her sister trying to give Mama an apoplexy? If so, she seemed to be succeeding. Amelia watched with alarm as their mother's face turned a deep, dark shade of red as she sputtered, "That is the outside of enough! Sit!"

Julia wiped the smile from her face and trooped back to the sofa. Reluctantly, Louisa followed her, and both girls sat and listened dutifully while Mama deplored their lack of manners.

Amelia drifted into her own thoughts until the scolding no longer penetrated them. She could still see Mama gesticulating and talking animatedly, but she was out of focus and indistinct, a minor distraction.

Julia was right. Mr. Winter was handsome. Amelia had thought him so yesterday, in the dim stable. In the full light of the morning room, he was dazzling. He was tall, with broad shoulders and a solid chest that suggested this was no idle fop, but a man who was prepared to work. His dark tan also spoke to long hours outside in the sunshine. His hair curled over the collar of his coat. She had thought it ebony dark yesterday, but now she could see layers of mahogany and gold there, too. Today, his eyes were more green than brown, and they sparkled with a hint of mischief that drew her to him in a way she had never been drawn to anyone before.

Not that anything could come of that. Though he had been civil today, her behavior in the stables yesterday must surely have given the man a disgust of her that would prove fatal to any friendship between them— other than the kind Amelia would never want. It did not make her feel better to realize this was entirely her own fault.

Had she but known the gentleman would be staying

in the area, instead of passing through, never to cross her path again… But, no. Amelia was too honest to say that knowing his connections would have made her behave any differently. Abraham Sutton had held the power to hurt her sister, and Amelia was duty-bound to protect her. And although she regretted that Mr. Winter had witnessed her fall from grace, she consoled herself with the thought that it really didn't matter. Like all of Lord Rotherton's guests, Mr. Winter would doubtless stay a month or so, then move on. She could endure a few weeks' embarrassment when in his company, surely? Especially since their paths would probably not cross very often.

All was not lost. After today, she was reassured that he would say nothing of their first meeting to anybody else. She was also certain Papa did not know Mr. Winter had been present in the stable or he would never have allowed the man over the threshold. Which meant she could still hope to regain her Season.

Relieved, she returned her attention to the conversation going on around her in time to hear Louisa grumble about being sent back upstairs to her governess. Her youngest sister pouted and dragged her feet but, ultimately, had no choice but to obey.

Once she had gone from the room, Mama turned to Amelia and Julia. "Run upstairs and dress properly," she commanded. "We have visits to make. Our neighbors will need to know about the arrival of Lord Rotherton's relative. It is not news we can, in good conscience, keep to ourselves."

Amelia and Julia exchanged glances. Humor danced in Julia's eyes. "Do you not think the gentlemen will have visited others today, Mama?"

"Well, of course they will have called on some," agreed Mama, with a frown. "But there will be others who are missed. Time constraints will see to that. Come, come, ready yourselves."

Amelia sighed and pitied the man. Before Mama was finished, there would be an onslaught of interested mamas and adoring chits from all over the district laying siege to him. Unaccountably, that thought made her stomach churn, and a strange ache lodged in her chest. She put it down to her compassion, for what else could it be?

Mama tapped her forefinger against her lips as she thought, then grinned. "We must give a dinner to welcome him."

Amelia winced. Such a dinner would, she knew, be a disaster. The man already knew her true nature. He would, doubtless, spend the entire evening watching her closely, waiting to be entertained by her latest faux pas. Just the knowledge that he was observing her would be enough to guarantee that such a thing occurred. The compassionate ache in her chest turned into the sharp pain of humiliation and despair.

"And," Mama went on, oblivious to the fact that at least one of her daughters was less than enthusiastic about her dinner party, "we could stop two gaps with one bush if we also invited Mr. Summersby."

Julia looked askance at that. "I do not feel— comfortable in his presence, Mama."

"Why ever not, child? What on earth is there about him to discomfort you?"

Julia opened and closed her mouth several times, then seemed to accept that, whatever she said, Mama would dismiss it, so she shrugged her shoulders and said nothing.

"It is an excellent idea," decided Mama with unarguable finality. "When two such gentlemen come into the neighborhood at the same time, it is an opportunity not to be sneezed at." She narrowed her eyes, thinking. "And, it may well work in your favor, Amelia. One gentleman can be interested in a lady's company, yet say nothing, dragging his boots, as the saying goes. But when there are two gentlemen rivalling each other, the one can be more easily persuaded to come up to scratch in timely fashion. I know, from your papa, men love the thrust and cut of competition."

Amelia closed her eyes, pained by her mother's plotting.

"Of course, I have no worries that Mr. Summersby would, eventually come up to scratch," Mama went on, and then she spent some minutes extolling his virtues. He was, she asserted, more handsome and more dignified than the average gentleman. He had a better manner and his breeding was evident. He was, after all, the son of a viscount. Although just a plain mister now, he would one day have a title, and Amelia could do no better than to encourage him.

Amelia groaned inwardly. Oh, Mr. Summersby was personable enough. He was gentleman-like in his ways, never rude, even in the face of the clearly unwanted attentions he received from Mama. His politeness marked him as different to his friends, who always left Amelia feeling that her family were nuisances whenever their paths crossed. He was also always impeccably turned out, and he looked every inch the respectable member of Society that he was. But still, there was *something…*

"So," said Mama, who had obviously continued speaking while Amelia gathered wool. "After visiting our friends, we will call at Frantham Manor. Having seen Mr. Summersby only yesterday, Amelia, you will be much in his thoughts, I make no doubt. One should always be prepared to press such an advantage."

Amelia glanced at Julia, whose expression conveyed sympathy for her sister, combined with relief that the sacrificial lamb was not to be herself.

Nor would it be Amelia, if she had anything to say to the matter. "He may be busy, Mama," she pointed out. "With his father so ill, he will have responsibilities to the estate, and…"

"La!" Mama waved a hand through the air, dismissing the argument. "He has men of business to do that for him. The estate can manage without him for an hour. Besides, we are simply doing our Christian duty, calling to enquire after his father. He cannot fault us for that. Now, wear your blue dress. It is most becoming on you. Julia, you must wear your green one. Not the mint green, the slightly darker one."

"Mama!" Julia objected. "It does not suit. It makes my skin look…" She searched for the right word. "Grubby," she finished, at last.

"For goodness' sake, girl!" Mama swatted away Julia's objection like a troublesome fly. "You do have some silly notions in your head. That dress is a pretty color, and very fetching. More importantly for this day's purpose, it is exceedingly modest. It would not do to have the gentleman's entire focus on you now, would it? You are far too young and beautiful to be throwing your future away on a mere viscount. Besides, it is only right that my oldest daughter should be matched before her younger sister."

Julia grimaced at Amelia, who bit her lip to stop the giggle her sister's expression threatened to release. Then, realizing that Mama's mind was made up and there was no use to say more, both girls left to change.

As she climbed the stairs, Amelia prayed that Mr. Summersby had no interest in her because, if he offered, she must, in all good conscience, refuse. She had a dreadful feeling Mama would not take that news well at all.

****

Josh and Rotherton parted ways just before Frantham Manor came into view. Rotherton continued along the road toward the stone pillars that marked the manor's gateway, while Josh followed a narrow track through the woods and up into the back end of the estate. He secured his horse where it was unlikely to be found and climbed the hill to the mausoleum at the crest of a small hill. Built of limestone with lead roofing, the building looked more like a tiny chapel-of-ease where the living could worship than like a final resting place for the carefully chosen dead.

The chapel door, a wide oak door studded with iron, slid open silently on well-oiled hinges, which Josh presumed was due to Hicks' diligence. Josh wondered if his father had ever realized what a wonderful asset his valet was.

Inside, the chapel was long and narrow. At the far end was a stained-glass window depicting two women weeping before an empty tomb, while a magnificent angel pointed them away from the grave. In front of that window was a rarely used altar table, a candlestick and communion plate sitting in the thick dust on the tabletop, their once gleaming beauty hidden beneath layers of grime and oxidation.

To one side of the altar was a grilled gate which, until yesterday, Josh had thought was kept locked. Just inside that gate, torches sat in sconces, waiting to be lit by whoever needed to go down the rough stone steps into the crypt where generations of Summersbys awaited the day of judgment.

Josh's boot heels rang out on the sunken flagstones, and their echo broke the still peace. A small gasp sounded, making him stop dead, every muscle tensed and ready.

A woman scrambled to her feet and away from the altar rail where she had been kneeling. She was dressed in the plain gray skirts of a housekeeper, although she seemed far too young for such a responsible position. Her hair was severely pinned beneath a neat cap that emphasized her lowly status, yet she held her head high, warily defiant. Her fingers clasped and twisted at her waistline, betraying her nervous agitation.

"Forgive me, madam," Josh said with a bow. "I did not mean to startle you."

"No, sir." Her voice was soft and mellifluous, and told Josh she had been better educated than most housekeepers would have been. She lowered her eyes, but he got the impression it was because she had remembered she ought to do so, rather than because she was humble.

"May I ask why you are here?" Ordinarily, Josh would not have cared one whit to find a person here in his family's private chapel. Hell—or rather, heck, since he was standing on consecrated ground—he would usually not have objected to finding the whole damn—

dashed—band of the Royal Sussex Regiment making use of the place. Today, however, he needed no prying eyes.

"It was peaceful," she answered his question. In her tone, he sensed an admonishment to him for destroying that peace. "I wished for somewhere to be alone with the Lord."

Josh's conscience pricked him sharply. The woman was not doing any harm here. He was a dast—a knave of the lowest order—to deprive her of the solitude she sought.

Be that as it may, he had a task to do, and he could not be seen doing it. So he hardened his heart and said, "This is private property."

The woman nodded once, accepting the truth of that. Her face paled, though, and her bottom lip gave the tiniest tremble. Josh looked away, guiltily. When this was finished, he would seek her out and invite her to use the chapel whenever she wished to do so.

For now, though, he watched and waited while she left, softly closing the door behind herself.

As soon as she had gone, he made his way through the crypt gate and down the steps, stopping only to light a torch to carry with him.

The sarcophagi of his ancestors lay in neat rows, three high, in alcoves either side of him. Josh tiptoed past them, not because he expected his footsteps to alert any living danger to his presence, but because it seemed the thing to do, a respect for the long-dead.

The last coffin still bore the sheen of newness on its wood. Josh stroked it lovingly, tracing the name of his brother on the brass plaque as he said his own, very personal goodbye, silently lamenting all the missed chances to be with Humphrey, the mistaken belief that there was plenty of time. He swallowed, patted the coffin, and made his way to the far end of the crypt.

Here, a small metal ring hung from the wall on a chain. He looked around at the shadows and darkness as if seeking out spies, then pulled on the ring. There was a low, scraping growl as the false wall moved and the hidden tunnel to the house revealed itself.

Going through the tunnel was easier today than it had been last night, although the walls were still so close together they made his heart beat wildly, and in places the roof was too low for him to stand upright. Josh had never considered himself claustrophobic, but this long, dark tunnel with no light shining at its end and no room to move his arms away from his body left his throat clogged with a fear that made him want to vomit. He thanked God for the torch in his hand, without which, he acknowledged, if only to himself, he might have turned tail and run, doubtless injuring himself badly as he hit his head on the low-hanging rocks in his panicked retreat.

Yesterday, this passageway had been draped with spider webs, so ancient they were as solid as any curtain. He had had to bat them away, sometimes hitting them two or three times before they dislodged, slowing him down enormously. Today, thankfully, the spiders had not replaced them and he could move forward without becoming sticky with gossamer, or needing to spit it out when it invaded his mouth on a careless breath.

Even without the webs, he was relieved when he climbed the steps at the far end of the tunnel and let himself into the tiny chamber behind the hearth of a disused room. He looked around, making sure there was no one to mark his entrance, hung the torch in a sconce to await his return, and vigorously brushed at his clothes to clear the worst of the dust and cobwebs. Then he sneaked out of the room and made his way through the house to the library, using the servants' corridors that Hicks had shown to him last night.

The library contained a small alcove, set into a wall behind the shelves of dusty books. Into this alcove a past viscount had built a desk and cupboards to hold his papers, and from then on it had always been used to conduct estate business.

Which made it the most logical place to begin the search.

Chapter Nine

After visiting several of their neighbors, Mr. and Mrs. Bell went to Frantham Manor. Amelia and Julia sat either side of Mama, facing forward in the coach while Papa sat with his back to the horses, a resigned expression on his face.

He had not wanted to make this trip, claiming he had far too much to do to be gadding about the countryside, calling on neighbors who probably did not want his company any more than he wanted theirs.

Mama had pursed her lips at that. "It is the least you could do for us, I would say," she answered him. "You were supposed to have called at the manor before now, so that we ladies could visit them, and they us, without raising eyebrows. Since you have been remiss in your duty, you will need to do it today. It is especially important now, after you have decreed Amelia shall not have a Season. We must ensure she takes whatever opportunities are thrown in her path."

Papa gave Mama a steady and inscrutable stare. "My dear," he said, after a few moments' thought, "I cannot see any reason for your consternation. There is no hurry to marry Amelia off. She is but eight-and-ten years old, hardly in her dotage. You talk as if she were in danger of becoming an ape leader at any moment."

"Hmm." Mama glared at him for a moment, then raised her chin disdainfully.

"Besides," Papa continued, his face impassive and his voice even, "far from neglecting my duty to you, I visited Frantham Manor, at your behest, when Mr. Summersby first arrived from India. You told me that if I did, that gentleman would come to call and pay attention to one of my daughters. To hear you say it, I believed he was all but ready to make her a viscountess without any further effort or expense needed from me. And lo! madam. Here I am, several months later. I still have three unwed daughters, no viscountesses, and Mr. Summersby's first call upon us is now long overdue." He cocked his head to one side as he thought for a moment. "I will allow," he said, "that he has not made a call upon anybody else in the district either, but that does not signify. I did my duty. Your promises were not delivered."

He winked at Amelia, who bit her lip to stop the giggle.

Mama fixed Papa with her steeliest glare. "You must have said something to offend him," she decided, at last. "Which is precisely why we will accompany you this time."

Papa's expression did not change. He simply raised one eyebrow.

Mama changed tactics. "What manner of neighbor would we be," she asked in her sweetest voice, "if we did not make an effort to go and enquire after Lord Frantham's health?"

Papa shrugged his shoulders. "We have no need to make a nuisance of ourselves for that. I can ask Lord Rotherton how Lord Frantham is at any time, and he will gladly tell me."

"Do not be difficult." Mama folded her arms tightly

across her chest and stared at him until he capitulated.

He must be wishing he had stood his ground then, for now that the visit was underway, things were decidedly uncomfortable. Mr. Summersby and his friends, Mr. Sykes and Mr. Harcourt, sat on one side of the room, while the Bell family sat on the other side. They resembled reluctant peace delegations from warring nations rather than neighbors trying to be friendly.

They were in a sitting room, a large room with French windows that would have let in a great deal of light, had there been a great deal of light to let in. Outside, the sky was low and dark, and the clouds threatened snow, reducing visibility inside, but no effort was made to improve things by using the lamps in the room. As had happened yesterday at the Golden Goose, Mr. Summersby was polite, if a little distant, his conversation limited to remarks about the weather and the state of the roads in winter. Mr. Sykes added little more to the conversation, and Mr. Harcourt said nothing at all. Amelia realized she had never heard him utter a word, and she wondered idly if perhaps he hid a speech impediment.

Sitting beside Amelia, Julia clasped and unclasped her fingers, a clear sign that she was not happy and wished to be gone as soon as good manners would allow. Mama, however, seemed in no hurry. She enquired after Lord Frantham's health and managed to express both sorrow at his continued illness and happiness that his son could soon take up the title, within the same sentence. Before anybody could answer her, she went on, "I suppose you are kept busy making plans for the future, Mr. Summersby?"

Julia gasped sharply at the crass question. Amelia closed her eyes and sighed inwardly.

"That is to say," Mama corrected herself, "you must have been making them for some time. After your poor brother's demise, when you became the heir, you must have given some thought to setting up your nursery."

Amelia lowered her gaze so that nobody could see her dismay. Her cheeks burned, making her thankful for the poor light.

"Before he can do that," said Mr. Sykes, "my friend would need to be married. He is not married, hence no nursery." His voice was smooth and sweet, like liquid honey, and it coated his easy smile. The effect should have been seductive, but Amelia was somehow repulsed by him, and a shiver cascaded down her spine.

"Well, of course," said Mama with a little laugh. "I realize that, Mr. Sykes. But Mr. Summersby is not getting any younger, is he? And with his father so frail, well, he will need to get a wife fairly quickly, don't you think? Do you plan to go up to Town for the Season, Mr. Summersby? Or," she grinned, slyly, "mayhap you have your sights set on somebody closer to home?"

Mr. Summersby looked dazed, and somewhat overwhelmed. Mr. Sykes raised an eyebrow at Mama, while Mr. Harcourt sat, watching, his face devoid of expression. Of the three of them, Mr. Harcourt frightened Amelia the most. His silence and the way he stared at them, as if he was seeing right down into their very souls, made her shudder. She turned to Papa, her eyes wide, pleading that he do something to end this excruciating meeting.

Papa gave a slight nod, and Amelia relaxed, sure he would soon have them back in the carriage and on their way home, until he asked, "Does your home still boast a most splendid library, Summersby? It has the reputation of being one of the finest book rooms in Sussex, if not in the whole of the south of England."

What? He wanted to discuss the library? Could he not see the need to retreat from this disastrous call?

"Yes," Mr. Summersby answered him. "The present viscount and his father were both avid collectors of books, and the collection is without par."

Amelia had been frowning at her father, but Mr. Summersby's comments caught her attention. *"The present viscount and his father"? Not "my father and grandfather"?* It was a strange turn of phrase, to be sure. Odd.

"Books are very important to a man, are they not?" Mama said. "A man must read to broaden his horizons. I wonder, though, do you like a lady who reads, sir? Or do you prefer them to take up more ladylike pastimes?"

"Perhaps you would allow me to visit it?" Papa spoke quickly, saving Mr. Summersby from having to answer. "I have heard so much of it, and I long to see it."

Mr. Sykes grimaced and opened his mouth, and Amelia thought he would object. Before he could, though, Mr. Summersby glanced at Mama, stood, and nodded at Papa. "Capital idea. Come now. I shall endeavor to show you around, although you will appreciate I am no expert." He and Papa left the room with alacrity.

Mama thinned her lips. This was clearly not part of her plan. Her expression made plain that if the gentlemen thought to outwit her, they were in for a shock. Mr. Sykes made to get up to go with Mr. Summersby and Papa, but Mama stopped him skillfully. "Mr. Sykes—and Mr.

Harcourt, of course—while my husband is gone to see the books, perhaps you would be so kind as to tell me about your voyage home from India? I know I will find it fascinating, and Miss Julia was saying just the other day how much she would like to hear a sea-going story."

Mr. Sykes sat down, reluctantly.

"Yes, Julia loves the sea," Mama continued. "Although my older daughter is not at all interested in tales of sea voyages, are you, Amelia?" Amelia narrowed her eyes, wondering what Mama was up to now. All became clear with her next sentence. "Amelia takes from her father, do you see? Like him, she adores books. La! I should have thought of it before. Amelia, darling, why do you not accompany your father to the library and see it for yourself?"

Amelia stared at her mother, horrified. Beside her, Julia did the same. Mr. Sykes began to object, and even Mr. Harcourt seemed to take more interest in the way of things.

"I am sure Mr. Summersby will not object to your being there, my dear, and with your papa to chaperone you, there can be no impropriety. Go, go, go, child. If you hurry, you can catch them. They cannot be but twenty feet along the corridor."

"Mama…"

"Don't argue with me, girl. While you sit here, prattling at me, they are getting farther away, and then Mr. Sykes will need to summon a servant to show you the way, which will be an inconvenience, I am sure. Do not dally. Go!"

Embarrassed and ashamed, Amelia stood and walked from the room. Mr. Sykes glared at Mama with daggers in his eyes, but, caught up in her minor triumph, she did not seem to notice. Disingenuously, she asked about the voyage again as Amelia shut the door.

Papa and Mr. Summersby were not in the corridor. They must have walked more quickly than Mama had allowed. Amelia sighed heavily. She could not go back into the room. It would simply cause more awkwardness. Surely, it could not be too difficult to find the library? She would show her face, admire the books, and return.

She found a large dining room and a smaller breakfast room before she discovered the library. At each room, she opened the door cautiously, not wishing to disturb the gentlemen in the conversation she imagined they would be having. The quiet of the library surprised her. She'd thought her father would be enthusing loudly over the volumes within. Perhaps he was struck speechless by the literary splendor of the place. She went farther in, looking for him.

It really was a magnificent book room. The walls were lined, floor to ceiling, with shelves, all of them filled with books. More bookshelves stood freely in the middle of the floor, giving the room a labyrinthine air. It smelled of leather and musty pages, and glue.

After a minute's wandering between the shelves, she had not found them. Perplexed, she stopped and listened more carefully. Perhaps they had taken a less direct route and would arrive presently, she decided, since she still could hear no quiet voices discussing favored tomes and prized possessions. Instead, she heard the sound of papers rustling. Adopting her brightest smile, apology for her presence ready, she made her way toward the noise.

She weaved between two tall bookcases and turned a corner of the L-shaped room, walking into a small alcove which was evidently used as a study. A large window took up most of the far wall, a cushioned seat built below the panes, so that one could sit in comfort and admire the view of the gardens and the vast swathes of undulating fields beyond.

A huge desk took up most of the space, although there was also a tall cupboard, in which she supposed important documents were safely filed. A chair had been pushed away from the desk, as if it was in the way. Several piles of paper covered both desk and chair, none of them neatly stacked. And there, going through one of those piles of paper, was Mr. Winter.

Amelia was not aware of having made a sound, but something alerted him to her presence. He whirled around, startled, legs bent, shoulders hunched, ready to face the threat. Recognition crossed his face, and he straightened, taking some of the menace from his stance, but his gaze did not waver.

Thoughts and questions tumbled over one another in Amelia's mind. Was he a criminal? Was he dangerous? She shivered. Then, determined not to let him see he had made her nervous, she raised her chin defiantly, took a deep breath and asked, "What do you here, sir?"

He swallowed, hard. "Miss Bell, I..." His voice was deep and thick, his expression uncertain. He pressed his lips together and glanced at the papers in his hand.

The danger in the situation was not lost on Amelia. He did not look like a threat, but then, he did not look like a burglar either, and yet here he was, rifling through a desk that was clearly not his own. What if he was desperate to get away? To stop her calling out for help? She swallowed, unsure which unsettled her most, this man's presence as an intruder in the house, or the realization that she wasn't afraid of him.

She should be afraid. Her father and Mr. Summersby had disappeared, and there seemed to be no one to rush to her aid. This man was bigger and stronger than she was, she who was all that stood between him and arrest, prison, perhaps even transportation, or the gallows.

That thought made her tense. Her breath caught and apprehension churned in her stomach as she pondered what to do. Mr. Winter stood absolutely still, one hand anchoring papers on the desk, his gaze fixed on her. His eyes were a swirl of color, now the brown of tree bark, now the green of the wood beneath. His jaw stiffened, which made his cheeks seem leaner, and his lips pressed into a thin line. He seemed annoyed that she had caught him, but there was no guilt in his expression.

"Where...where is your cousin?" she asked at last, more to fill the awkward silence than to know the answer. It was an absurd question, she knew. If Mr. Winter had set out to burgle the neighborhood, he was hardly likely to bring the local magistrate with him! At that moment, though, it was the only thing she could think to ask.

He surprised her by answering, "He is visiting Viscount Frantham. I believe he reads to him."

"I see." Her voice was amazingly steady, considering every nerve within her tingled and every muscle trembled at being here, like this, with him. She took a deep breath and raised her chin. "And you have perhaps come to find him a book?"

Mr. Winter opened his mouth to speak, then closed it again and looked down at the desktop. Beside the piles of paper, his leather gloves lay abandoned. Amelia followed his gaze, noticing his bare fingers. They were long and lean, the skin sun-darkened like those of a laborer, but his nails were short and well-tended, as a gentleman's should be. A few dark hairs curled at his wrist and disappeared into his sleeve.

"Miss Bell," he said, carefully, "I know it is a lot to ask, but I—" He took a deep breath before he continued. "I would prefer that people not be made aware of my presence here."

Amelia glanced at the papers strewn across the desk. "I can see you might."

"I am not a thief." His eyes pleaded with her to believe him and, strangely, she found she did. Amelia could not begin to guess why he should be sneaking about in the library at Frantham Manor but, as her initial shock wore away, she realized there had to be more to this than she could yet understand.

She glanced around the room. Nothing seemed to be missing. There were no telltale marks on the furniture where an ornament had been removed, no gaps in the shelves to show the disappearance of a valuable tome. And while Mr. Winter was certainly rifling through things he had no business touching, those things were papers, not jewels. Surely, a thief would not spend time going through the library when there must be richer pickings elsewhere in the house?

Mr. Winter watched her closely. His eyes had darkened until they were more brown than green. Suddenly, Amelia wanted to lose herself in them and never break free.

And there she went, being all poetical and missish again. What was it about this man, that the merest sight of him turned her from the sensible, practical person she knew herself to be, into a quivering hen-wit?

She blinked to break the spell. He was still watching her, imploring her with those compelling eyes. She stared into them for a second longer, then forced herself to look away.

"You should hide, sir," she whispered. "They will be here at any moment."

Mr. Winter pushed the piles of papers haphazardly into the desk drawers before moving to the window. Amelia shook her head, her eyes wide with horror. He was going to be caught! She could see from here that the window was locked. He would never open it in time, not without alerting somebody to his presence. Even if he could do so, how would he close it again to cover his tracks? How would he cross the grounds without being seen by those armed men?

But to her astonishment, he did not attempt to open the window. Instead, he lifted the cushioned seat below it, revealing it to be the lid of a deep box, built into the wall. Amelia watched, speechless, as he crawled into the tiny space, folding himself down into an awkward and most uncomfortable-looking position, before pulling the cushion back into place. Then he was gone, and the seat looked as if it had never been disturbed.

For a second, she stared, hardly able to believe what she had seen. Then she heard voices coming along the corridor toward the library. Papa and Mr. Summersby were talking in a friendly fashion, laughing with each other. The sound of them brought Amelia to her senses. Quickly, she moved out of the alcove and stood by the bookshelves, trying to look innocent—something she did not think would be easy for her this day.

At the last moment, she saw Mr. Winter's gloves,

lying forlorn and forgotten on the desktop. She stared at them, stupidly, as if she expected them to jump up and hide themselves.

In the corridor, Mr. Summersby mentioned the door, wondering who had left it open. Papa said the outside air was bad for the books. They came inside and the door clicked closed behind them.

Amelia snatched up the gloves and shoved them into her pocket.

Chapter Ten

Papa looked startled to see Amelia as he rounded the bookcase and came face to face with her. Behind him, Mr. Summersby frowned, confused. Amelia smiled brightly at them and fought the urge to glance over her shoulder at the window seat. "There you are, Papa," she said. "I thought I should find you here already but, as you see, I arrived first."

Her father raised an eyebrow. "I asked Mr. Summersby to show me a painting his father acquired last year," he explained. "It's by Mr. JMW Turner. I'm sure the name means little to you, my dear, but I have to tell you, Mr. Turner is considered one of the foremost artists of our time."

"I believe I may have heard his name," Amelia said, although she wasn't certain of it. "Was the painting all you hoped?"

Papa hesitated. "It was not as big as I thought it would be. Somehow, when a painter is become acclaimed, one thinks of his works as towering giants, almost too big for the wall that holds them. This one was small, and rather delicate. And all the better for that, truth be told."

"I agree," said Mr. Summersby. "When a picture is too big, the detail can become overwhelming. The wood becomes hidden by the trees." He glanced toward the door as if he expected somebody else to join them. If he believed his friends would come, Amelia thought wryly, he had no idea how strong Mama's determination could be. Amelia clasped her hands in front of her waist for an instant. Her forearm brushed against the bulge of the glove in her pocket and she prayed it did not show in the line of her dress. Her chest tightened and her shoulders were stiff with the anxiety of it.

"This truly is a magnificent library," Papa said, his voice a reverent whisper. He looked up and down at the books on the shelves, his passion for them sparking in his eyes. "Tell me, sir," he asked Mr. Summersby, "had many books been added while you were away? There must have been some wonderful ones to greet you upon your return home."

"I don't know... I daresay a few... I..." Mr. Summersby was decidedly uncomfortable. He glanced at the books. "I have not had much opportunity to peruse these shelves of late." He cleared his throat. His words became more clear-cut, his accent more expensive, and Amelia realized his earlier statements had not been of the same quality, the vowels rounder, the consonants coarser. "Reading is a great love of mine, but when there are other considerations, it must needs be put aside."

A cold finger of suspicion clawed at Amelia's spine. The man did not know his own library? Then Papa agreed with him and lamented his own lack of time, and Amelia wondered if she was mistaken. Papa was not a stupid man, and he showed no doubts about Mr. Summersby. And while Amelia had never warmed to the man, she had to admit she had never suspected him of actual wrongdoing before.

She was clearly allowing herself to be misled by the doubts Mr. Winter had planted in her head. But who was to say that Mr. Summersby was the villain here? She had surmised that Mr. Winter was an actor, working for the side of law and order. But he had not said so. What if she had jumped to the wrong conclusion?

An instant later, she dismissed the very idea. Lord Rotherton had introduced the man just this morning, which meant that, whoever he was, he had the earl's blessing. It would take a great deal to persuade her that Lord Rotherton was involved in anything nefarious, which meant she had no choice but to give his cousin the benefit of the doubt and ensure his hiding place was not discovered.

Nervously, her eyes flicked to the window seat. It looked as solid as ever. Nobody would ever guess a man hid beneath it. She dragged her attention from it before her companions remarked upon her interest.

Papa wandered farther into the library. He ran a loving finger over the leather spines of a dozen books on one shelf, then traced the gold lettering embossed on another, before letting his gaze travel up, over the shelves and toward the ceiling. His expression was rapt, as if, in these books, he had seen the gateway to paradise itself.

Mr. Summersby followed Papa. He said nothing, although several times Amelia thought he was about to do so. His face was thoughtful, and a little troubled. Once, he licked his bottom lip, took a deep breath, then glanced at the library door before sighing and keeping his silence.

Amelia walked behind them. The gloves in her pocket seemed to grow, forming a lump that could not be missed if the gentlemen but looked her way. Any moment now, they would be too big for her pocket to contain, and must fall to the floor, betraying both her and Mr. Winter.

She looked over at the window seat yet again. Then, realizing that her nervous glance would give him away more surely than if she had pointed him out, Amelia turned her back to him and made a show of examining the books at her eye level.

Goodness, but subterfuge was exhausting! There were so many things that might give her—or Mr. Winter—away…a look, a word, a blush. Guilt and worry ate at her until she thought she must collapse from them. Yet, at the same time, she felt strangely elated, eager for more.

The two men wandered the library for what seemed an eternity. Papa asked questions. Mr. Summersby answered them, usually vaguely, his disinterest in the books and their provenance obvious. Amelia followed behind them and tried to seem at ease.

Finally, having done a circuit of the whole room, they found themselves at the door again. Papa thanked Mr. Summersby for his kindness and called Amelia to come. "Your mama will begin to fret if we are gone much longer," he said.

The last thing Amelia believed Mama would do over their prolonged absence was fret. Still, she followed Papa out of the library and into the corridor. Her forearm brushed the glove in her pocket once more, and Amelia's eyes widened in horror. How could she possibly go home with a man's glove secreted about her person? If she were caught with such an item—well, her reputation would certainly never recover from that. But how on earth was she to remove it and return it to its owner without either Papa or Mr. Summersby seeing it?

An idea came to her and, in her own inimitable fashion, she launched it into being before she could think it through. She fumbled to undo the clasp of the brooch on her spencer, then secreted the tiny jewel in her fist before giving what she hoped was a dismayed cry.

"My brooch," she said. The two men turned and stared blankly at her. She gave a tight smile. "The clasp is always coming undone, Papa."

"Is it?"

Amelia felt the prickly heat of bright crimson fill her cheeks as she told the untruth. "It must have come off. In the library, for I definitely had it earlier." She smiled, then sobered, convinced her grin showed off her guilt. "I shall go and find it."

"No matter," said Mr. Summersby. "I shall look for you."

"Oh, no!" Amelia winced at the panic in her voice. "I mean, I would not put you to the trouble, sir. I have an idea where it may have fallen, and it will doubtless be quicker for me to find it than for you, since you do not know where..." She trailed off, aware that she was rambling. She widened her smile again and prayed she looked more honest than she felt. "Do you go on to find the others. I will run back inside, find the brooch, and catch up to you before you know it."

"We can help."

She shook her head. Her smile was fixed now, becoming a grimace.

"Don't be a goose, Amelia," said Papa, and the two men turned back to the library with her. She shivered with dread, and her heart beat so loudly she was amazed they could not hear it. Nausea churned in her stomach as she wracked her brains, wondering how she would resolve this without being caught herself, or causing Mr. Winter to be caught. Of all the scrapes and situations Amelia had ever managed to be embroiled in, and there were more than a few, this was without doubt the worst.

Please, God, she prayed silently. *Please help me. If you help me, I'll...* There must be something she could promise the Almighty if He came to her rescue this once.

"I'll look over here," said Papa, heading toward the far right-hand corner of the room. Mr. Summersby took the left-hand side. And, suddenly, Amelia was alone at the entrance to the alcove. With a hurried "thank you" to the benevolent God, she hurried over to the desk, pulled the gloves from her pocket, and put them where she had found them.

"God speed, Mr. Winter," she whispered, and hurried back out into the main library. "Found it," she called, when she was far enough away that the two gentlemen were unlikely to look into the alcove as they passed. She held up the little brooch and pushed a smile into place.

"Be more careful, please," said Papa, and he ushered her from the room once again. "We will get that clasp mended as soon as we can."

"Yes, Papa," she answered, and she walked meekly between them, back to the sitting room.

****

Josh put his eye to the tiny hole under the rim of the window seat and tried to see as far as he could. He had first used this hiding place as a small boy escaping the boring lectures of his tutor. Then, of course, he had had room to maneuver, unlike now, when his shoulders were jammed in hard, his arms brushing against too-close walls which stole his breath and made his heart beat erratically. His legs were tightly folded under him, making his thighs ache and his calves sting. They had cramped once already, and it had taken everything within him not to move to ease the pain. He'd sent up a silent thanksgiving when the spasm died, leaving the bittersweet pain of the bruise.

He could see most of the alcove, although the free-standing bookshelves cut off his view of the rest of the library. Gray-blue light spilled from the window above his hiding place, drawing patterns on the carpet and forming grotesque shadows that changed the shapes of the chair and desk legs. He couldn't see the top of the desk.

The moment he had shut the seat down upon himself he had remembered his gloves, which he had removed to allow him better access to the sheaves of papers in the desk drawers. He'd thrown them carelessly onto the desktop, where they now sat proudly, waiting to be discovered by the men, whose voices had become loud and clear enough for individual words to be heard. He grimaced, swallowed a curse, and awaited discovery.

At the last second, he saw Miss Bell snatch at the desktop and then move away from it, pushing the gloves into her pocket as she did so. Josh was torn between wanting to kiss her for saving him and wanting to shake her for putting herself at risk. If she should be found to have a gentleman's gloves about her person, even if they never connected those gloves to an intruder...especially if they never connected those gloves to an intruder...

Josh smiled, wryly. He may not have known the lady long, but he already knew she would not have contemplated doing otherwise. Everything the lady did, it seemed, was reckless and impulsive. Whether that was a good thing or a bad, Josh wasn't certain, but she had saved him this time.

He waited for an eternity while the gentlemen toured the library. Mr. Bell came into his line of vision and stared at the books as if they were holy relics, now reaching out to them, now pulling back, as if he thought himself unworthy of touching them. The light of true love shone in his eyes. Josh guessed he barely remembered his companions.

Mr. Summersby was ill at ease. Which he should be. The man wanted these people to believe this was his home, that he had been born here, had spent his formative years playing in the halls, sliding down the bannisters and hiding in the corners, when it was evident he had not. The smallest questions were deflected and unanswered, although there were several times when Summersby looked as though he would say something. Each time, he chewed his bottom lip and took a deep breath. Then he glanced at the door, sagged, and said nothing.

The trio moved away from the alcove, beyond the bookshelves, and out of sight. Josh heard their voices, the soft click of their boot heels on the polished wooden floor. His back spasmed. He held his breath against the groan he needed to release, and he prayed they would hurry up and leave.

At long last, the library fell silent, and the air took on an empty quality, as if it missed the presence of living things. Floorboards began to creak and pop in protest at the abandonment. Josh gave one last glance around through the peephole, making as certain as he could that everyone had gone, before he released the latch and opened the seat.

He crawled out and spent a moment on all fours on the alcove floor, gratefully stretching his muscles and breathing in the unfettered air. His feet tingled in a way that was not quite painful but was definitely not pleasant, and it was some moments before he dared try to stand upon them. Mayhap, he thought, he should be a little less confident of using his childhood hideaways now he was full grown.

His gloves were back on the top of the desk where Miss Bell had hastily returned them, crumpled and creased from being shoved so tightly into her pocket. He picked them up and stared at them, his fingertips stroking the downy kid leather, a smile playing on his lips.

Miss Bell had certainly taken him by surprise, which probably showed that, Rotherton's confidence in him notwithstanding, Josh was not the right man for a successful subterfuge. He had been so completely engrossed in his search of his father's desk, skimming his eyes over papers and ledgers, learning the goings-on at the Frantham estate and looking for patterns, that he had not heard her approach. Had she screamed at the sight of him, or tried to call for help, he would have found it dashed awkward, to say the least. More, Rotherton's investigation, and the chance to bring the imposter and his friends to justice for any wrongdoing, would have been lost. At best, the villains might have escaped. At worst, Josh's father, if not himself and Rotherton too, could have been placed in even greater danger.

But Miss Bell had not screamed or called for help. Not by a single word or action had she made any effort whatsoever to alert anyone to Josh's presence. In fact, by hiding his gloves from them, she had helped him. Why?

He pulled the gloves through his curled fingers and tried to make sense of it all. It was clear to him that Miss Bell did not trust Mr. Summersby, though surely she could not suspect the man of being an imposter. So was her distrust instinctual? That sixth sense which his mother had always called "female intuition"?

For his part, Mr. Summersby had not behaved as Josh had expected either. The man was clearly distracted by something, though what, Josh could not begin to guess. His discomfort gave Josh a feeling that whatever was happening here at Frantham was deeper even than Rotherton had supposed. And if that were so, the truth needed to be unearthed as a matter of urgency.

Josh pressed his lips into a tight, thin line and thought everything through. From what little he had seen today, the man calling himself Summersby might prove to be the weak link that would allow them to break the chains and free the truth. But that would not be Josh's task. All Josh had to do was provide the information Rotherton needed. The earl would do the rest.

He put his gloves back on. The action made him think of Miss Bell, and involuntarily, he smiled. He could see her now, snatching up his gloves, trying to look innocent, and only succeeding in looking all the more guilty, at least to him. The young lady was clearly not practiced in the art of dissembling. She blushed far too easily, her soft, creamy cheeks turning a bright, almost glowing pink that made her eyes sparkle like diamond-cut sapphires and her hair shine like a bright, gold halo. Several times before she left his line of vision she had glanced guiltily over at the window seat. He had willed her to look away, to focus her attention on anywhere else before she drew her companions' attention to him. At each nervous glance she had bitten her bottom lip, leaving the imprint of her top teeth in its plump, red surface. Josh had wanted to reach out to her then, to tell her to stop marring its beauty. In his mind's eye, he pictured her looking up at him while he smoothed the teeth marks away with his finger. He saw her, eyes drawn to his as he lowered his head, closing the gap between them until he could brush his own lips tenderly over hers. She would taste of summer fruits and dainty cakes, and something else, something he could not put into words, something deliciously, indefinably, uniquely, Miss Bell.

Josh could almost taste her now, on the air she had so recently breathed. His stomach muscles constricted and there was a hardening in his thighs, tightening his trousers. The discomfort brought him to his senses. Annoyed with himself, he tried to ignore the ache and instead concentrated his attention on the job he had to do. He pulled open the desk drawer with rather more force than was necessary, then thumbed through the papers again, hoping against hope that something would strike him on this second glance.

Most of the documents pertained to the estate. His glance was cursory, but he saw nothing that made him think things were not in good order. As he had thought, the Frantham lands were not a source of vast wealth, certainly not enough to attract fraudulent claimants, although they were a long way from being poor. The yields looked to be good, the buildings seemed to be in a decent state of repair, and the accounts were healthy. But there was nothing to suggest a reason for Summersby and his friends to have tried to take over here.

After he finished searching the alcove, Josh made a cursory tour of the bookshelves, looking for he knew not what. Nothing seemed out of place. No books seemed misshapen by papers hiding between their leaves, and the thin veil of dust which hung over most of them had not been disturbed in a very long time.

With a sigh that mixed resignation with irritation, he left the room, checking the corridor carefully before sneaking across it to head back to the west wing.

He was almost at the servant's staircase when a door clicked open farther along the corridor and Mrs. Bell's trilling laugh escaped the room. Josh froze, horrified. He was still too far from the staircase to make it there before he was discovered, but he had gone past the point of no return to the library.

Mrs. Bell said something. One of the gentlemen replied. Josh darted into a shallow niche and squeezed behind a tall, marbled plinth on top of which rested an impressive Grecian figure. He pressed himself as far back into the niche as he could, held his breath, and hoped the dark corner, and his luck, would hide him.

Seconds later, two footmen came through the green baize doors that separated the servant's part of the house from the main. Josh tensed as they neared him, but neither noticed him. They passed by and went to help the departing guests into their coats. Josh closed his eyes in relief.

Summersby and his friends were friendly and light as they watched their guests leave. As soon as the door closed behind them, however, all pretense at conviviality disappeared.

"Blasted woman!" said Sykes, his words clipped by his gritted teeth. "She's like a dog with a bone." He glared at Summersby. "Get rid of her."

Josh stiffened. The threat was clear in Sykes' voice.

An image came to mind of Amelia, her eyes wide with fear as Sykes bore down on her, a threatening snarl distorting his features, and it was all Josh could do not to rush out there and thrash the man for so much as suggesting it. He took several deep, silent breaths before his blood came off the boil.

In the hallway, Summersby looked helplessly from Sykes to Harcourt, and then at the footmen, whose faces remained impassive. "I fear that would be easier to say than to do," he said, in answer to Sykes' command. Josh's eyes narrowed and his jaw tightened. They were all as bad as each other.

"I don't care." Sykes took two paces away from Summersby, turned, and paced back. Summersby took a nervous step backward. Harcourt sniffed and examined his nails. Josh frowned at their reactions. This partnership suddenly seemed less than equal to him. He watched and listened avidly.

"We cannot have that woman visiting here whenever she pleases, making a nuisance of herself," continued Sykes. "The old hag has a voice that could flay the skin from an elephant, and a careless tongue to match it. Some of the 'pearls of wisdom,' " he sneered the last three words, "which she imparted to us this morning leave me in no doubt we cannot rely on her discretion. And I am convinced she sees far too much."

"I do not see what—" Mr. Summersby's words ended in a faint cry as Sykes pushed him back against the wall, his forearm at Summersby's throat, forcing the other man's head up to an uncomfortable angle. Mr. Harcourt continued to play with his nails. The footmen exchanged glances but otherwise showed no reaction. Josh narrowed his eyes. This was not what he had expected at all.

"We have worked too hard," said Sykes, his voice dangerously low. "*I* have invested too much to have that interfering baggage spoil my plans at the eleventh hour."

For a moment, they were frozen in place, a menacing tableau in the expensively appointed hall. Then Sykes straightened and released Summersby, who stood up straight and adjusted his cravat. The footmen looked ahead, as if they wore blinkers. Harcourt seemed bored.

"What exactly is the plan?" asked Summersby, after a minute. Sykes turned the iciest of stares onto him, and Summersby flinched. "I...I wanted to know how to prevent her from ruining it."

Hidden behind the plinth, Jonathan willed Sykes to answer, to reveal everything he and Rotherton needed to know to put an end to this. Of course, it would never be so easy.

"You," Sykes said, "should remember what curiosity did to the butler."

Summersby swallowed, hard, leaving Josh in no doubt that was a reference to Grayson, his father's long-serving butler who had, according to Hicks, met with a freak and fatal accident.

Sykes turned to Harcourt and snapped his fingers. Harcourt picked up two hats and gave one to Sykes, putting the other on his own head before reaching for gloves.

"We will be back for dinner," said Sykes to Summersby. "I suggest you use the time to think of ways to discourage the odious Mrs. Bell and her pretty chicks." He and Harcourt left the house.

As the door closed behind them, Summersby sighed

and shook his head in an attitude of defeat. The footmen smirked at him, but he made no attempt to reprimand them. Instead, he turned on his heels and went back into the sitting room, shutting the door with a decisive click.

The footmen walked back along the corridor toward the green baize door, their conversation murmured but noticeably gleeful. Once again, they passed Josh's hiding place without seeing him.

Josh waited a few seconds, then carefully eased out from behind the plinth, headed to the servants' staircase, and made his escape.

Chapter Eleven

Mama could barely contain her joy on the carriage ride home. "Such a personable man," she told Amelia and Julia several times, her smile wide. "His manners are impeccable."

Amelia darted a glance at her father, who sat opposite them, his back to the horses. Not by the merest twitch of a muscle did his face betray his thoughts, but Amelia fancied she saw exasperated amusement in his eyes.

"I cannot approve of the company he keeps," continued Mama, her smile flattening. "Mr. Sykes can only be described as surly, would you not agree, Julia?"

"Yes, Mama," Julia answered, dutifully.

"You and Amelia had the best of it, being invited to go and see the library," Mama told Papa. "'Twas an invitation you did well to accept. I am so pleased, too, that Mr. Summersby saw fit to include Amelia on your little excursion. So often, unenlightened gentlemen do not like a woman who enjoys reading. I just knew Mr. Summersby would be different."

Papa's eyes met Amelia's for the briefest of seconds, before he looked back at Mama. Amelia's lips itched to form a smile. She pressed them tightly together until the urge passed.

"His only fault, as far as I can see, is that he has been a bachelor for far too long. He enjoys the bachelor ways too much. On top of which, he has lived out of England these many years, which cannot have benefited him in the least. We will need to re-civilize him, I make no doubt. But there, it is not an impossible task. I have every confidence you will prove its equal, my dear Amelia."

Amelia's eyes widened in alarm. How had the conversation moved in such a direction, so quickly?

"Yes," Mama agreed with herself, oblivious to the horror on her eldest daughter's face. "Remind him of the proper ways of an English gentleman, but do it subtly. Make him think he has reminded himself. Gentlemen do like to think that everything was their own idea."

Julia gave Amelia a sidelong glance. Papa raised an eyebrow, but he did not rise to the bait.

"Then," Mama went on, picking imaginary pieces of lint from the lap of her coat, "once we have tamed him a little, we can encourage him to be rid of the odious Mr. Sykes, and his other companion, Mister... Oh!"

"Harcourt," supplied Julia.

"Mr. Harcourt. A veritable dog-in-the-manger, he. Do you know, the man never said a word all morning? Made no attempt at polite conversation at all, if you please. Not even a hello."

"Mayhap he is unable to speak," suggested Papa.

Mama thought for a moment. "Oh, well. If that is the case, he is acquitted. But it does not signify. Once Amelia has brought Mr. Summersby up to scratch, both of those other—gentlemen—will be gone."

Amelia grimaced. She did not wish to bring Mr. Summersby up to scratch. Truth be told, she did not wish to bring anybody up to scratch at the moment, and certainly nobody who lived in this neighborhood. Marriage was something she had always believed would be hers one day, but only to the right gentleman, and only after she had enjoyed her Season. Her Season may have been postponed—she refused to believe her father would be so cruel as to deny her forever—but surely the loss of a year did not mean her prospects were damaged beyond repair?

It seemed Papa agreed with her. His eyelid dipped in what could have been a conspiratorial wink before he answered Mama, "Amelia is but eight-and-ten years of age, Letitia. Surely, there is no great urgency to marry her off just yet?"

"Spoken like a man," snorted Mama. "No urgency, indeed! Much you gentlemen know of the years of planning and hard work that is required to find a suitable husband, even if one is lucky enough to be the parent of an Incomparable. And heaven alone knows, Amelia is hardly an Incomparable."

Amelia swallowed, trying to ignore the pain in her chest at Mama's callously tossed words. She knew she was not as pretty as her younger sisters, but surely, her own mother had no need to voice that fact.

On the other side of the seat, Julia glared at Mama, then gave Amelia a look of apology. Amelia's return smile was half-hearted.

"I cannot agree with you," said Papa. His eyes glittered a warning at Mama, who had the grace to look shame-faced. "Amelia is, in my opinion, a prize of the highest order. Any man would be fortunate to have her. But not until she is ready. You will say I am selfish, my dear, but I find I do not wish to give her into the care of any other man so soon, no matter how personable he may be. Unless," he held up a hand to stop Mama's protest, "unless he is an exceptional man, worthy of her in every way."

Mama sniffed, but said no more.

Papa's defense of her made Amelia feel better. As did the knowledge that, in one respect at least, she knew he was right: she wasn't ready for a husband. Knowing Papa thought so made her wonder if that had played a part in his decision to cancel her Season, a decision she suddenly saw in a whole new light.

Amelia had thought of the months in London only in terms of the fun she would have, mixing with other young ladies and being introduced to exciting gentlemen. There would be picnics and promenades, balls and dinners, musical soirees and visits to the theatre. She might even have been granted vouchers for Almacks, and permission to dance the waltz there. Amelia had looked forward to all of these things, and the myriad new dresses she would have required; dresses that would have shown her figure to its best advantage and made her feel like a princess.

Her parents' expectations, she realized, were completely different. To them, the fun and the fripperies were no more than accessories, things one must have in order to succeed in the real endeavor. For Mama, that was simple: Mama wanted a husband for her oldest daughter, preferably one with a title so she could boast to her friends, and a fortune that would see Amelia comfortable for the rest of her life.

As for Papa, he wanted... Amelia was not certain exactly what Papa wanted, but one thing she did know: he would not spend a fortune to be disappointed. Which meant, if she did have a Season, he would wish to see her wed by the end of it. And, if he truly thought her unready for marriage, it was no wonder he took the chance to cancel everything.

Amelia stared out of the carriage window at the winter scenery rolling by and imagined the husband she hoped one day to have. Ideally, he would be handsome, although she was fully aware that physical beauty was naught but froth. The most handsome of men could be ugly deep within, and no woman would want a husband with an ugly soul, no matter how fine his face. Besides, beauty was completely in the eye of the beholder. At Christmas, Julia had taken a liking to one of the guests staying for the season at Rotherton Hall. The subject of Lord Rotherton's friend had filled every conversation with Julia for weeks, and she had wandered around looking as silly as a moon-calf. Amelia had studied the man, wanting to know why he captivated Julia so, but try as she might, she saw nothing about him that was anything more than ordinary.

In which case, she amended, her own future husband should be handsome, if only in her own eyes.

Hopefully, he would also be tall. Amelia was not overly tall herself, but she was not petite, either, and she would prefer her husband to be taller than she was. If he could stand head and shoulders above her, so much the better.

A picture came to mind of Mr. Winter. He was handsome, certainly, and tall. In the stable, she'd had to look up to see his face. He had long legs, with well-shaped calves that needed no padding. His waist was trim, his stomach flat, and his shoulders broad and strong. With his dark hair and arresting eyes that seemed to change from green to brown according to his mood, he was certainly a perfect fit for Amelia's own requirements.

He had no title. Nor was he likely to inherit one, as far as Amelia knew. Not that Amelia wanted a title, she didn't care one way or the other. But Mama cared very much, and a dutiful daughter would at least try to please her mother. So, a title it was, then.

As for Papa, he would undoubtedly wish the man Amelia married to be rich, although not because he was greedy, or that he felt money made a man superior in any way. Papa was simply a man of the world. Before Amelia's first dance at the Assembly Rooms in Rotherton two years ago, Papa had gently, carefully, made her aware of the dangers that awaited a young lady with a sizeable dowry. Amelia's portion was twenty thousand pounds, and that could buy a woman a great deal of misery if it attracted the wrong man. If the man who offered for her was already rich, her fortune would, most likely, not be his first consideration. Amelia found it hard to disagree with Papa's logic.

Titled and wealthy, then, as well as tall and pleasing to the eye. Those seemed most reasonable requirements. But there was one other condition, far more difficult to fulfill and yet of paramount importance. For as long as she had dreamed of finding a husband, it had been the one thing on which she refused to negotiate. Without it, nothing else would mean a thing, and it was this: the man she married must love her, exactly as she was. He must cherish the bride he was getting and not hope to mold her to his tastes after the ceremony. Amelia could not even contemplate marriage to any man who might try to squash her sense of fun or expect her to be a dull pattern-card of a Society woman. He would never expect her to perform dutifully on the pianoforte for their guests, or paint insipid pictures of delicate flowers whose only value would be in the way they hid damp patches on his entailed walls.

Amelia gasped at the image which formed once more. The man she saw was undeniably tall and handsome, with hazel eyes and a smile that was warm and sensual and full of promise. But as far as she knew, Lord Rotherton's second cousin was not rich and titled. No. He was just a plain mister, far from wealthy, and totally unsuitable in every way. Why, he might even be a criminal!

She thought of that moment when she had disturbed him in the manor's library today. He should not have been there, that much was undeniable. The guilt in his expression was plain to see, the clandestine nature of his actions making him suspect, at the very least. Yet Amelia had hesitated no more than an instant before deciding she would not betray him. Since that moment, she had thought of almost nothing else, her thoughts circling around, wondering if she had done the right thing, justifying her decision in every way she could: he had not been stealing, had left untouched things of obvious value, which surely spoke of a higher, purer motive.

Amelia snorted at that thought. Ordinary theft might not be his motive, but she could hardly describe what he'd been doing as pure. He had, after all, been going through the estate's private papers, perhaps in an attempt to harm the viscount. Although Amelia could not like Mr. Summersby, she had every respect for his father, and it did not sit well with her that she may have helped cozen the sick, aging nobleman.

"Must you make such an unladylike noise, Amelia?" scolded Mama. "You sound like a pig at the trough." Amelia realized with dismay that she had snorted out loud. How was she to explain that?

In the next second, Mama explained it for her. "I hope you haven't caught a chill, girl," she said, and she moved her body sideways, creating a space between herself and Amelia and squeezing Julia into the corner of the seat. "Although, even if you have," she continued, "a difficulty breathing through the nose should not be solved by snuffling and snorting. Use your handkerchief, but gently, mind. Otherwise you will redden the tip of your nose."

"Yes, Mama." Amelia pulled her handkerchief from her pocket and made a show of dabbing daintily at the skin around her unblocked nose while she silently cursed the mysterious Mr. Winter, at whose feet she felt able to lay this latest dressing down.

At the time, she realized she had assumed Lord Rotherton had been party to his actions. Now, however, as she examined the event with the cool eyes of hindsight, she began to wonder. What if the earl did not know what his cousin was doing? For all she knew, Mr. Winter made a habit of sneaking into places where he did not belong. Although, if that were the case, he was clumsily inept. Amelia had caught him in the act when she had employed no stealth or subterfuge. Which meant he was either very bad at his chosen profession or, more likely, considering he wasn't already in Newgate awaiting the gallows, today's foray had been his first.

Amelia frowned. There were easier places to burgle. Frantham Manor was well guarded, and those guards were armed, so this could not have been a crime of opportunity, but a deliberate act. And if Mr. Winter were looking for something specific, he likely had his cousin's blessing.

"I knew he couldn't be bad," she mused.

"What's that?" asked Mama, letting Amelia know she had again spoken aloud. "You mustn't mumble, Amelia. If I've told you once, I've said so a thousand times."

"Sorry, Mama."

Mama glared at her a moment longer, then went on with her plans. "Once you are mistress of the manor, you will want to completely refurbish it. I see no point in being a viscountess if you must sit in gloomy discomfort. Those dark walls, and all those uncomfortable wooden chairs—you will need something upholstered. And as for the window seats! Why anyone would want to sit under a draughty window is beyond me."

The window seat! Mr. Winter had gone straight to it. He had known it would provide him with a secure hiding place. He *knew* the manor!

Amelia's spirits rose. There was intrigue and adventure aplenty here. She straightened, her mood lightening, lips twitching with the urge to smile. Mayhap she could help? She could...

Papa frowned at her, sobering her, reminding her she needed to regain his trust if she was ever to have her Season. She could not help. She could do nothing, for intrigue and adventure belonged to childhood. They certainly had no place in the life of a proper young lady.

She quickly reminded herself that the same could be said of a tall, well-made stranger with hazel eyes and secrets to spare.

Chapter Twelve

Josh strolled toward Rotherton, losing himself in his memories. His childhood here had, on the whole, been a happy one, spent wrestling with the village lads in the woods and fields surrounding the town, or fishing with his best friend, David, now Lord Rotherton, in the streams. In the town itself, they'd played knock-down-ginger on those houses with no gardens between the doors and the street, rattling the door knocker and running away, then trying not to give away their hiding places with their giggles at the frustrated complaints of housekeepers who'd got better things to do with their time than play silly games.

Bigger than the nearby hamlet of Frantham, Rotherton boasted an array of shops, a forge, the Golden Goose Inn, and the Assembly Rooms. The High Street was better maintained than the roads in many other rural towns, although the winter weather had already gouged holes in its surfaces, and thick mud collected between wheel ruts carved by laden carts and a twice-weekly stagecoach.

Fourteen years, and it was as if Josh had last seen it yesterday.

In a square near the forge, four men played a game of horseshoes. Three of them wore the livery of the outdoor staff on the Frantham estate, which piqued his interest, so he wandered across to watch them. It

133

occurred to him that he might glean something from listening to their conversation while they were relaxed. The odds were long, he knew, but Josh had ever been an optimist, ready to embrace an opportunity. That approach had served him well in India, and made him and his partner very wealthy men. If it now helped him gather the information he needed to end whatever was happening at Frantham Manor, he'd be able to take ship and return to the life he'd built there.

The fourth horseshoe thrower was not in Frantham livery. His clothes were homespun, the clothes of a laborer, although they were not stained with evidence of heavy physical effort. He was thickset, and he crossed the game area with a swagger. As he bent to pick up the horseshoes scattered around the peg, he pushed his hat back, and Josh recognized Abraham Sutton, parish constable. He sniffed his distaste for the man.

At the same moment, Sutton saw Josh, and he sneered. "Here, lads," he called, and he backed his words with a nasty laugh. "We're being watched." He gave a mocking bow. "And not just by anybody, either. We're being watched by a toff of the highest sort. Boot kisser to an earl, no less." He laughed again. The Frantham men exchanged glances, and Josh tensed, unsure from their expressions whether they disliked Sutton's taunts or intended to join him in any attack on Josh.

"Want to join us, Mister Winter?" Sutton put emphasis on the word *mister*. "It'd do you good to throw something other than your cousin's cash around, I reckon."

"Leave him be, Abe," said one of the Frantham men, and he turned back to the game.

"We were warned, no trouble," added another.

Sutton opened his mouth, presumably to argue, but the man glared a warning at him. "And that goes for you too. Unless you want to wash out other people's stables forever."

Josh said nothing, but raked his disdainful gaze down from Sutton's face, over his barrel chest, and to the toes of his worn and scuffed boots. Then he turned his back and moved away, his step deliberately relaxed.

Behind him, Sutton snarled. The Frantham men murmured fiercely at him. Sutton muttered that it was all right, they could unhand him, he wasn't going to do anything stupid. Josh grinned to himself.

A few moments later his grin faltered, then returned more brightly when he saw the Misses Bell follow their mother out of one of the shops. He bowed in greeting and the three ladies curtseyed, the young ladies doing so more enthusiastically than their half-hearted Mama.

"How lovely to see you," he told them, and silently cursed himself for saying something so inane. The sisters exchanged what looked like amused glances. Mrs. Bell made a dismissive sort of grunt.

"Good morning, Mr. Winter," said Amelia. "How fares your cousin?" She looked to right and left. "He is not with you?"

"I believe he has some business to attend to."

"It is good that you are able to fill your time without him by studying your surroundings. Do you find much of interest in your search of the place?"

Josh grinned. "I believe I will do so."

"I wish you luck. Although you shouldn't need it. This is a very helpful neighborhood. If you seek something specific, you have but to make it known, and there are those who would gladly aid you in any legitimate search."

"A kind offer indeed. But I often prefer to explore alone."

"Alone, sir? Or with your cousin? Tell me, does he give his blessing to your most thorough explorations?"

"Amelia, what are you talking about?" interrupted her mother. "Why on earth would Lord Rotherton need to give his blessings to Mr. Winter's perambulations? He is free to wander at will, I make no doubt. And he is more than capable of finding his way unaided around a town the size of Rotherton." She gave a trilling laugh and turned to Josh. "It hardly compares to somewhere like London, with all its twists and turns and what-not, does it?"

Beside her, Amelia blushed. The deep pink rising through her cheeks made her eyes seem bigger and bluer, and the dark lashes surrounding them were impossibly thick and long. A few curls escaped her bonnet and rested on those warm cheeks, shining like spun gold. She pulled her bottom lip beneath her top teeth, worrying at it, and Josh had the sudden urge to reach out and touch it, to cover it with his own lips and soothe where she had bitten. The world around her shrank into the background until he saw nothing but her face. The delicate perfume of summer flowers seemed to fill him as their eyes met, and held. His trousers became uncomfortably tight, and it was all he could do not to reach out and take her into his arms, and embarrass both of them.

Something grabbed his arm, pulling him back to the moment, and Mrs. Bell asked, "May we count on you and Lord Rotherton?"

The question pulled Josh's attention back to the conversation, where it should have been all the time. He tried, in vain, to piece together the rest of her speech in order to know what she had asked of him. His eyes darted guiltily from Mrs. Bell, whose smile was bright and slightly disconcerting, to Amelia. She, however, had cast her eyes down, leaving him alone and at a loss.

It was Julia Bell who came to his rescue. "I am sure Mr. Winter is uncertain of Lord Rotherton's plans, Mama," she said, and there was laughter in her voice. "He cannot accept an invitation to a dinner party without referring to Lord Rotherton's diary."

A dinner party. Josh smiled gratefully at Julia. Her eyes danced with amusement. She was clearly fully aware that he had not listened to her mother. The quick glance sideways at her elder sister told him she was also aware of the reason for that.

His face heated, and his cravat suddenly became too tight. He fought the urge to push his fingers between the restrictive cloth and his throat to make breathing easier.

"A dinner party, did you say?" Rotherton spoke from immediately behind Josh, startling him. How a man as big and solid as the earl could move so silently baffled and slightly concerned him.

Mrs. Bell beamed at the newcomer. "My lord," she said through a smile so broad it was a wonder her words could be formed at all. "How do you do?" She curtseyed, and her daughters followed suit. Rotherton bowed and stepped forward to stand by Josh's side.

"I was just telling Mr. Winter we are having a dinner party on Thursday," Mrs. Bell told Rotherton. "A number of our neighbors have already accepted: the vicar and his lady, Mr. Summersby and Mr. Sykes, my particular friend, Mrs. Ashton and her family. I hoped we could expect you to join us, also?"

"We would be honored," said Rotherton. At his words, Amelia looked up, and for an instant Josh fancied he saw dismay in her eyes, before she hid it behind a coldly polite mask.

Josh frowned. Did she not wish them to join her family at dinner? Was it because of what had happened in the library yesterday? That thought brought him up short. 'Twas no wonder she was coy, when to her his actions at Frantham Manor must have seemed suspect, to say the least. She probably thought that if he came to dinner, he would leave with his pockets filled with cutlery.

Mrs. Bell took Rotherton's arm and strolled along the High Street, telling him some tale he seemed to find very amusing. Her youngest daughter walked demurely beside them. Josh offered his arm to Amelia. For the briefest of moments, he thought she would not take it. Her eyes widened and her cheeks glowed, redder than ever, and every inch of her seemed to thrum with the contemplated horror of touching him. Disappointment at her reaction hit him like a fist to the solar plexus.

He began to drop his arm. If the lady did not wish his touch, so be it, although he fully intended to engage her in conversation. He could see no way of her avoiding that, at least. But just as he lowered his forearm, she surprised him by wrapping her tiny hand around it. Even through her glove and his sleeves, he felt the warmth of her fingers, as clear as if her skin was bare upon his.

That thought conjured up images that had no place in his head while he was out walking with her in public. He swallowed, and tried to think of something inanely polite to say to her.

Amelia beat him to it. She glanced up at him, then

looked away again, her discomfort plain. "I…" She gave a dainty cough to clear her throat. "I feel I should tell you, Mr. Winter, that I have a great respect for Viscount Frantham."

Josh nodded. "As do I." She looked up at him again, one eyebrow raised, and he felt compelled to say more. "The viscount is a good man." *If a little solemn and severe for my taste.*

"Yes, he is. He was kind to me when my family first came to the neighborhood." She smiled, softly. "He learned that I liked to ride, so before my father built his stable, he permitted me the use of one of his mares."

That did not sound like his father. "He did?"

"He did. And when the stables were built, he sent his man to help Papa choose the horses he would buy. Now that he is unwell, I would not see anybody hurt him."

This time, when she looked at Josh, her gaze did not waver. In her eyes, he saw the fierce determination of a tiger about to defend its cub. Josh only wished he could inspire such loyalty.

"I kept your confidence yesterday," she continued. "I don't know why I did that. Perhaps I shouldn't have done. But it seemed the right thing to do at the time."

"It was."

Amelia waved her free hand, dismissing his statement. "You were clearly looking for something in particular. I must now ask, if you found that item, would it harm Lord Frantham in any way?"

"On the contrary, Miss Bell, I hope it will be of great benefit to him."

She sighed then, and it seemed the weight of the world had fallen from her shoulders. Josh would not have been surprised to learn the poor woman had agonized for hours over her decision to help him. He patted her hand, reassuring her. "You care for him very much."

"He is a friend, sir. Of course I care for him."

Josh nodded, then asked a question he had no right to ask, but which, he realized, had been plaguing him since she had startled him in the library. "And his son? The Honorable Mr. Summersby?" The word Honorable threatened to choke him. There was *nothing* honorable about the man now using that name.

"I do not know him," said Amelia, after a brief pause. "He only arrived in the area a few months ago and, with his father being so ill, he has not been much out in Society."

"He is coming to your dinner party," Josh pointed out. "Mayhap you will be able to become better acquainted with him then."

The distaste that showed briefly on her face made him happier than it should have done. She quickly covered it with a mask of indifference. "It makes no matter, really. I shall go to London for a Season, if not this year, then most certainly next. From there, I will marry and move to my husband's home, which could be anywhere in Britain. Most probably, Mr. Summersby's path will rarely cross mine after that, so there is no reason to be anxious to become better acquainted with him."

The elation Josh had felt when he had seen her dislike for Summersby deflated at this reminder that she would marry in the future. His spirits sank further when he realized her walk along the aisle would doubtless happen quickly. She was a young woman of good family, intelligent and well mannered, and more than a little pleasing to look upon. The bucks in London would climb over each other to get to her. The thought of that left a bitter taste in his mouth, and a heavy lump in his chest.

He had no reason to feel that way. It wasn't as if he could offer for her himself. Josh did not belong in the rarefied world of the *ton*, with its delicate maidens and genteel ways, and over-exacting expectations. Truth to tell, he had never fitted in there, but now, after his years in India, he would be more *de trop* than ever. India had toughened him, made him a man, and although it had brought him riches beyond his wildest dreams, it had also roughened him, and left him unsuitable for a Mayfair drawing room.

When the mystery at Frantham was solved and his father was safe, Josh would return to India, to the place he now called home. He had a partner there, and a thriving business, friends, and everything a man could need.

But India was not for everyone. He glanced at Amelia. A beauty like hers would not do well there. Her beauty was soft and delicate, with a complexion that made him think of roses in their first bloom, and eyes that sparkled like the sun shimmering on a summer sea. No. Amelia Bell needed a temperate clime, not the scorching sun that would bring out freckles and peel her nose before the heavy air in Madras turned her cheeks to tanned leather and her golden silk hair to straw.

Still, he couldn't help but regret that their paths in life were so completely different, and destined to cross for such a short time.

****

I shall go to London for a Season? I will marry? Amelia could scarcely believe she had said such a thing. His smile had slipped for a moment at her words, his expression freezing before he managed to hide behind his mask of impassivity. The memory of it mortified her even now, several hours later, as she sat in the ladies' sitting room with her sisters, a small piece of embroidery in her hands. The heat in her cheeks had nothing to do with the fire burning merrily in the hearth and everything to do with those moments in town this morning.

Papa had always told her she was too outspoken for her own good, and now she had proved it. Even as she had spoken the words, Amelia had known better. It simply was not done for a young lady to discuss her ambitions so openly with a gentleman. It could be construed as angling for an offer—not that she believed Mr. Winter would take it as such. He was a distant relative of an earl, and probably penniless to boot. He had to know that any offer of his for a woman such as Amelia would not be looked upon kindly by her family.

Which was, she could admit to herself now, a shame, for in all other respects Mr. Winter presented the very ideal of a husband. He was tall and handsome, and did not his very appearance speak to his suitability? His flat stomach and trim form were those of a man who did not overindulge, while his powerful chest, broad shoulders, and well-shaped legs suggested that he was capable of hard physical work should the need for it arise. He held himself well, his erect posture and the proud set of his jaw giving him a presence she could not define but which she instinctively recognized. This was a man who was clearly comfortable in his own presence, and that, in turn, made Amelia comfortable, too.

After she had blurted her intention to marry, she had glanced up at him, surreptitiously. He looked straight along the street, seemingly oblivious to her faux pas, no censure in his expression, which made her want to sigh with far too much relief. His cheeks were flat, his nose straight, and his chin strong, but it was his lips that truly caught her attention. Full, yet firm, she couldn't help but wonder what they would feel like, kissing hers. Would his be a gentle kiss? Soft as a butterfly's wing? Or would his be a more solid kiss, his mouth hard against hers, taking control? Would his lips part, his tongue sliding irresistibly against her lips, making her want to let him in, to feel the taste of him?

Her eyes widened, and she dropped her embroidery to the floor in shock at the wantonness of her thoughts. Quickly, she scooped up the piece and smoothed it in her lap, staring down at it as if examining her uneven stitches and hoping against hope that neither of her sisters would remark her distraction. Seconds passed. Neither Louisa nor Julia said anything, and Amelia let go the breath she was holding.

She stabbed the material with her embroidery needle. She could not believe the direction of her own thoughts! To even think in such a way about kissing a man! For while it was true she had been kissed before—twice—she had never solicited those kisses, nor had her imagination lingered over them afterward. She hadn't even enjoyed them much, if she was honest, and yet somehow she knew his would be different. The very thought of him kissing her made her lips tingle with eager anticipation, while her breasts grew heavy and her nipples peaked, rubbing in a not-unpleasant way against the lawn of her chemise. There was a strange feeling between her legs, too: not quite an ache and not quite an itch, not quite a good feeling, but certainly not a bad one.

Experiencing such sensations in the middle of the

High Street had made Amelia blush deeply. She had felt the heat under her skin, burning her cheeks and prickling all the way up to her hairline. Cursing her too-fair skin, which showed embarrassment so clearly, she glanced up at him and willed the icy air to cool her face quickly, before he saw. Alas, he had turned his head at that very moment. His eyes, more green than brown today, and framed by impossibly long lashes, shone with amusement, the wretch!

Trying to seem calm and indifferent, Amelia had taken a deep breath and looked for a safe topic of conversation with which to distract him. The weather. Yes, that was it. She would ask how he found the English weather after so many years in India. She cleared her throat.

"Will you and Lord Rotherton be going up to Town for the Season?" The question was out before she even knew her mind had formed it. Her heart skipped as mortification took her over. With a question such as that, the man would surely think she had set her cap at him now.

"Alas, no. My stay in England is, I think, destined to be a short one. By the time the Season begins properly at the end of March, the winter storms should have cleared the Bay of Biscay and it will be safe to sail. Which will mean I can return to India."

"Return...?" The word flew from her, filled with shock. "But—but I thought—you have only just arrived here."

Mr. Winter smiled. "I came for a specific purpose. Once that is done with, I shall return home, probably never to leave there again."

Amelia's stomach lurched then, the way it had when

one of her beaus had driven his gig too fast over the hump-backed bridge across the Rotherton brook. Mr. Winter was *leaving*? Although why that should matter so much to her she couldn't fathom. She barely knew the man, and what she did know of him made her very...uncomfortable. Why, she had hardly welcomed the idea of him coming to dinner at her home, had she? When Mama had invited him, Amelia had been at such a loss as to what to do, she had been unable to look at him. Her thoughts and wishes were such a jumble. She had wanted him to refuse for her peace of mind, but when it seemed as if he would do just that, her heart had plummeted and her stomach churned. When Lord Rotherton had accepted the invitation for him, Amelia had been astonishingly pleased. And that disconcerted her more than anything else, for why would it matter whether he came or not?

Unless, of course, she hoped his presence would thwart Mama's all-too-obvious matchmaking attempts between Amelia and Mr. Summersby.

Mr. Summersby was, Amelia knew, the reason for this sudden flurry of social activity on Mama's part. Amelia's mother fully intended Amelia would marry the viscount's heir, and this dinner party was merely one weapon in her arsenal. Amelia could only be thankful that propriety meant her mother could not simply invite the man on his own but was compelled to find other guests to fill her table.

"Penny for them?" Julia's cheerful voice startled Amelia out of her reverie and brought her back to the here and now of the sitting room. As she jumped, she stabbed her thumb with the embroidery needle, and she hissed a sharp breath, then sucked at the injured digit.

Thankfully, it didn't bleed.

Julia grinned. "You were wool-gathering. Was it, I wonder, about a certain gentleman who is newly arrived in the area?"

"No!" Amelia looked around in horror, wondering what Louisa would have to say to Julia's remarks. The last thing Amelia needed was for her loose-lipped youngest sister to begin spreading such a tale. Louisa was, however, not in the room. Nobody was, other than herself and Julia.

"Louisa had to go upstairs for her French lesson," Julia said, blithely. "I never thought she would leave, and I have been dying to ask you."

"Well, it's a very silly question and a quite absurd notion." Amelia dropped her embroidery into her lap, all pretense at doing it gone. "Quite absurd. What can possibly have made you think that?"

Julia's grin widened, and there was a satisfied gleam in her eye. Amelia mentally kicked herself for protesting too much.

"If it is any consolation, my dear Millie," said Julia, looking as if giving consolation to Amelia was the last thing on her mind, "he was distracted by you, too." Amelia looked up, sharply. Julia's eyes shone as she nodded. "He was incapable of speaking, so lost was he in admiration of you."

"Don't say such things." Amelia picked up her embroidery again and stitched furiously.

"'Tis true," insisted Julia.

Amelia sighed and began to undo the stitches she had just put into her work.

"It was a very good thing Lord Rotherton was there to come to his rescue," continued Julia, looking as innocent as she could manage. Which, in Amelia's opinion was not very innocent at all. "And it's a very, very good thing that he will dine with us on Thursday. It will give the pair of you an opportunity to speak to each other properly, instead of standing about like two newly minted statues."

Down went the embroidery again. "We did no such thing!"

"Ah, but you did." Julia's laugh, usually so sweet, grated on Amelia's nerves today. "You'll have to do much better than that, you know. Like this." She put down her own embroidery and stood, hands clasped in front of her waist and head tilted at a demure angle. "Oh, Mr. Winter," she said, breathily, "may we take a turn about the room? There is much I wish to say to you, and walking will give us a modicum of privacy." She fluttered her eyelashes.

Amelia gave her a flat look and spoke in the haughtiest tone she could manage. "Contrary to what you seem to believe, Julia Margaret Bell, I am a respectable lady. Anything I could possibly wish to say to Mr. Winter, or any other gentleman, for that matter, will not need privacy. I would happily say it in full hearing of Mama and Papa, and everyone else."

Even as she said the words, though, she knew they weren't true. There was one subject which was best not discussed in front of an audience, although it wasn't the subject Julia was imagining, if her naughty grin was anything to go by.

Mr. Winter was embroiled in some adventure at Frantham Manor, and it drew Amelia like a moth to a flame. She longed to join him in it, to help the ailing viscount, yes, but also for the opportunity to spend more time with Lord Frantham's self-appointed champion.

That brought her up sharply. She could not mean that. Must not mean it. If Papa thought, even for one moment, that his eldest daughter was thinking such thoughts about an unsuitable gentleman like Mr. Winter, Amelia was likely to find she wouldn't just lose her Season for this year, but for every year. Far from meeting and marrying some dashing man about town who would sweep her off her feet while falling deeply in love with her, she was likely to find her future secured—in a nunnery!

But surely, she thought, she could join Mr. Winter on his oh, so enticing adventure without compromising herself or ruining the family name?

She knew he searched for something at Frantham Manor, something which would benefit Lord Frantham, if Mr. Winter were to be believed. And Amelia found she did believe him. There was something about the way he spoke, the expression in his eyes, a softening when he mentioned the older man that told Amelia he cared a great deal for the viscount and his wellbeing.

If that was the case, then Amelia was certain she could help. Mama's determination to bring Mr. Summersby up to scratch meant that Amelia was likely to become a frequent visitor to Frantham Manor. It would certainly be easier for her to access the house than it would be for Mr. Winter, and once inside, there were any number of legitimate reasons for her to wander away and look about her. If she was caught, Mr. Summersby would undoubtedly accept that she had lost her way, or become distracted. But should Mr. Winter be caught there—he would probably find himself in a great deal of pain.

That thought strengthened her resolve. From now on, she would engage Mr. Summersby in conversation at every opportunity, hoping to glean from him any useful facts. She would look for clues and be of great use to Mr. Winter's investigation.

Her satisfaction at her decision must have shown in her smile, for Julia narrowed her eyes, warily. "What devilment are you about?" asked her younger sister.

"Devilment?" Amelia blinked and tried to look innocent.

"Amelia Jane Bell…"

Amelia held up her hand to stop her sister's words. "I may well take a turn about the room with Mr. Winter after all," she said. "Should the opportunity to do so arise. But I assure you, it will all be above board and proper."

Julia struggled to contain her grin. "Will you take a turn with Mr. Summersby as well?"

No! Amelia drew herself up to her full height and raised her chin, haughtily. "A lady waits until she is asked."

"Fustian! You'd take a turn with him soon enough, if you liked him. But it seems to me you prefer Winter to Summer." Julia giggled. "Strange that their names are the opposite of each other, isn't it?" Then she sobered and patted Amelia's arm, her expression giving her the appearance of a dowager aunt, experienced in the ways of the world, rather than of a younger sister who knew even less than Amelia did. "I can help, you know. If you…"

Julia's mouth clamped shut as the door swished open and Mama glided in.

"Oh, good, I have found you two together," said

their parent. "I need you both to come and look at some bolts of cloth that have been delivered. There is such an array of colors, and I can never decide which ones to choose. Your father will be furious if I take the lot, so you must come and advise me on which to buy."

She turned and left the room again. Dutifully, her daughters followed her.

Chapter Thirteen

Amelia smoothed down the front of her gown, pushed her brightest smile to her lips, and went downstairs. The first guests would be here at any moment, and it wouldn't do if she was not there to receive them. Besides, the sooner this dinner party began, the sooner it would be finished, and life could, hopefully, return to normal.

If only she did not feel the weight of all Mama's expectations. Mama had got it into her head that Amelia was the perfect bride for Mr. Summersby, and nothing Amelia could say or do would shake the notion loose. To her mother, the man was ideal: heir to an ailing viscount with a respectable, if not grand, fortune, and since Papa had put an end to hopes for a more *tonnish* match this year, Mama decreed that this was the best Amelia could hope for.

Amelia did not agree. True, this Season would not be hers, but she was still only ten-and-eight, hardly at her last stare. Waiting a whole year to get to London was vexing but it would soon pass, and Amelia would not be the only girl who did not have her come-out until she was ten-and-nine years old. It could even work in her favor— she would be a year more mature and so able to stand apart from the simpering school misses, which in turn might make it easier for her to catch the eye of the best the *ton* could offer.

Besides, even if she had been allowed her Season this year, there was no guarantee she would have taken. Lots of girls did not do well on their first outing to the capital. For an example of that, she need look no further than Catherine Ashton, a neighbor who would accompany her parents to the dinner this evening. Catherine was one-and-twenty now, a pretty brunette who had now braved two Seasons with not a hint of a betrothal.

Her failure was not because of any discernible character flaw that Amelia could see, either. Catherine was certainly not unmanageable, the charge too often laid at Amelia's own feet. Amelia was, said Papa, too brash, too hoydenish and prone to scrapes. No man in his right mind would ever make an offer for such a fright of a girl.

Catherine was none of those things. She was quiet and obedient, respectfully behaved at all times. In short, she was Amelia's exact opposite, a thought that gave Amelia a good deal of hope, since it proved that the ton could as easily reject a pattern-card of respectable womanhood as it could reject everything else, and that in turn indicated that any failures may not be solely due to herself.

The little knub of satisfaction that formed in her breast at the thought of Catherine's failure made Amelia squirm with guilt. She resisted the urge to rub at her chest to dislodge the shame she felt for such emotions. Catherine was a lovely girl and an old friend. Amelia did not wish unremitting spinsterhood upon her, and lauding her friend's difficulties was far beneath her.

Guests began to arrive, and soon the parlor was filled with those who had secured Mama's invitation. It was to be a small dinner, with just fourteen to sit down, although this had more to do with the lack of suitable dinner guests in their sparsely populated neighborhood than any real attempt at restraint on Mama's part. As well as Amelia, Julia and their parents, Catherine and her parents, the gathering was to be made up of the vicar and his sister, Mrs. Rawlins, a widow newly come into the area, Mr. Summersby and his companion, Mr. Sykes, Lord Rotherton, and Mr. Winter.

Amelia sighed and once again wished the evening over.

Mama wasted no time. As soon as Mr. Summersby arrived, she maneuvered Amelia so that he was beside her, unable to ignore her. He was clearly as uncomfortable about this as Amelia was, and the situation was not helped when Mr. Sykes stood nearby, close enough to hear even the quietest of whispers between them, while he himself never said a word. He didn't need to do so. His imposing presence, and the wary way in which Mr. Summersby glanced at him before he said a word, ensured that his silence dominated the entire conversation.

Not that it was much of a conversation at that. Amelia held back a heavy sigh as they established that Mr. Summersby's father was well, and that the winter had not been as harsh as it might have been thus far.

She was about to ask him some inane question about his horse when the air in the room seemed to sharpen and crisp. A shiver ran up her spine, not unlike the tingle she'd felt as a little girl when Julia had run her fingernail lightly up and down Amelia's back. The tiny hairs at the nape of her neck seemed to stand on end. Had it been summer, she would have expected a thunderstorm.

Beside her, Mr. Summersby and Mr. Sykes did not seem to notice. They merely stood as they had been standing, the one looking awkward, the other bored. A quick glance showed that the Ashtons and Mr. Burgess, the vicar, had made no notice of the strange atmosphere, either.

Amelia straightened her shoulders, giving them the tiniest of shakes as if that could dislodge the tingle within. She half turned and looked over her shoulder at the door, as if compelled to do so.

In a strange, silent, slow motion, Lord Rotherton entered the room and smiled at Mama, whose face lit with the pleasure of seeing him. He bowed and turned back to the door, just as Mr. Winter came through it.

The air shimmered around him, softening his outline, the hard planes of his face, the solid wall of his chest, now hidden behind a dark waistcoat shot through with silver thread.

The waistcoat made Amelia frown. His clothes as a whole were impeccable, expensively tailored, and they fit far too well to be borrowed from his cousin. Lord Rotherton was as tall as Mr. Winter, but his shoulders were narrower and his limbs longer and thinner. Had he loaned his cousin that beautiful coat he wore, it would have fitted ill, probably to the point of absurdity.

Which meant they were Mr. Winter's own clothes. Which in turn meant he was not the poor relation, as everyone had supposed. Amelia felt glad for him as she mused that mayhap his pockets were not as to let as the gossips would have her believe.

Or mayhap, she argued with herself, he had prevailed upon his cousin to fit him with a decent suit to save himself from embarrassment. After all, the *on dit* about Rotherton's relatives was that none of them had a feather to fly with, and were it not for him, every last one of them would have drowned in the River Tick long since.

Not that it was any of her business how Mr. Winter acquired his wardrobe, or who paid for it, she reminded herself. Her cheeks heated and she took a deep breath, pushing her curiosity deep down inside herself.

The welcoming smile Mama had bestowed upon Lord Rotherton faded, then dropped at sight of his cousin. Amelia winced at the curtness of her parent's greeting. Titleless he may be, and for all anyone knew, penniless. But based on Amelia's encounters with him thus far, he was a fine, upstanding gentleman, with far more to commend him than could be found in the viscount's heir standing beside her. If only Mama could see below the surface sometimes.

Then again, Mama was not the only one who could not seem to see gold beneath the tarnish. Mrs. Ashton bustled past Amelia, leading Catherine, to whom she whispered furiously, "We might as well make his acquaintance, although his prospects are so poor. I don't know what Mrs. Bell was thinking, sitting you next to a ruffian such as that. Why, you only have to look at the darkness of his skin to see he is no gentleman. That man has labored in fields, you mark my words. My poor Kitty. You are worth so much more."

"I don't mind, Mama," answered Catherine.

"Well, *I* mind." Mrs. Ashton sighed. "Be polite, of course, but don't become too familiar. Maintain a distance, and this evening shall soon pass."

Incensed at Mrs. Ashton's callous dismissal of Mr. Winter, Amelia turned back to him again. This time, their eyes met and all thought flitted away from her, like butterflies rising on summer air.

For a long moment, she stared at him, unable to do more. His eyes were more green than brown tonight, and framed by lashes so long and thick she wondered they did not weigh down his eyelids. The lamplight played on his hair, leaving gold and silver strands gleaming against his dark head.

He bowed his head toward her slightly. So slightly, in fact, that had Amelia not been watching him closely, she might not have seen the movement at all. Even so, the acknowledgement made her cheeks heat and her pulse speed up. She lowered her eyes for a moment, then raised them again. He still watched her, a half-smile playing on his lips, and a twinkle of mischief in his eye. It was as if he knew exactly what she was thinking, knew the way she felt.

Amelia turned away, nonplussed. Of course he knew no such thing. No man could know another person's innermost thoughts and emotions. He was merely teasing her. She would simply refuse to look at him, and put paid to that!

She gave her attention to Mr. Summersby, who continued their conversation about the weather, mentioning the poor climate of the last two summers. "Dreadful," he said with a sad shake of his head. "Although last year was not as bad as sixteen was, so we may live in hope that things will improve. In sixteen, the poor were dying in their hundreds from the hunger, the cold and wet. London's markets were bare of produce, and there were riots in the streets."

Mr. Sykes glared at him. Mr. Summersby swallowed, hard. "So I was told," he mumbled.

Amelia glanced at the two men. That Mr. Sykes was angry with Mr. Summersby was not in doubt, though she could not fathom why. Surely he could not object that his friend had a care for those less fortunate than himself? It was a gentleman's Christian duty to be compassionate. Just as it was a lady's duty to ease tension when she came across it.

"Was the weather unseasonal in India?" she asked.

The two men exchanged glances. Mr. Sykes shrugged and made a small noise that sounded suspiciously like a grunt. Mr. Summersby smiled at her. "India is always unseasonal, Miss Bell. We would not have her any other way. But may I say, you are looking particularly fine this evening? The color of your dress makes your eyes shine brighter than ever."

"Why, thank you," she said, and the three of them lapsed into another awkward silence, which was thankfully broken when they were called in to dinner.

Amelia found herself at table between Mr. Summersby and Mr. Ashton. The older gentleman kept her entertained throughout the first course with a humorous recounting of a recent visit to the nearby town of Lewes and the characters he had encountered there. When the second course was served and she had to turn to her other companion, his diffidence was almost painful. She tried several times to begin a discourse, but he seemed unwilling to answer any of her questions, other than in the most vague terms.

Across the table, Mr. Winter talked amiably with Mrs. Rawlins. Amelia watched them for a moment. She knew very little about Mrs. Rawlins, other than she was a widow who had arrived here three months ago and taken a cottage in the village. The smallness of the dwelling and the fact she employed just the one maid indicated she was a lady of meagre means, although she was clearly gently reared. Amelia knew the lady gave nothing of herself away easily—Mama had complained of her secretive nature after calling upon her. Amelia suspected that was, in part, the reason the widow was invited tonight; the convivial setting might cause her to tell them more about herself.

For now, though, she spoke quietly to Mr. Winter. The pair smiled, and a dimple appeared in his cheek. He replied to her, and she chuckled. Amelia wished she could have heard what he said.

"It is good to see you returned to the fold, Mr. Summersby," said Mama, and all other conversations ceased. Amelia glanced at her sister, Julia, who looked as wide-eyed as Amelia felt. Surely Mama did not intend to dominate the table this early in the meal. At the far end of the table, Papa sighed, but he said nothing.

"Thank you," said Mr. Summersby. He bowed his head and concentrated on cutting into his fish.

"I daresay, you have missed such gatherings as this while you were so far from home." Mama's words were not a question, and Mr. Summersby made no attempt to answer her. Julia rolled her eyes. Amelia frantically searched her mind for something to say, to draw his attention back to her so that the rest of the diners could resume their own social niceties.

Before she could, however, Mama did ask Mr. Summersby a question. "Tell me, sir," she said. "Do you miss India?"

****

"Do you miss India?"

The question made Josh's breath catch in his throat,

and his pulse spiked. He looked up from his dinner plate, only too eager to answer. *Yes. Who wouldn't?* He opened his mouth, then closed it again as he realized the query was not aimed at him but at the false Joshua Summersby, who sat across the table looking decidedly uneasy.

"You must be so glad to be back here, though, to be home in the civilized world?" persisted Mrs. Bell.

Josh blinked. Did the woman think India uncivilized?

"Oh, indeed," agreed Mrs. Ashton, nodding sagely. "These foreign climes are all very well, but they must become exceedingly tiresome after a time."

Across the table, Amelia grimaced. Beside her, Mr. Ashton smiled indulgently at his wife. "I should think, my dear," he said, "that Mr. Summersby might beg to differ. He would no doubt paraphrase the late, great Dr. Johnson, and tell you that when a man is tired of India, he is tired of life."

Mrs. Ashton studied her husband for a moment, then laughed. "You are a wit, Mr. Ashton."

Around the table, others joined in with the laughter. Josh exchanged glances with Rotherton, who gave the tiniest shrug of his shoulders before feigning laughter of his own. Summersby, Josh noted, did not seem to see the humor. Instead, he was tense, his back unnaturally straight and his shoulders raised, as if he expected to jump up from his chair at any moment. Curious, Josh watched him more closely.

"Is it very hot there?" asked Mrs. Bell as the laughter died away.

Summersby glanced at Sykes. Sykes nodded, almost imperceptibly. Summersby smiled and nodded at Mrs. Bell. "Yes," he said, "it is. Hot and exceedingly arid. Not a pleasant climate for those used to the temperate English summers."

Arid? To what part of India did this man claim to have been? In the northwest of the country, in Rajputana, perhaps, he might have found himself in the Thar desert, which could be described as arid for many months of the year. Although, even then, travelling to that region would have taken him through many other provinces, with a vast array of climates, not one of which could have been described as "exceedingly arid." For example, in Madras, where Josh had been based, and where most Europeans first came ashore, it was anything but arid.

"Whereabouts in India were you?" asked Catherine Ashton. She turned and smiled at her father. "When we return home, we will be able to look it up in your book of maps."

"Capital idea," nodded her father.

Summersby swallowed and looked as if his cravat was too tight. All eyes were on him now, everyone waiting for him to answer.

"I was—I spent most of my time in India in…" He picked up his napkin and dabbed at his mouth as if he had just finished a morsel of food. Another quick glance at Sykes, whose mouth puckered as if he had been eating lemons. Summersby smiled. "In Madras," he finished.

Josh's eyebrow shot up. It was all he could do to stop himself proclaiming the man a liar and a charlatan right here at the dinner table. A small movement to the side of Summersby caught his attention. Amelia was staring at him, blue eyes wide and pleading, as if she willed him not to say what he was about to say. The tip of her tongue touched the center of her top lip and the curls arranged so artfully around her face quivered, as if every part of her reached out to beg for his silence.

He schooled his face and gave her the briefest of smiles. She relaxed and smiled back. Triumph flowed through him. He turned away from her before anyone else could notice their silent communications, and Rotherton caught his eye. The earl gave a tiny shake of his head in warning. Josh's nod of agreement was almost as invisible.

Exposing Summersby as a fraud to this gathering had a certain allure. It might well send the man and his cohorts fleeing into the night, thereby rescuing Josh's father from whatever was happening at Frantham Manor, but it would not help Rotherton to end the entire game. Much as Josh was tempted to stop everything here and now, he had no way of knowing if his father would be safe if the villains were not finished completely. The imposter would keep for now.

He looked back at Summersby, then at Amelia beside him. She looked down at her plate quickly. A few seconds passed. She looked up again, saw him still watching her and looked away again.

Lord, but did she know what she did? He thought not. The woman was too innocent to know how her shy glances teased him, how he longed for her to glance up at him, just once more. He watched her, waiting, willing her to meet his gaze...

"Weren't you, Mr. Winter?"

Mrs. Bell's sharp tones cut through the haze surrounding him, startling him so much he almost dropped his fork. He turned to give her his attention, and winced at the way she bared her teeth at him in an expectant smile. He had no idea what she had just asked him, and she was clearly waiting for his answer. All he could do was incline his head and hope it was the correct non-verbal reply.

"And did your path cross Mr. Summersby's during your time there?" she continued.

From the corner of his eye, Josh saw Rotherton give the smallest shake of his head. A warning? If so, he did not need it. He knew what the earl required of him. Instead, he hoped fervently that "there" meant India, and prepared to answer his hostess.

Before he could say anything, though, Amelia joined in. "I believe India is a very large country," she said. "It must be more than possible to spend many years there and still not encounter a specific person, such as Mr. Summersby."

"That is indeed true." Summersby sounded as relieved as Josh felt.

"This fish is delicious, Bell," pronounced Rotherton. "Did it come from your own river?"

Mr. Bell answered him, and the conversation moved on. People turned back to their neighbors and spoke quietly, the low hum of their voices punctuated by chuckles and occasional exclamations, backed by a chorus of chinks as silverware met china. Josh chanced one more look at Amelia and saw her watching him. He smiled a thank you for her intervention. She batted her eyes, using those delectable lashes to say he was welcome.

If only that were true, he thought, as the servants brought the meat course.

The gentlemen did not stay long at their port before they joined the ladies in the drawing room. Actually two rooms divided by wide doors that opened to create a larger space, it was long and narrow. To one end were a collection of chairs and sofas, all upholstered in delicate shades of blue, embroidered with gold thread that picked up the gilt on the arms and legs. Dotted around the room were occasional tables on which rested tiny tea cups, within easy reach of the chattering ladies.

At the other end of the room, Josh could see the pianoforte. Miss Ashton sat at it, playing a lively air proficiently. Julia Bell stood nearby, ready to turn the pages of her music. Much of the rest of that room was hidden from him by the dividing walls.

Amelia was to one side of the main room, perched on a chair with legs no wider than a splinter. Josh marveled that the dainty piece took even her meagre weight. He felt sure it would not have survived his bulk.

Summersby and Sykes entered the room and looked around. Mrs. Bell gestured with her head that Amelia should get up and make them welcome. Amelia pretended not to notice, which, Josh told himself, gave him no satisfaction whatsoever. If he felt anything about the exchange, it was merely amusement that the matchmaking Mama's plans were so easily thwarted. He certainly did not want to crow triumphantly. Nor was his joy tempered by the realization that, in preventing Summersby sitting near her, Amelia had also prevented Josh from doing so.

Amelia took care to look everywhere but at her mother. Josh could see that the effort was costing her. Her whole body quivered with barely contained agitation, the slight fidgets of her feet making her skirt flutter around her ankles. She folded her hands in her lap, then unfolded them and reached for her tea cup, sipped at her drink, put the cup down, and refolded her hands in her lap. Then she did the whole thing again. Josh wanted to reach out to her, to take her tortured fingers in his and calm her. He wanted to tell her all was well, even though he had no way of knowing whether that was true.

Miss Ashton finished playing. Her mother and a few of the other ladies applauded politely, then continued their conversations. Julia and Catherine sat down, heads together, speaking softly. Amelia sipped at her tea again and seemed to try not to look out of place.

Josh could stand no more. He pushed a friendly smile onto his face and walked across the room to her. "Do you play, Miss Bell?" he asked, indicating the pianoforte. She started, as if she had not seen his approach.

"A little."

"You play very well, Miss Bell," said the vicar. "False modesty is as bad as vanity, you know." He softened his criticism with a kindly smile.

"Then, would you allow me to turn your music for you?" persisted Josh.

"Splendid idea," said the vicar, clapping his hands. "Something bright and easy to follow, if you please." He leaned forward, conspiratorially. "I am partial to Dibdin myself."

For a moment, Josh thought Amelia would refuse the request. Then she nodded once, stood, and walked quickly to the pianoforte. "I will play, if my sister and Miss Ashton will sing. Their voices are sweeter than mine."

Julia and Catherine made their way back to the instrument and took their places. Amelia found the music for the song "Sound Argument."

"Remember to sing it in Scottish accents, my dears," called Mrs. Bell. Josh grinned. It was a common ploy.

Apparently, singing a folk song in a false accent could protect the lady's reputation, although he had never fathomed quite how.

Amelia played the first few bars, and the other girls began to sing. Behind them, she spoke to Josh in a sing-song voice that would hide their conversation from the ears of others.

"Did you find what you sought in Frantham Manor?" she asked.

Josh gave her a sidelong look. He didn't wish to discuss this with her, especially not in a crowded drawing room.

"Mayhap you need help from somebody who knew the family," she continued, matching the words to the tune perfectly. Josh raised an eyebrow, unsure whether to be impressed with her rhythmic abilities or dismayed at her interference. "I have known Lord Frantham for some years now," she sang. "If I knew what you seek, if I knew what you seek, if I knew what you seek, I might have seen it."

She played a few bars to separate the verses.

"I can manage," he told her, his words clipped, his annoyance plain. He did not need or want this young lady pushing herself into a situation that could, at best, see her ruined, or at worst, be dangerous to her.

"'Twould be easier for me," she sang. "I have ready access to the manor which is denied you."

"No."

She ignored him. "It would cause no comment were I to visit his lordship. I can go to the library to find a book to read to him. And what would anyone care if searching for the right book took me all day? There are so many books. So many places to look for them."

"No."

Julia and Catherine sang the next lines, and Amelia joined in with them. "I grant, the best blessing we know is a friend, for true friendship's a treasure."

Josh glared at her, then joined in softly on the next line. "Oh, taste not the dangerous pleasure."

Amelia colored slightly. "Thus friendship's a flimsy affair."

He gritted his teeth at her. "If my friendship were flimsy," he hissed, "I would let you continue with your absurd plan."

"It is not absurd."

The girls sang, robustly. "Nor anything pleasing but trouble."

As they repeated the line, Josh sang to Amelia. "Nothing pleases you but trouble."

Her color deepened. He reached over and turned the page, ready to begin the third verse.

"You are being unreasonable," she told him.

"Not I." He did not dare look at her. If he did so, he would undoubtedly pull her into his arms and shake her. Or kiss her senseless. He didn't know which. Both would be disastrous.

"All I need to know is what to look for."

Would the woman never give up? "I forbid it."

"You cannot," she told him, and a victorious grin played upon her lips. "I am not your responsibility."

"For which I thank God at every moment."

She pursed her lips and glared at him. In front of her, Julia and Catherine sang the final lines.

"That with all respect for the fair, I'd advise him to sigh and live single."

He turned his glare upon her and joined in. "I'd

advise him to sigh and live single."

She sniffed and concentrated on playing the final bars on the pianoforte.

****

Amelia stood and Julia took her place, Catherine beside her. As they began to play something else, Amelia took her music to the cupboard at the side of the room. She was far too flustered to sit with the rest of the party. She needed to calm herself before she could re-join them. How dare he presume to tell her what she may and may not do? He was not her father, to dictate her behavior and control her actions! And then to insult her, when she was only trying to help him!

"One of these days," she muttered, "no one shall forbid a woman her part in an adventure by virtue of her sex."

The deep voice behind her made her jump. "Until that day, there will be no adventure for you."

She turned her head and glared at him. His determination showed on every line of his face, his narrowed slash of a mouth, his hard eyes. A muscle jumped in his cheek. It made her pulse skip, and caught her breath. The defiant retort withered on her tongue. With an effort, she turned away from him. Perhaps, if she could no longer see him, he would not affect her so.

From here, the rest of the room was hidden from her view, only Julia and Catherine at the pianoforte visible to her. It should have relieved her for, if she could not see the gathering, then they could not see her, could not witness the effect he had upon her, the uncertainty she felt by dint of his nearness. She lowered her head and concentrated her attention on the drawer full of music manuscripts before her.

Julia and Catherine sang the chorus of their song.

"Promise me you will not carry out your foolhardy plan?" His words were no more than a whisper. His breath stirred the tiny curls at the nape of her neck and sent shivers along her spine. She took a deep breath and stiffened her shoulders.

"How is it any more foolhardy than yours?" she answered him, defiance making her tone sharp. "Were it not for me, you would have already been caught, and with not even the flimsiest of reasons to cover your presence."

He made a small noise. Whether it signified that he was angry at her continued argument or that he was conceding the point, she could not tell.

"For certain, Mr. Winter," she went on, "left to your own devices, you would now have nothing but your connection to Lord Rotherton to protect you from a spell in jail, or perhaps even transportation. Whereas, I may come and go…"

"No! I forbid it!"

She whirled to face him, face hot with fury. Drawing herself up to her full height, she glared at him, anger all but exploding from her. "You forbid it? You forbid it?" She poked her forefinger into his chest as she sputtered the words. "No, sir, you do not. You cannot sway me, and I will not be denied. I do and say what I will, and you cannot stop me. You do not have the right to—mmh!" The last sound was a squeak of surprise as his lips pressed against hers, cutting off her words.

The kiss was hard, at first, punishing. His lips were firm against hers, the rasp of his chin rough against her own smooth skin. He tasted of the brandy he had drunk, laced with tea, and the sweet icing on the biscuit he had eaten with it. His cologne wrapped itself around her—exotic flowers, silk and cotton, the scents of places far, far away. His hands rested on her shoulders, warming her skin. Of their own volition, her hands touched his chest, her fingers pressed against the watery cool of his waistcoat, the hard warmth of his body below it. She could feel his heart beating, faster and louder than she would have dreamed possible.

The kiss softened until his lips caressed hers. His hands moved round to her back, drawing her closer to him. Her own arms moved up, encircling his neck, her fingers threading between the short hairs at the back of his head. She leaned in closer to him, felt the heat of his body against hers, the hardness of him pressing against her stomach. It should have shocked her, repelled her. Instead, it thrilled her.

His tongue moved against the seam of her lips, begging her to open. She did so and he slipped inside, the warm taste of him filling her, making her want more. Her heartbeat sped and her knees weakened, and if he had not held her, she would have melted into a puddle on the floor.

There was a small mewling noise, and she realized it was her as she pulled him closer, closer…

Julia's voice, so sweet a moment ago, became strident, slightly off key. "Shall my signal be," she sang, loudly, while her fingers pounded at the keyboard. "And this shall be my song. Blow high, blow low, let tempests tear the mainmast by the board. My heart with thoughts of thee, my dear, should keep love well stored."

The incorrect lyrics in the final line jolted Amelia back to reality. She was in Mama's drawing room, with several of her neighbors no more than a few feet away from her. If one of them had stood, approached the pianoforte, they would see her, kissing Mr. Winter for all she was worth!

She untangled her fingers and pushed him away. Immediately, he broke the kiss and took a step back from her. His breathing was as ragged as hers, his chest rising and falling heavily. He swallowed, hard, turned from her, stood admiring a painting on the wall, his hands clasped behind his back.

Amelia touched her fingers to her lips. They felt swollen, tingling as if stung. Her pulse skittered unevenly, and her face was hot. She turned toward the pianoforte and saw Julia glaring at her. Amelia lowered her own gaze in shame. The music in her hands shook. She turned to the drawer and slid it into place, taking deep breaths to calm herself. Julia's singing became sweet again.

"There you are," said Mama as she moved from the populated part of the room and approached Amelia. "Have you found another piece you wish to play?"

"Er—no." Amelia could not believe how breathless she sounded. "I am happy to listen to the others."

"Well, if you wish it," said Mama. "Though it is a shame. Yours is such sweet playing. However, it speaks well of you to let the others shine. Come and sit with me, and tell Mrs. Ashton how well Catherine does." She pushed her arm through the crook of Amelia's elbow and led her back to the main room.

From her seat beside Mama, Amelia watched Mr. Winter move back into the crowd. He moved slowly, admiring pictures around the walls, as if trying hard not to draw attention to himself with sudden movement. At last, he sat down, on the edge of a chair in the corner. For the first time, Amelia noticed how tiny the furniture was in this room. The spindly legs on the chair seemed hardly adequate to hold the gentleman's frame, and she half expected them to splinter and deposit him in a heap on the ground. His back was ramrod straight, and he fairly quivered with tension. His hands pressed against his knees, as if they could stop the nervous bounce that now and then escaped. He fixed his gaze on the pianoforte, concentrating as if his entire life depended on her sister's performance.

Which, mused Amelia, it very well might.

****

Riding home in Rotherton's carriage, all Josh could think about was Amelia. He should never have given in to the urge to kiss her, especially not in such a dangerously public place. But then, if he was honest with himself, he hadn't really given in to the urge to do anything. It was as if some strange force had taken control of him, body, mind, and spirit, so that he acted instinctively.

He should be grateful that nobody, save her sister, had seen him take her in his arms in that way, or he would be marching inexorably toward the altar right now. And how disastrous that would have been, for her more than for him. Vivacious and pretty as an English rose, she had the promise of a future. In the next year or two, she would meet a man worthy of her, one who would cherish her and give her the life she deserved. That life was most definitely not growing sallow and old before her time in the sub-tropical humidity of Madras. It would break Josh's heart to see the rose wilt, perfume souring, the vividness fading away until all that was left were dried and withered petals. He should keep his distance at all costs.

But then, he was beginning to realize, she was a stubborn little minx, and she had got it into her head that she could help with the problems at Frantham Manor. How, in all good conscience, could he keep his distance when he knew that would simply encourage her to run headlong into a situation she was not at all equipped to handle? Intrepid she may be, but she was also vulnerable. Which, in turn, meant that he must keep a weather eye on her. He groaned at the realization.

"That sounds as if your thoughts are profound enough to give you indigestion," said Rotherton. He sat back on his seat, hands clasped across his stomach and a knowing grin lighting his face.

If you only knew.

"So," continued the earl, "now that you have met him, what did you think of our esteemed Mr. Summersby?" He flicked an imaginary piece of lint from his coat lapel. "He does not seem to have fond memories of India."

Josh snorted. "The only India he has any memory of at all is the tea he was served at breakfast."

Rotherton nodded. "Thank you for not pressing the issue tonight. I know you were tempted, for your father's sake."

"Following your plan is the only way to ensure his complete and lasting safety." Silently, Josh added, *And to ensure Miss Bell does not do something reckless in the meantime.*

Rotherton's smile was grim. "May it be resolved quickly," he said.

Josh nodded his agreement.

Chapter Fourteen

Amelia woke to a room that was still bathed in the blue-white light of early morning, although the chill of dawn had been pushed back by the cheerful fire already lit in her hearth. For some time, she lay still in her bed, her feet toasty beneath the heavy blankets, while her mind replayed the events of the night before.

Specifically, The Kiss.

The very thought of that kiss made her lips tingle, and she touched her fingertips lightly to them, half expecting to find them swollen, their texture somehow different to the way they had felt yesterday morning. That they were still smooth and warm, still the same shape and size as they had ever been, was a complete surprise, especially when she could still taste him, still feel the warm confidence of his skin against hers, his tongue caressing hers until her insides quivered and her nipples stood to attention. The soft cotton of her nightgown was heavy against them, an irritant that was as pleasurable as it was discomforting. A strange ache between her legs made her squirm in an effort to release it, which only served to make the cotton stroke her nipples the more.

She closed her eyes and took a deep breath, telling herself it was absurd to feel this way about such a little thing as a kiss. After all, it was not as if she had never been kissed before. She had been. Twice. Although neither of those snatched moments had made her feel remotely like this. The kisses in her past had been wet and uncomfortable, the smell of stale breath, the rough stubble of a man in need of a shave. There had been absolutely no similarity between them and the kiss she had received from Mr. Winter last night.

Amelia tried to tell herself it was the danger, the thrill of being somewhere they might be caught. The little alcove to the side of the drawing room may have seemed private, but it would have taken little to change that. If one of Mama's friends had walked across to where Julia played the pianoforte, they would have been unable to miss the spectacle of Miss Amelia Bell being thoroughly compromised and bringing scandal on the family name once again. And if Papa or Mama had seen... Amelia shuddered at the thought.

Part of her wanted to rail at the unfairness of it. After all, she had not invited Mr. Winter into the alcove, had not asked him to kiss her. He had taken her by surprise, and it did not seem right that she, an innocent, should have risked censure and ruin. Amelia made a face. If she was honest, that was not a valid defense. He may have initiated the kiss, she may not have seen it coming, but she was not an innocent. She had kissed him back, an equal partner as she wove her fingers through his hair and pulled him closer to her. Had it not been for Julia's strident singing bringing Amelia back to reality, she might have stayed within his arms a lot longer, and given away far more than a kiss!

It had taken several moments after they broke apart before she was composed enough to return to the main part of the room and take her place in company. Judging from the wild-eyed look on his face, the raggedness of his breathing and the way he had stared at the unexceptional painting on the wall, he had felt the same way. Then, for the rest of the evening, every time she chanced a look in his direction, he was staring at her, as if he studied everything about her. Heat rising through her cheeks, she had lowered her eyes quickly, determined not to glance at him again, not to give him any encouragement. Seconds had passed. Sometimes more than a minute. Then, finally, she had been compelled to look up again as a moth is compelled to fly to a flame, only to look away again in confusion at his relentless stare.

She would have liked to tell herself he stared because he found her irresistible, but she knew that was not the truth. Gentlemen did not find young ladies like Amelia irresistible. Attractive, yes, she was not so unaware that she did not know some found her attractive, even with her too-wide mouth and her turned-up nose. Others made it clear they found her engaging. They would talk with her at soirees and enjoy her company, her willingness to find joy in the dullest of occasions, and her sense of humor that allowed her to see the absurd for what it was. They would dance with her at the assemblies and know her for a gracious and forgiving partner who didn't complain when they trod on her toes or threw her around the dance floor like a rag doll. She could be relied upon at dinner to converse intelligently. But there was a world of difference between being good company and having a man fall at her feet, his eyes filled with devotion and voice lost in wonder of her.

"Not that I would want a man to behave in such a fashion," she muttered. "He'd be a candidate for Bedlam if he did, and that's a fact."

Still, to be treated like a goddess, just once, would surely be wonderful. To be raised onto a pedestal like some valuable work of art, rare, precious, and fragile.

That last thought made her scowl. Mr. Winter seemed to think she was fragile, even if she was neither rare nor precious in his sight, and she hadn't found it wonderful at all. In fact, it had been downright infuriating, being forbidden to do things as if she were a child.

And why? She was in far less danger than he would be. The viscount's library was open to her in a way he could only dream of. Even the horrid Mr. Sykes would not question her presence, for surely he could not cavil at someone wanting to read to an ailing nobleman. She had to admit, she had never before gone without her parents, but she didn't feel that would be too remarked upon.

That Mr. Winter thought such a simple task beyond her capabilities smarted. That he would deny her even such a dull adventure as this, simply because she was female, made her all the more determined to defy him.

There was no time like the present. This morning, straight after breakfast, Amelia would visit Frantham Manor and prove the man wrong about her. She would find whatever it was that was out of place or incriminating in that library, and then present it, with a victorious flourish, to the sheepish Mr. Winter.

She would show him. She threw back her blankets and rang for her maid.

Two hours later, she set off, taking a shortcut through the fields and woods that separated the Frantham estate from the small town of Rotherton. She wore a woolen walking dress in ivy green, and the deep juniper color of her coat seemed to make it warmer, although the dew on the coarse grass dampened her hem until it wrapped itself, cold and uncomfortable, around her calves, and her toes chilled inside her wet half boots. The sky was still an unremitting gray, but there was now a glow to the air, as if the sun threatened to break free at any moment. A small breeze played around her, brushing against her cheeks and tugging at the brim of her dark green bonnet. It rattled the leaves on the holly bushes that bordered the final field and shimmered the surface of a dark brown puddle. Amelia hopped over the muddy water, landing on the grass on the other side with a little skip to steady herself. A few more yards and she would reach a narrow opening in the holly hedge, through which she could move from the field to the driveway leading to the manor. The route was muddier than using the proper road, the ground a little less steady, but going cross-country took well over a mile off the journey.

She squeezed through the opening, and her coat caught on the bush. Not wanting to pull the thread, Amelia grimaced and stepped backward to free herself, putting herself out of sight of anybody on the drive. She pulled carefully at the bush, trying to unthread her coat. She'd just managed to extricate herself when she heard Mr. Sykes speaking to someone on the drive. Her lip curled in dismay. She did not care for Mr. Sykes at the best of times. Now, no doubt, he would accompany her to the manor house and she would be forced to make polite conversation with him.

"It can't stay there," he said now, his voice gritty with an angry sneer. "It will get damp, and then it will be useless."

Amelia nearly groaned out loud. The man was

clearly in a sour mood. She prayed he wouldn't want to escort her, and she wouldn't have to be polite to him.

"It was the only place we thought it would be safe," grumbled Mr. Sykes' companion. His was not a voice Amelia recognized, but the words had a strong Sussex burr to them. "Don't want no look-seers finding it and blarting about it to one and all, do we?" continued the man. "Ain't nobody likely to go out to Marshy Meadow in January."

Amelia straightened, her head cocked to one side as if that could help her to hear more. She frowned. Why would anyone *want* to go to Marshy Meadow? On the edge of Rotherton, the place was cold and inhospitable, even in the height of summer, set as it was on the edge of the river, under sheer cliffs of chalk. The ground was always wet and spongy, difficult to walk across without falling into thick, dark mud that had the consistency and stickiness of honey. As a child, Amelia had lost a boot there, and by the time she'd limped home, her feet were bruised and her stockings beyond repair. Since Papa had forbidden her to go anywhere near the boggy meadow in the first place, she had been sent to bed without any tea, and she had been made to use her meagre sweet allowance to save for a new pair of both boots and stockings. Amelia had thought it harsh punishment indeed, but it had worked. She had never played in Marshy Meadow again.

And now, the man on the drive had hidden something there? He would be fortunate if it didn't sink, to be lost forever.

"There's a very good reason why no one goes there," Sykes snapped. He sighed, a loud, rasping noise full of anger. "Get out there and bring it back."

"It'll likely take three or four trips to bring it all," complained the man. "And the ground won't take the wagon far into the meadow, so we'll have to carry the stuff almost to the gate."

"I don't care."

"I suppose we could use the wide-wheeled wagon, and careful how we spread the load..."

"I don't need to know the logistics!" Sykes' voice dripped contempt. "Just do it." Amelia stiffened at his tone, and her hands came up defensively, even though he had not seen her and could not be directing his anger at her. Feeling foolish, she lowered her arms again.

The heels of a man's boots rang against the driveway's hard surface as he strode briskly away. Muttering under his breath, the second man walked in the other direction, past where Amelia was hidden. Instinctively, she shrank back into the hedge, thankful she had worn a green coat today, which meant he was far less likely to see her.

As soon as he had gone by, she peered out. A quick glance showed her that Mr. Sykes had completely disappeared around a bend in the drive, while the other man marched toward the gate, shoulders hunched, every movement filled with fury.

Amelia thought for a moment. He was going to fetch something that was hidden, something neither he nor Mr. Sykes wished others to discover. Could this be what Mr. Winter had been searching for?

Now Amelia was torn. Should she follow the man out to Marshy Meadow and try to discover exactly what had been hidden? Or should she fetch Mr. Winter and direct him to the hiding place?

Of course, whatever the man had hidden might have

nothing to do with Mr. Winter's search. It would, therefore, be a waste of his time to bring him out until she was certain it involved him. She told herself her reluctance to fetch him had nothing to do with her certainty that, while he investigated, he would insist she stay behind.

She glanced after Mr. Sykes once more. Satisfied he was gone, she set off after the second man.

He didn't expect to be followed. Not once did he turn around to make sure he was alone, and he made no effort to hide his progress, all of which made Amelia's task easy. They left Frantham Manor and made their way along the road away from the village. The road was more of a track, a thin strip of hardened mud, with two deep ruts running either side of a raised center where grass grew. Pot holes of various sizes made the ground uneven. The lush green grass on the verges seemed to tumble down the sheer drops into the deep ditches that ran along under dry stone walls separating them from the fields beyond. Some of those fields were a deep green, dotted with sheep and cows. Others were a dark brown, cleared soil, ploughed and ready for planting when spring arrived.

The fields gave way to woodland, where trees grew closely together, their branches twining into a messy tangle. Brambles, bare and forlorn now, grew around the edges of the wood, as if standing guard, denying all access, while ivy clung to the tree trunks like a protective blanket. In the distance, Amelia could hear the dull roar of the river.

About a mile from the manor gates, a small cottage stood to one side of the road, its flint walls capped by a low, pantiled roof. The shutters over the tiny window were in need of repair, the paint completely peeled away, and the wood soft and crumbling where rain had made it rotten. The door looked no better, and moss grew on the uneven stonework. The building had an unlived-in air, yet this was where the man stopped and pounded on the door. Amelia crouched down on the verge and held herself absolutely still, praying he would not turn and see her.

The door opened and the man went inside. Amelia half ran, half crept forward, as close to the window as she dared, hoping to glean more information, but all she could hear were muffled voices. She scrunched her face in frustration, then rushed to find a hiding place when she heard the unmistakable rattle of the door latch. She made it to the back of the house and hid behind a pile of wood. In a small shed, a cow lowed, and a goat bleated.

The man came into the yard with two companions, both dressed in the smocks and coarse breeches of laborers, their legs below the knee bare, their feet encased in cumbersome clogs.

"You get the wagon," said the man from the manor, "and meet us there. We'll start hauling it out."

"Going to be a long day for us, I reckon," answered one of his companions.

"Aye," said the other. "Bloody nobs. Do this. Do that. Never think of our backs breaking, do they?"

"Mr. Sykes ain't no nob."

"He'd like to be, and that's the same thing."

"No, it isn't. We'd all *like* to be..."

"Oh, quit your jawing and get that wagon hitched." The man from the manor almost barked the order at the other men. He pointed at one of them. "You come with me," he said, and the two of them walked back out to the road while the third man went into the barn.

It seemed an age until the wagon, drawn by a sorry-looking ox who had definitely seen better days, rattled past Amelia and headed out along the road after the other men. She stood, then grimaced at the pins and needles pricking at her foot and the ache in her leg from so long in an awkward position. She rolled her ankle first one way, then the other, and scrunched her toes up in her boot to get the circulation going again before leaving the yard and following the cart at a discreet distance. The road she walked along was narrow, only a little wider than the wagon. Hedges grew high on each side, with here and there a tree to break their uniformity. She could hear the dull roar of the rushing river in the distance, its volume swelled by the winter rains. Amelia shivered, awed by the power behind the sound.

They left the hedges behind, the road edged by more dry stone walls, and she saw the fields beside the lane. Beyond them were the tall chalk cliffs that flanked the river. They stood against the sky, their sheer white sides daubed with lines of green. At their base were hefty pieces of chalk, evidence of more than one rockfall.

Those cliffs were the reason this part of the land was so prone to flooding. Once the river rose, they restricted its path, keeping the overflow trapped between them like tea is trapped by the sides of a cup. The ground never had opportunity to dry fully, and was always spongy and squelching beneath one's feet, which was why the locals called it Marshy Meadow. No good for planting crops or for putting livestock out to graze, the land lay fallow all year, ignored by all and sundry. Which, Amelia allowed, made it the perfect hiding place for the nefarious goings-on of Mr. Sykes and his cronies. Except, as far as Amelia knew, there was no hiding place on the flat expanse of land.

The ox pulled the wagon through the gate that led into Marshy Meadow before the driver pulled to a stop. Amelia crouched down to hide, pressing herself against the wall and thanking everything that was holy that she had worn a dress and coat in green today. She would not have blended so easily with her surroundings if she had worn blue or, God forbid, red. Green allowed her to creep nearer to the gate to see what the men were doing.

"I can't get this wagon across here," said the driver. "It'll sink."

"I know that," said the man who had been at Frantham. "But you needn't think you're sitting there while me and him do all the fetching. Come on, put your back into it."

Muttering obscenities, the driver trudged into the meadow.

Cautiously, Amelia watched them walk across the uneven ground, now and then stumbling. As far as she knew, the meadow ended at the water's edge, and the cliffs meant there was no other way out. She couldn't see anything in the field that looked out of place, either, and she frowned, trying to make sense of their actions. Then she started, eyes wide, as the third man appeared on the sheer side of the cliff. He stood about three feet from the ground, dark against the white of the chalk. Under both arms he carried what looked like casks. The driver took them from him and headed back to the wagon. Amelia darted across the meadow's entrance and hid behind the wall on the other side, reasoning they wouldn't see her here when they left. As long as they went back the way they had come, that was.

The men moved between the cliff and the wagon several times, each time thudding more casks onto its wooden bed. Amelia longed to know what was in the wooden barrels, but she did not dare to investigate further. Most likely, they were filled with brandy, and the last thing she wished to do was to fall foul of smugglers. People still talked about the Hawkhurst gang and their vicious reign of terror, and that had been seventy years ago! She would stay put until they were gone, learn exactly what it was they were up to, then tell Lord Rotherton of it, so that he might do his duty under the law.

Amelia wondered if his cousin would come out here with him. It was the sort of duty she imagined Mr. Winter would be proud to do. She could see him now, fighting the villainous leader of the gang, subduing him and bringing him to book, the strength of him easily keeping the ruffian down, his commanding presence ensuring the gang's surrender before he stood tall, straightened his coat and pushed back his tousled hair...and then, no doubt, scolded Amelia for being anywhere other than in her own sitting room, embroidering flowers onto doilies. She scowled at the memory of him last night, towering over her, glowering and saying, "I forbid it." As if he had the right to do any such thing. And then, when she defied his arrogant order, to take such a liberty as to kiss her!

She put her fingers to her lips as if, somehow, she could feel the imprint of that kiss there. The warm scent of him washed over her, so real and strong she looked around to see if he was behind her. He wasn't, of course, and she exhaled sharply, feeling foolish, relieved and, at the same time, disappointed.

Which was silly. She wasn't here to gather wool

over him. She was here to discover what these men were about, to do her part in bringing smugglers to book, and to help her friend, Viscount Frantham. Putting Mr. Winter firmly from her thoughts, she concentrated all her attention on the three men trudging back and forth from the cliff to the wagon, carrying heavy barrels on their shoulders.

Finally, the driver declared the wagon would take no more, and they must transport this first load and come back for the rest. Crouched small, pressed against the wall and hardly daring to breathe, Amelia watched them travel back along the road to wherever they would store their ill-gotten gains next, then made her way across Marshy Meadow to see what she could learn before she went for help.

Her boots squelched over the muddy field, sinking deep more than once, so that the cold wet spilled inside them, soaking her feet and clinging to her stockings. Her hem grew heavy with mud, and she shuddered, wondering what were the chances of her getting to her room and changing before Mama or Papa could see her bedraggled state.

"You really should think these things out before you act," she scolded herself as she reached the cliff. "You wouldn't attract half the trouble you do if you used your brain—oh!" The last word was an exclamation as she found an opening in the rock. About three feet above the ground, it was tucked into a crease in the cliff face, so that it wasn't immediately obvious unless one was actually searching for it. From what she could see, it went back a few feet before it was swallowed in darkness, but there was no doubt in her mind—this was where the barrels had been.

She looked down at her coat and sighed. She could either save her clothes or she could find out what was in the cave. "I've come this far," she whispered, but she unbuttoned the coat in an attempt to save it from the worst of the damage before she hauled herself up over the chalk.

The narrow entrance to the cave went back a few feet, then seemed to end in a solid wall but, on closer inspection, she saw that the path merely turned a sharp corner and carried on down into the cliff. At the end of the second tunnel she could see a flickering light and she made her way to it, to find herself in a large cavern with a high roof and hard packed floor. A torch flickered in a sconce that had been hewn from the wall of the cave. The room contained about two dozen barrels and a couple of chests. A few knives with wicked blades and a couple of sharp farming implements were piled against one wall. Awed, and a little frightened, Amelia wandered around the chamber, unsure where to start.

She lifted the lid on one chest and the pungent scent of tobacco filled the air. She was right, then; they were smugglers. Was this the evidence Mr. Winter had searched for at Frantham Manor?

Moving farther around the edge of the cave, she reached a place where the wall disappeared into another opening, even narrower than the entrance to the cave. She squeezed through and found herself in a smaller cave, dimly lit by a shaft of sunlight falling from a hole in the rock several feet above her. There was nothing stored in this cave, so she returned to the main chamber.

The men would return soon, and move more of their cargo. Amelia knew she must not be here when they came. More, she must get a message to Mr. Winter before it was gone. She hurried toward the cave entrance but tripped on the uneven floor. As she fell, she knocked one of the barrels. It wobbled and the lid dislodged. Instead of the expected brandy spilling out and soaking into the floor, there was a trickle of dark powder.

Amelia took off her glove and gingerly reached toward the powder, took a handful. It was coarse against her skin, some pieces sharp, others smooth and round. It had a brittleness about it, and yet was hard, too. It smelled faintly of charcoal with a whiff of something sharper behind it, not unlike the smell of the necessary at the Golden Goose. She wrinkled her nose, dropped the powder back onto the pile, and pulled on her glove. The sooner she reported this finding to Mr. Winter, the better she would feel.

Propriety demanded she go home and write him a note, asking him to meet with her, but she didn't think they had enough time for that. She had no way of knowing how far the smugglers were taking their contraband, or how long they would be gone. It would not do for it all to have disappeared before she could show it to Mr. Winter. The quicker she could tell him her news, the better. So, with only the slightest twinge of anxiety about her reputation, she ran toward Rotherton Hall.

She was almost there when she encountered the very gentleman she sought, walking along the lane. He stopped when she called out to him, and waited for her to catch up.

"I need...you...to come...something to...show you," she told him, then took several deep breaths and willed her heartbeat to slow down.

He frowned. "To show me?"

She gestured with her hand that he should follow her. He looked set to argue with her, but she held up her hand. "No time," she said. "You must see," and she walked back the way she had come. His boot soles scraped against the road, then sounded, clear and firm, as he followed.

They reached Marshy Meadow, and she showed him where the cave was, following him down the narrow passages to the large chamber. There were fewer barrels in here now, indicating the smugglers had already returned for a second load. Amelia took him to the barrel she had upended and showed him the powder that had spilled out.

"I thought it would be brandy in the barrels, but it isn't. Unless brandy turns to powder in certain circumstances?"

"Not that I know of." He crouched beside the barrel, removed his gloves, took a handful of the powder and smelled it. "Smells like gunpowder to me."

"Gunpowder?" Shock and horror made her voice a squeak. "What is happening here? Why would Mr. Sykes have need of gunpowder?" She looked around. "So *much* gunpowder."

"I'd like to know that myself." He stood up and dusted the powder from his hands, his mouth set in a grim line, determination and worry in his eyes. He caught her watching him and smiled. "'Tis probably nothing," he told her. "Part of their normal cargo each week, I shouldn't be surprised."

Amelia arched one eyebrow, and her tone was disbelieving. "Gunpowder? You think the gentlemen bring this amount of gunpowder into England every week? And what, pray, do you think they intend to do with it? Blow up the Houses of Parliament?"

Mr. Winter looked sheepish. "Not every week," he said. She glared at him, and his shoulders sagged in defeat. "I would think this is an unusual cargo," he admitted. "We should inform Lord Rotherton. He can haul them in and question them, while you go home, where you will be safe." She bristled as he led her toward the cave's entrance.

"I am perfectly capable of looking after myself," she said. "I found the cave, and the contraband, did I not? Without help and without detection. I would remind you to…"

He turned around and shushed her, one finger to his lips. Incensed at his rudeness, she opened her mouth to give him a piece of her mind, but his eyes hardened, his finger pressed his lips harder, and his mouth took on a thoroughly determined line. Puzzled, and a little hurt, she closed her mouth again.

Then she heard what he had heard, and her pulse sped up again at the sound of men's voices, coming toward them across Marshy Meadow.

Chapter Fifteen

Josh looked around frantically for somewhere to hide, but he could see nowhere. He didn't much like his odds, three of them to one of him, especially when he must also protect Amelia, but it didn't seem he had a choice. At least he had the element of surprise.

"This way," Amelia whispered, urgently. She grabbed his arm and pulled him toward the rock.

Josh frowned. "What are you doing?" There was no hiding place along the back wall of the cave. The men would be bound to see them there.

"I discovered it earlier. Come on."

He watched in amazement as she squeezed into a crack in the cave wall and disappeared. Outside, the men sounded as if they had reached the opening to the cave. With a last glance in their direction, Josh followed Amelia through the fissure.

It was a tight fit. He had to exhale sharply and contort his body to get through, making it in the nick of time as the men's boots scraped the cave floor behind him.

He found himself in a smaller cave, lit by slivers of natural light that made the damp walls shine and reflected in a puddle that had formed on the uneven ground. Amelia stood in the center of the tiny chamber, looking pleased with herself.

"We should be safe here," she whispered, so softly

he almost could not hear her.

In the outer cave, a man complained loudly that he'd got water in his boot. There was a grunt, a slight thud, and the sound of running water.

"Don't empty it there, you'll get the powder wet," said a second man. "Honestly, there are times when I think God missed you out completely when it came to brains."

"I got no brains? I'm not the idiot as stored this lot here in the first place."

"Oh, be quiet and start taking it out. You're like an old woman, finding fault with everything."

They carried on arguing, the scrape of wood against rock and the grunts as they picked up the barrels punctuating their words.

A soft rustling behind him caught Josh's attention and he turned to see Amelia sit down on the cold, hard ground. "It took them an hour to load up the last wagon," she whispered. "I don't intend to stand here all that time."

"You will ruin your dress," he warned.

Amelia shrugged. "Won't be the first time that's happened. Mama has come to almost expect it of me."

Josh grinned and sat down close beside her. He told himself he needed to be close to her so they could talk without the men in the other chamber hearing them. If it weren't for that, he would have sat elsewhere, given her distance. He was merely thinking of her safety, that was all.

They were so close he could hear her soft breathing and feel the warmth of her body next to his. The scent of her seemed to fill the air, a soft, flowery perfume, mixed with the cold wintry air trapped in her hair. His thighs tightened and there was an urgent ache low down in his stomach as his arousal began.

Of all the inappropriate...

He bit down on his bottom lip and closed his eyes, willing his body to behave.

He'd almost got his errant feelings under control when Amelia shifted, coming closer to him, so that her arm touched his and her leg pressed against him, and he groaned as his manhood grew again, pressing against his trousers. It hurt like the devil, and he bit his bottom lip to stop the agonized cry. Praying the light was too dim for Amelia to notice, he unbuttoned one side of the fall of the trousers and slid his hand in to readjust himself.

"Do you get spiders in caves?" she asked, and she leaned even closer to him.

"What?" To his own ears, his voice sounded strained, strangled.

"Spiders. I think one just crawled over my hand." She shuddered. "I hate spiders."

"They won't hurt you—"

"Don't say that! Papa says that. It's not helpful." She gave a tiny squeak and slapped at her leg, making her gown rustle and billow. She wiggled her legs and slapped again.

Josh glanced at the entrance, worried that the men would hear her. She slapped again, and he reached around her waist and hauled her onto his lap. It would be sheer torture, he knew, but better that than those ruffians should discover them here, where he was outnumbered and trapped.

"What are you—"

Needing to silence her, he did the only thing he could. He covered her lips with his, catching her exclamation of surprise in his mouth. Amelia stiffened in his arms, and he braced himself, ready to be pushed away, perhaps even slapped. Then she relaxed against him, her fists unclenching, hands pressed against his chest as she returned the kiss.

She tasted of fresh winter air, and her skin was as cold as the chalky cave, but her mouth was warm beneath his, her breath as ragged as his was becoming. She gave a soft moan and lifted her arms, winding them round his neck, knocking his hat away before her fingers played through his hair.

He pulled her closer, so that her breasts pressed against his chest, hardening his body even more and pulling a reluctant groan from him. He burned with the need to touch her, to pull her closer still, until she was part of him, and he was part of her. Desperate for more, for a taste of her, he drew his tongue across the seam of her lips until she opened for him, allowing him to thrust into her mouth. His tongue scraped over the deliciously sharp edge of her teeth before finding her tongue, moving alongside it in an exquisite, torturous dance.

Josh's hands stroked her back, her shoulders, her neck, and his fingers found her hair, as soft and smooth as silk. Her bonnet fell away, hitting the floor with a soft thud, and then came the soft pattering of a dozen hairpins raining down, freeing the long tresses, which tumbled over her shoulders. Even in the dim light, her hair shone, drawing him. He gathered it in his hands, and growled at the feel of it, cool and heavy. He deepened the kiss, and she shifted, pressing against him as if she tried to climb inside him, and flashes of lightning sparked behind his eyes.

His lips left hers, and she gave a sigh of displeasure

that made him want to crow in triumph. Instead, he feathered kisses along her jawline to her throat, her neck, her ear. She threw back her head and arched her back to give him access. His hand moved of its own volition, stroking her neck, her shoulder, her side, until his palm settled on the sweet curve of her breast.

He unbuttoned her coat and pushed it aside so that all that was between them was the soft wool of her high-necked day dress. He caressed her through the gown, smiling when he felt her nipple harden and grow beneath his fingers.

It wasn't enough. With an urgency he could not fathom, he wanted to touch her, the warm softness of her, skin on skin, to feel her flesh shiver beneath his hands. Bringing his mouth back to hers, he fumbled with the buttons on her dress, opening it, exposing her beauty to him, then worked his fingers under the edge of her cotton chemise to the warm skin below. She moaned softly into his mouth and he surged on the sound as her fingers pushed deeper into his hair.

She was killing him! Exquisite pain shot through him, and he shifted slightly, clenching his stomach muscles and tightening his thighs against the ache.

He massaged her bared breast. The nipple grew, hard and erect and perfect, and he tweaked it between his finger and thumb. Amelia moaned, deep and low, and arched against him, pushing it into his hand. His heart beat erratically, his breathing tight, and every nerve within him was on edge. He kissed her neck, the little dimple at the base of her throat, and she clung to him, her face buried into his hair, her own breaths short and rapid. Her actions were innocent, unschooled, and more erotic than a touch from the most practiced of courtesans.

She was everything he wanted, all he could desire.

Josh lifted her up, pulled her against him, and his mouth found her breast. He suckled greedily, drawing the nipple deep. She tasted of roses and cotton, mixed with cold air and her own unique warmth. She gasped and pushed her hands deeper into his hair, pulling him closer, holding him there.

His other hand moved down, skimming her waist, her hip, her thigh. Instinctively, she raised her knee and he found her ankle beneath the hem of her dress, and stroked it through her thick stockings. Amelia squirmed against him, pressing closer to him, setting him on fire. He could feel her heart, the beats so fast they seemed to meld into one. He pushed the hem of her dress up. It rasped softly against her stocking as he lifted it up, over her calf, past her knee, his fingertips trailing it, feeling every twitch of her muscles, every jump of her nerves.

He reached the apex of her thighs, felt the springy curls guarding her center, the wet heat below them. She was panting now, writhing against his hand, pulling at his hair as if to drag him away from her, then pushing him close to her again, as if she couldn't bear even the shortest distance between them.

She was so close. So close. Any moment he would feel her shatter. It was what he wanted more than anything, he realized now, to feel her fall apart beneath his touch, to see her, eyes glazed with satiation as heaven pulsed through her, leaving her boneless...

"Wagon's full. We'll have to come back for the rest."

The loud voice in the other chamber brought Josh crashing back to reality. What the hell was he doing? What was he thinking?

He pulled back, his shoulders stiff with mortification, breaths rasping on his shame. Their eyes met and held for a moment, hers wide with fear and confusion, and he felt like the worst blackguard in England. His stomach churned, and his heart did a strange flip-flop as he watched her emotions flash across her face: confusion, hurt, embarrassment.

Amelia scrambled off him, and her knee caught him in the midriff, forcing the air from him on a soft, "Oof!" On her feet, she shook her skirts until they fell into place, covering her legs. Josh watched the shapely limbs disappear, and regret, large and solid as a peach stone, lodged in his throat. She tucked her breast back into its place and fastened the buttons on her bodice, then smoothed her hand over it as if checking all was well. Josh's mouth dried and his stomach lurched. He wanted to howl, to beat his fists against the stone walls of the cave until every iota of frustration and need was wiped from his body.

In the other chamber, a second man continued the conversation, forcing him to silent stillness. "Does Mr. Sykes want all of it?" he asked.

"S'pose so. He ordered it, and he must know how much he needed." A boot heel rang against the stone floor, and someone grunted. "Aye, well, it isn't him as has to haul it everywhere, is it? Bleedin' toffs and their orders. Hide it here, move it there. Never satisfied, are they?"

"Oh, stop moaning. You're getting paid for it, aren't you?"

The voices grew fainter as the men moved away, until they faded altogether.

Josh sat back, his shoulders resting against the wall.

The cold damp seeped through his coat, icing his skin. His erection began to subside, and his heartbeat steadied as rational thought returned. He could not believe he had acted in such a crass manner! Amelia Bell wasn't some penny harlot to be tupped in an alley. She was a lady, gently reared and innocent. A virgin. Josh had had no right even to kiss her, let alone to...

Amelia crouched beside him and gathered up her hairpins, then fumbled with her hair, piling it on top of her head and shoving the pins in firmly. Josh winced at the forcefulness of her actions, surprised she didn't make her scalp bleed, and relieved when she finished the task without apparent injury. She snatched up her bonnet and jammed it on her head.

Josh closed his eyes as shame washed over him. He'd taken advantage of her, her innocence, the circumstances in which they found themselves. No wonder she was angry with him. She should be angry. He should be horsewhipped. He'd had absolutely no right to do what he had done. The only saving grace was that those men had spoken before he had made things any worse.

He regretted his actions, his lack of control, but in all honesty, he could not regret what had happened. Having Amelia in his arms, kissing her, touching her, had been—heaven. He would remember the feel of her against him, her curves, the soft sounds she made as she rose higher and higher—those things would remain with him forever.

But not regretting it did not mean he should not apologize. No matter how he felt about what had happened between them, the fact remained that he'd had no right to take liberties with her. He must apologize, and the sooner the better.

He cleared his throat. "A thousand pardons," he said, "I should not have… All I can say is I am sorry. I—please be assured it will not happen again."

****

Amelia stood and stared at Josh, her eyes so wide they hurt. In the dim light she could make out little more than his silhouette, but that was enough. She watched his shoulders slump, his head bow with the shame and regret that should have been hers. He had kissed her, yes. But instead of pushing him away and showing outrage as she should have done, she had kissed him right back! Mayhap her father was right—she was not ready for a Season, for surely, no lady would have behaved as Amelia had just behaved.

Heat flushed her cheeks as she relived the last few moments. She'd felt his warm lips against hers, his rough cheek rubbing against her smooth one, and she had pulled him closer. She had hugged him to her, her fingers playing in his thick, dark hair, reveling in the feel of it, his loose curls warm and soft and wrapping around her fingers. His lips against her neck had sent shivers rushing down her spine, and a delicious, wonderful, indescribable ache to the place between her legs.

His calloused fingers had pressed against the soft flesh of her breast, and oh! the wonder of it when he'd sucked her nipple into his mouth, sending darts of desire through her entire body. It had been the most magical moment of her life, and all he could do was apologize for it!

She had felt him against her when they kissed. His body had hardened, and there was no mistaking the growls of pleasure, or the musky scent of his arousal. He had not been indifferent while they were...doing what they'd been doing.

But afterwards. Afterwards, he had spoken to her in the same tone he might have used to speak with a maiden aunt at a garden party: steady, polite, a little distant, as if what had just happened between them was a mundane, everyday moment. Which, for all she could say, was exactly what it was to him.

Nonplussed, and if she was honest, more than a little insulted by the ease with which he could put their kisses and caresses behind him, Amelia suddenly had a desperate need to get out of the cave and away from him. She rushed across the few feet to the opening in the wall and squeezed herself through it.

"Amelia," he called after her. "Amelia. Wait."

"They're getting away from us," she called back. Her voice, she noted, gratefully, was even and matter-of-fact, betraying nothing of all that boiled within her. If only she could stop her eyes from burning with tears she refused to shed, and dislodge the lump of coal stuck fast in her throat, then all would be well.

"I suppose that's what one gets for being so wanton," she muttered as she stepped into the larger cave. All but a few of the barrels had gone now, and the chamber had an empty, hollow feel. Her footsteps echoed as she crossed to the corridor that led outside.

"Amelia!" Josh grunted as he came through from the other cave. Unsure she could keep her feelings from her face, she kept her head turned away.

"We should follow them," she said.

"There's no need. Thanks to you, we know they're taking the barrels to Frantham Manor."

"Then that is where we must go."

"No." His tone was uncompromising. Amelia whirled around and glared at him, shocked and angry. He sighed. "It could be dangerous, Amelia," he told her, as if she hadn't been able to fathom that for herself. "I don't want you anywhere near—"

"You don't want?" All the frustration and anger bubbled up inside her and threatened to explode. "You don't want?" She advanced on him, poking her finger sharply into his chest. He grunted, though whether with pain or surprise, she could not say. "What matter is it to me what you don't want?"

"Amelia—"

"If not for me, *my* intrepid efforts, you would not even have known about this cave, or the gunpowder, or anything else." He had backed away from her as she continued to poke him, and now stood against the wall. She put her hands on her hips and gave him her angriest glower. "I found this, and I can find out its intended purpose."

"No, you can't," he replied, clearly as determined to win this battle as she was. "These men are dangerous. You need to stay far away from them."

She drew herself up to her full height, which was still several inches shorter than he was. Her spine stiff, eyes narrowed, she spoke through gritted teeth. "I am not a piece of porcelain, liable to crack at the slightest knock."

"You are a lady—"

Amelia snorted her derision, and he pursed his lips.

"You are a lady," he repeated. His tone was that of an adult explaining facts to an exasperating child. "Quite apart from the danger you may face, you have a reputation to consider. If you become embroiled in a scandal… Amelia, you would not thrive as my wife. Therefore, I cannot, in good conscience, marry you."

Humiliation burned through her, stoking her anger. *Of all the arrogant, presumptuous…* "Nobody asked you to," she hissed. Then she turned on her heel and marched away, out of the cave and away from the infuriating, overbearing man, before he could break her heart any more than he already had.

Chapter Sixteen

Amelia was still angry that night as she lay in her bed, although the fury within her had shifted. She was no longer angry at Josh—well, not as angry as she had been earlier, anyway, although she suspected it would be a long time before the discomfiture his words had caused her would fade.

I cannot, in good conscience, marry you.

"That is all to the good," she muttered to the shadows her candle flicked across the wall. She tossed onto her side, pounded at her pillow to make it more supportive of her neck, and relived, yet again, those moments in the cave, the kiss they'd shared, the warmth of him pressed against her, his fingers stroking deliciously at her sensitive flesh, the way her heart pounded as if it would push its way free of her chest, her body on fire.

I cannot, in good conscience, marry you.

What did he think? That she was so desperate to gain a husband she would grasp the first gentleman who didn't run fast enough away from her?

"I don't want to marry him, either," she said, and pounded the pillow once more. "An absurd idea. He is the most unsuitable man I've ever met."

That was true. Josh—Mr. Winter—was the very opposite of everything she must look for in a husband. He had no title, nor was there one in his future. There was no fortune behind him, either. It was well known that Lord Rotherton had no money to speak of, and if he, the head of his family, had none, it stood to reason that his less elevated cousin certainly hadn't.

Only the poor could afford to marry for love. Not that she loved Josh Winter, of course. She enjoyed his company, yes, but then she enjoyed the company of many people. People who had not kissed her, and touched her, and…

She threw another punch at the pillow. She was not attracted to Josh Winter. He was bossy and overbearing, dictating her behavior as if he had the right, deciding where she could and could not go.

"Too dangerous for me, indeed," she sneered. He would have said it was too dangerous to follow those men to Marshy Meadow, as well. But it wasn't, and they'd learned a little more of their villainy. "You wouldn't know about the gunpowder if I'd stayed back and been a mouse," she said. She huffed, then spoke through gritted teeth. "I am no mouse, Mr. Winter. I could show you a thing or two…" Amelia bit her bottom lip, thoughtfully. "I *could* show you," she decided.

Amelia would go to Frantham and discover what was going on, then bring the information to him. He would have to admit she was capable, then, would he not? That she was not the delicate hothouse flower he thought her, but a robust human being who could weather an adventure as well as he.

A grin spread over her face, forcing a chuckle from her. She would go tomorrow… Botheration! Tomorrow was Sunday. There would be church, then a quiet day at home. Visiting would not be appropriate. Monday morning, Mama was taking her to Tunbridge Wells for a fitting at the dressmaker, although why it was still necessary when she would not have a Season at which to wear the dress was beyond Amelia. That may be, but she knew better than to think Mama would be persuaded to cancel the appointment.

She turned to her other side, kicking at her covers in frustration. She had to go to Frantham Manor and find the truth, and she had to do it soon. Every day she delayed could mean the information came too late. Sitting up, she smoothed the pillow flat where her punching had caused it to bunch, then lay down and watched the candle shadows.

Monday, after nuncheon. The dressmaker's visit would be finished with, and Amelia would be free. What better time to take herself for a walk. And if she found herself near Frantham Manor, so be it.

Satisfied with the plan she had made, she closed her eyes and tried to sleep.

****

Over dinner that evening, Josh told Rotherton about the cave and the gunpowder. He did not mention Amelia's part in the escapade, not wanting to risk her reputation. He didn't think for a moment that Rotherton would gossip about her, but Josh didn't want the earl to think any ill of her, either. Although why people shouldn't think ill of the little minx was beyond him. His mind conjured a picture of her as she had been today, her hair up in a haphazard golden topknot, eyes bright with adventure and smile full of devilment. The man who won her would, undoubtedly, be run ragged. A sharp pain shot through his chest at the realization that that man would never be himself, but some milk-faced Englishman with a title and an estate to lay at her feet.

He frowned. Josh was English, albeit his skin was darker than most, thanks to fourteen years in the sun. One day, he would have a title and an estate. It might not be the largest estate in England, but then again, those years in India had helped him amass a fortune that few aristocrats could rival. In other words, he was as eligible a suitor as anyone else.

But to take her to India...

Josh put a forkful of food into his mouth and chewed absently. He loved India, and the country had been more than good to him. But, he realized, it no longer pulled at his heart the way it had done. He had planned to return, but now he wondered if he truly had to do so. His partner was more than capable of handling their business affairs in Madras, and they had been discussing finding an agent to look after their interests here in England. Perhaps Josh could stay and take on that role. He could be close should his father need him, while retaking his place in Society, and paying his addresses to Amelia...

"Are you sure it's at Frantham?" Rotherton asked, pulling him out of his reverie. His face must have shown confusion because Rotherton grinned and added, "The gunpowder. Are you sure it's at Frantham?"

Josh swallowed the food he had chewed tasteless. "I'm certain of it."

"I fear the need to discover their plans is becoming more urgent." Rotherton circled the rim of his wine glass with the tip of his index finger while he thought. "I don't like this development at all."

Neither did Josh. Storing gunpowder in the house was reckless and dangerous, not least to Josh's father, who couldn't escape should there be an accidental explosion. The thought of his father in peril brought with it the overwhelming urge to see the old man, to talk with him and see if they could make peace. At the same time, perhaps Josh could learn whether Hicks had learned anything from the other servants. He might even know where the barrels had been stored.

"I will visit my father this evening," he said. Rotherton raised an eyebrow, and Josh shrugged. "What better time to go? The mysterious Mr. Summersby and his friends will likely be in the dining room, sharing their brandy and cigars. They are very unlikely to visit the sick room at this hour, are they? I can get in and out unremarked."

Rotherton didn't look happy at Josh's plan, but he didn't try to stop him. "Be careful," was all he said.

****

Josh made his way through the tunnel and into the house, then moved silently along the corridor toward his father's chamber. The moon shone through the windows, bathing the corridor in blue light and picking out gold and silver threads in the ancient tapestries on the wall. The air was musty from misuse and heavy with the dust caught in the woven fabrics. The end of Josh's nose tingled, and he flexed his nostrils to stop a sneeze.

He was almost at his father's door when the handle moved and a sliver of light shone from inside the chamber. He smiled, expecting to see Hicks come out of the room, but the smile froze when he heard an unfamiliar voice say, "I am glad to see the viscount looking so well. I know Mr. Summersby will be relieved."

Josh looked back along the corridor and knew he did not have the time to get back to the door of the chamber he had just left. Not without making noise, anyway, and that would alert whoever it was as much as if they saw him standing there. There were no statues to hide behind, no alcoves, nothing. Unless…

He lifted the side of the nearest tapestry and wormed his way behind it. It draped itself over him, covering him and blocking out the light. Old dust and damp assailed his senses. He pushed the end of his cravat up over his mouth and nose, and hoped that would be enough to stop coughs and sneezes, while he prayed the darkness of the corridor would disguise the telltale bulge in the tapestry and the man would leave without seeing anything amiss.

Through the tiniest gap between the tapestry edge and the wall, Josh watched Sykes leave his father's chamber, followed by Harcourt. The door shut emphatically behind them. They looked at it, then laughed. Josh tensed, every muscle held absolutely still. He hardly dared breathe.

"He's a bulldog," said Sykes, shaking his head. "The most loyal valet in all England."

Harcourt grunted.

"No need to scowl, my friend," continued Sykes. "You will have your revenge on him." He looked up at the ceiling, then glanced up and down the corridor. Josh tensed a little more and willed himself invisible. Clearly, his wish came true, for Sykes looked away again, no hint of suspicion about him.

"I want several barrels in this part of the house," continued Sykes. "There must be no chance of that old man surviving." Josh gasped, and was grateful that his cravat caught the sound. A sick feeling hit his stomach. They planned to blow up his father? What had that sick old man done to them that they wished to murder him? Every part of him quivered with rage at the thought of someone doing his father harm. He wanted to reach out, grab Sykes, and tear him limb from limb. It took everything he had to remain still.

"Nor his busybody servant," continued Sykes. Harcourt grunted again, and Sykes chuckled. "I know. I would have liked to see them all go up together, but it can't be helped. We cannot ask our esteemed visitors to come to a sick room, can we?" He looked around again. "Pity, really. It's a nice house. And there are things in the main wing that I should have liked to keep, but if I remove them now, somebody is bound to notice. That nosy Bell woman would remark on the smallest sweetmeat dish. I'm sure she has taken inventory of the place. And she is bound to grace us with her presence at least once between now and Monday night." He sighed, heavily. "Ah, well. We all must sacrifice to the higher purpose."

Josh's nausea rose to his throat. If Mrs. Bell planned to visit, there could be only one reason: Amelia. Her mother would bring her here, throwing her in front of the man she knew as Summersby, oblivious to the danger. But while her mother did not know the danger, Amelia would be completely aware of it. What if she gave herself away, alerted Summersby and Sykes to the fact that she knew?

Oh, God! Josh forced the groan of despair down, along with the nausea. He would warn her not to come. No, that would do no good. If he did that, the independent-minded minx would doubtless become more determined than ever. *Lord, save me from stubborn females.*

Sykes had said something about esteemed guests, too. Josh did not know who these guests could be, but when you added their presence to the plans Sykes had for blowing up the house—Josh knew instinctively that he and Rotherton would need reinforcements if they were to thwart the man's plans. Rotherton would likely have to call in the militia, for it was certain the bumbling parish constable could not handle this.

That constable, the boorish Abe Sutton, had been with some of Sykes' men the other day, and they had seemed thick as thieves, which made Josh more than a little wary of asking Sutton to have his back. Besides, the man was a useless bully; he'd shown that when he attacked Amelia—and came off worse. The thought made his lips twitch beneath his cravat. She had certainly not surrendered meekly to the man. Josh could still see the spark of anger in her eyes, the determined set of her jaw, and he had no doubt that, had he not come to her rescue, she would have rescued herself, and Sutton would have been the sorrier for it. His smile broadened. That was, surely, the moment when he began to fall in love with her.

Love? His smile dropped at the thought. Every muscle tensed and every nerve stood to attention. Love. Did he love Amelia Bell?

The answer was as clear in his head as a church bell and had him grinning like a lunatic. Yes, he did. He loved Amelia Bell! He wanted to shout his joy, dance like a madman at the full moon, proclaim it to the world. It took all he had to keep himself still behind the tapestry.

Then the smile faded and the joy left as he remembered their encounter earlier in the day. *'I cannot, in good conscience, marry you.'* The words had hurt her, he knew. Worse, he had gone on to treat her like a delicate little flower whose petals would fall at the slightest breeze—something she had proved, time and again, that she was not. She was determined and courageous, and more capable of looking after herself than many a man Josh had met. No wonder she was angry with him. How she must hate him for the way he had patronized and belittled her.

He would apologize, On his knees, if that was what it took. He would beg her forgiveness, and then...

"I know," said Sykes, startling Josh. Thankful that he'd done nothing during his wool gathering to alert the men to his presence, he dragged his attention back to the here and now, where Sykes had put his arm across Harcourt's shoulders. "Our Mr. Summersby is becoming something of a liability. I think he's been snooping around. Some documents in the library have been disturbed."

Harcourt nodded and made a gesture with his hands which clearly meant something to Sykes.

"Yes. You're right, as usual." He nodded and patted the other man's back. "Make sure he dies with his guests on Monday night. Now, then, show me where you put the barrels..."

Still talking, Sykes led his silent friend away. They turned the corner and were gone from sight. Josh waited a minute, until he could no longer hear the murmur of their voices or the scrape of their boots on the flagged floor of the ancient corridors before he dared to come out from behind the tapestry. He breathed deeply, enjoying air which was relatively fresh and free from mold, and thought of all he had just learned, and what it meant.

His first thought was to rush into his father's chamber and take the viscount and his valet out through the tunnel to safety, but if he did that, the plotters would know they had been discovered and would run to ground, only to surface somewhere else and cause harm to others. Josh could not live with those consequences, which meant he could not rescue his father just yet.

On the other hand, if he moved his father too late…

He paced a few feet along the corridor, turned and paced back, trying to think what to do for the best. He ran his hand roughly through his hair, as if that would dislodge an idea from his head. A few more turns up and down the corridor and he stopped at his father's door. Perhaps Hicks could come up with something.

Josh strode into his father's chamber, startling Hicks, who jumped up from his place beside the bed and stood, looking as if he was ready to take on Attila the Hun and his hordes. He recognized Josh, and his shoulders slumped with relief.

"It's you, sir," he said on a whoosh of breath. "I thought they'd come back." He frowned. "They may not be far away. If they see you…"

"They've gone," said Josh, and he waved a hand through the air, dismissing Hicks' concerns. He looked past the valet to the man in the bed, disbelief, shock, and heartache coursing through him.

His father was a shadow of the man he had been. He had lost so much weight that his body barely lifted the blankets, and his skin, papery and dry, was the same color as the snowy sheets and pillowcases he lay upon. His mouth was slightly open and drooped to one side, his lips wet, his breaths raspy. A dribble of what looked like gruel ran from the corner, down onto his chin. His eyes, the same hazel as Josh's, were rheumy, but still contained the spark of intelligent spirit Josh remembered so clearly from his childhood. His hair, which had been thick and dark when Josh left, was now wispy and white, and his scalp was dotted with liver spots, as were the backs of his hands.

It was all Josh could do to hide his shock. He swallowed hard, emotion clogging his throat and burning behind his eyelids. This was the man who had loomed large over his early years, indomitable and indefatigable, ruling all with a rod of iron. To see him reduced to this shell was heartbreaking.

Josh suddenly felt guilty, as if seeing his father in this weakened state was an intrusion. He looked away to the nightstand, where there was a half-finished bowl of gruel, illuminated by a single beeswax candle. Hicks picked up the bowl and sat on a stool beside the bed.

"If you don't mind, sir, your father needs to eat." He tried to spoon some of the gruel into the viscount's mouth, but the viscount lifted one thin arm and pushed the spoon away. He stared at Josh, and a first tear spilled from his eye and rolled over his cheek. Josh felt the itch as his own tears escaped.

Father lifted his hand higher, holding it out toward Josh. The effort the movement took was obvious, and Josh hurried closer to take the wasted hand. Father's mouth moved, as if he tried to form words. No sound came. Josh glanced at Hicks, an eyebrow raised in question, a plea in his eyes.

"He doesn't talk, sir," said Hicks. "But that—" He pointed to Father's lifted arm. "That tells you he is pleased to see you. That's the most he's done unaided for a very long time."

Josh sat on the edge of the bed and gazed at his father. Tears made his vision unfocused, so the old man seemed to shimmer before him, but there was no mistaking the lopsided smile. Josh lifted the thin, old hand to his cheek and held it there. "I am so sorry, Father," he whispered.

The older man's mouth worked a few more times, and then there was a raspy sound, as if something was being used for the first time in an age. He coughed, and tried again, and Josh heard the faintest whisper: "My son." Father's jaw slackened, then firmed again. "My son," he repeated.

Hicks gasped and stared in astonishment at his master. Josh kissed his father's hand, and wept.

An hour later, Father slept, exhausted by Josh's visit but clearly happy. Josh, too, felt as though a heavy burden had been lifted from his shoulders. He hadn't known how much he longed to reconcile with his father until today, and he was torn between gladness that it had finally happened and disappointment that it had taken so long. There were so many wasted years to make up. He prayed God would grant them time together now.

In hushed tones, he told Hicks what he had heard in the corridor.

"Those villains!" Hicks paced the floor near the bed, wringing his hands. "Those bounders! Those snivey hooks!" He turned to face Josh, his face wrinkled with anxiety. "What will we do?"

Josh glanced at his sleeping father. "Can he walk at all?"

"He hasn't done so."

Josh swore. "When the time comes, we'll need to get him out, and you cannot carry him."

Hicks thought for a moment. "I believe there is a bath chair in the attics."

"No." Josh shook his head, emphatically. "That

won't do. We need something that will go through the tunnel to the crypt."

"The tunnel?" Hicks' eyes were as wide and round as saucers. He opened and closed his mouth several times. Finally, clearly unable to think of something to say, he clamped his lips together.

"Yes," Josh said, "the tunnel. I want to get you both out of here without them knowing, if I possibly can. I wish I could do it now, but that's out of the question." He grimaced. "If only I knew the full extent of their plans for Monday evening. We need to time this correctly, or it will all be for naught."

Hicks nodded, thoughtfully. "As to carrying your father, I may have a solution. If I confide in Mrs. Hargreaves, show her the tunnel, she can bring her husband or her sons. Big, strong men, they are, sir. They'll carry my lord with no trouble."

"And I may know a way to learn more of their plans."

"How will you do that?" asked Hicks.

Josh grinned. "I will ask."

Hicks' eyebrows reached his hairline. "Ask?"

"Yes, Hicks, ask. Mr. Summersby may feel inclined to tell us all, once he knows what his compatriots plan for him. I will go to his chamber now and see if I cannot persuade him to join with us."

"What if he refuses?" Hicks spoke so quickly, he could hardly catch his breath. "What if he raises the hue and cry against you? He could kill you, murder us all in our beds!"

"Knowing your friends want you dead might make you change your colors, don't you think?" The more Josh thought about it, the more the idea appealed to him.

Summersby did not look comfortable in the position he had usurped. He may even have been coerced to it. Josh remembered seeing him threatened and taunted here, in the hallway of this very house, while the footmen looked on. That time, he had done as Sykes told him to do. Now, things might be very different.

"Perhaps. But what if you're wrong?" Hicks' voice was shrill with worry now.

The smile Josh gave him was designed to calm the agitated valet. "If I'm wrong, we will execute the alternative plan."

"What's the alternative plan?"

Josh didn't have the slightest idea. He promised to return, winked at Hicks, and slipped out of the chamber, leaving the poor valet wringing his hands and predicting doom.

As he crept along the corridors, hugging the shadows to keep himself invisible, Josh prayed Hicks wasn't proved right.

There were guests at the Frantham dinner table that evening, and Josh had to kick his heels in the corridor outside the master chamber for well over an hour. It gave him plenty of time to second guess himself, and he nearly walked away several times. It was only lack of a cohesive alternative that kept him in place until, at last, he heard voices as the guests took their leave. Moments after that, footsteps sounded, coming up the stairs.

Josh hid in an alcove and watched as Sykes escorted Summersby to the master chamber and opened the door for him. They shared pleasantries, but when Summersby went inside, Sykes pulled the door to and locked it, pocketing the key before sauntering back along the corridor and making his way downstairs again. Josh's hope rose. If they were locking him in, Summersby might not be a willing party to whatever they were doing. Which might also mean he wouldn't need much persuasion to answer Josh's questions. All Josh had to do now was enter the room and find out.

Years of sneaking back into the house after illicit night excursions now stood him in good stead. He could pick the back door lock like an expert housebreaker by the time he was fourteen, so this door held no challenge for him at all. He was in within seconds.

Summersby's eyes were wide, his shoulders stiff as he watched Josh enter his dimly lit room and close the door behind him. The man stood by the bed, cravat gone and shirt undone. His breathing was shallow and rapid, fists bunched, ready.

After a moment, he narrowed his eyes. "Winter?"

Josh gave him a drop-the-pretense stare. "We both know that is not my name," he said, and the imposter swallowed. "What I'd like to know now," Josh continued, "is your name."

"Summersby."

Josh pressed his lips together, angry.

The man shook his head and held out a hand, as if in supplication. "Truly," he said. "My name is Summersby. It's what attracted Sykes' attention in the first place. That, plus my likeness to you."

"Summersby." Josh's tone let the man know he was unconvinced.

"Benedict Summersby. We are third cousins."

Josh glared at the man, unsure whether to believe him or not. To his knowledge, he had no cousins; his father had been an only son. But it was possible there were more distant branches of the family, and there was no denying the familial resemblance.

Summersby clearly took Josh's silence as a cue to continue. "I'm an actor," he said. "Part of a touring troupe. We were playing the northwest, and doing badly, when Sykes approached me. He bought me a meal and told me he needed someone to impersonate the viscount's heir—you—for a few days. Said it was an urgent matter. You hadn't returned from India, and there were some things that needed settling quickly. Offered me fifty pounds." He snickered, humorlessly. "I never saw fifty pounds together in my life. Should have known it wouldn't be that easy." He sat on the edge of the bed, his shoulders sagging and his face haggard with his shame. "I was slow witted. By the time I realized what they were doing, it was too late. I couldn't make my exit. God knows I tried." He rubbed his hand wearily across his face, then pointed at the door. "Sykes usually locks that—"

"He did tonight."

"Then how…?"

"I had a misspent youth. What exactly are they doing?"

Summersby looked up at the ceiling, his face a mask of despair.

"That bad?"

Summersby nodded. "The worst. Treason."

Josh froze. He stared at Summersby, astounded.

Summersby sighed, heavily. "On Monday evening, we are hosting a small dinner. Very small. Just five of us at table: myself, Sykes, Harcourt, Lord Liverpool and the Duc de Richelieu."

Hardly able to catch his breath, Josh stumbled to the chair next to the hearth and sat down. The Prime

Ministers of both Britain and France were coming here? Together?

"They think they're coming to hold secret talks together, without the interference of their advisors." Summersby shook his head and clenched his jaw against his obvious distress. "They won't even have their usual entourage, 'to preserve the secrecy, don't you know.' "

Josh thought for a moment. "But why the secrecy? We are not at war with France."

"There are..." Summersby moved his hand in a *comme-ci-comme-ça* gesture, "delicate issues that need to be resolved. And both men have enemies. The meeting has been postponed twice because one or other of them has been targeted by an assassin."

"And on Monday night," mused Josh, "the attempts succeed."

Summersby slumped, rested his elbows on his knees so that his hands dangled between his legs, and gazed at the floor beneath his feet. "They'll lull them into feeling safe, then shoot them. After which we will disappear and, presumably, you will be wanted for the crime."

Josh nodded, deciding not to tell Summersby the true plan at this stage. He didn't know the man and could not predict how he would react to the idea of being blown up. If Summersby confronted the others or tried to escape, it could jeopardize the chance to thwart the plot and put Josh's father in grave danger. "What do they hope to gain?" he asked instead.

"With both men dead, the British and the French will point fingers at each other. There'll be uncertainty, mistrust, chaos. And in the midst of all this, they'll free Napoleon."

For a long minute, the two men were silent. The only

sounds in the room were the spit and crackle of the fire in the hearth, and the occasional hiss of the candle beside the bed. Outside, a fox barked. Josh's pulse beat, drumming in his ear, and his thoughts tumbled, one over another, through his head.

They wanted to free Napoleon? Were they mad? For years, the self-styled emperor's lust for power had caused suffering and misery to hundreds of thousands across the world. He had been brutal to all who stood in his way, massacring men, women, and children without remorse. That somebody would want to put him in a position to continue his murderous spree beggared belief.

It could not be true. Even if there were men fanatical enough to wish for his return, he was a spent force, the army he would need to succeed no longer under his command. And yet...his enemies had thought him gone forever before his escape from Elba. The speed and ease with which he'd regained power then had taken everybody by surprise. Thousands were killed or maimed before he was stopped. The world could not afford to give him another chance.

"You are sure?" he asked.

Summersby nodded, his face bleak. "I am sure. They idolize him, almost worship him, and talk of the day when he will rule over all of Europe. Including Britain." He rubbed at his face with his hands. "And I am a coward, for I have not even tried to stop them."

"Do you think you could have?" Josh thought the task would have been impossible. As well as Sykes and Harcourt, there were several armed men on the estate. Josh had no doubt they would be ready to quash any opposition to their plans.

"Maybe," said Summersby, quietly. "Maybe not." He raised his head, determination plain upon his face. "But coward or no, I am not a traitor. I will do what you need me to do."

Josh watched Summersby carefully, looking for telltale signs that he was lying. The man held his gaze for a moment, then sighed. "I am not a fool. I know the price of my part in this." He swallowed, and his eyes filled. "When I go to the gallows, it will be with my self-respect restored."

A minute passed. Two. A single tear escaped and rolled down Summersby's face. He made no attempt to wipe it away, made no attempt to move at all.

Finally, Josh made up his mind, and took the biggest gamble of his life. "Be ready," he said. Silently, he slipped out of the chamber, making sure to lock the door again.

Chapter Seventeen

It was Sunday afternoon. Outside, a gray sky hung so low it touched the tops of the bare trees. The ivy climbing the kitchen wall was dark, the grass washed out. In her room, Amelia paced, unable to settle. She'd told Mama she had the headache and had come upstairs to lie down. It wasn't exactly an untruth, she thought, ruefully, because the thoughts swirling in her brain and the emotions churning through her stomach were enough to start a pain in anyone's head.

A head, moreover, that was plagued with constant contemplations on the one subject she did not wish to contemplate: Josh Winter. What was it about that insufferable man that he invaded every waking moment?

It wasn't as if this seeming obsession with him could lead to anything. Papa would never let her marry a nameless poor relation with no prospects, even if the gentleman in question was willing to come up to scratch. Which Josh Winter clearly was not. He had, at least, been searingly honest about that.

Even so, when she had seen him this morning in church, her heart had skipped a beat and her breath caught in her throat. He had greeted her family and executed a perfect bow. Julia, Louisa, and Amelia had curtseyed, and Papa had inclined his head politely. Mama, however, had been cold, as if he were beneath her notice. Amelia's cheeks had burned with shame at the snub. Whatever he thought of it, however, remained a mystery. Not by so much as a blink did he react.

He sat beside Lord Rotherton in the front pew, directly in front of Amelia. She had been unable to concentrate on anything else. As the vicar exhorted his flock to put on the armor of Christ, Amelia watched Josh's back. She examined the way his too-long hair curled over his collar, and noted the breadth of his shoulders, filling his coat to perfection. Because he was in front of her and facing forward, she strained to hear him singing the hymns, although now and again, she heard a line or two. He had a deep rich voice; he didn't growl the words like Papa was wont to do, nor, thankfully, did he warble like Mama. Amelia found herself singing louder, hoping he would hear her. Would he think she had a pleasant voice?

That thought left her feeling guilty. She was supposed to be singing in praise of God, not to impress other people, so she raised her eyes heavenward and said a silent "sorry" to the Lord. It was an apology she repeated several times during the service.

Afterwards, she had hoped to spend a few moments in conversation with him and Lord Rotherton, but her attention was drawn to her sister. Julia was, once again, having difficulty with the unwanted attentions of Abe Sutton. The swelling around his eye had gone down now, and the bruise had faded, although there was still the faintest hint of yellow-green about his skin. He held his hat in his hand, crushing the brim and trying to flirt. Julia looked pained, but could not pass him to safety, so Amelia walked over to rescue her.

She put her arm firmly through her sister's. "Mama is asking for you," she announced, before giving Abe the coldest stare she could manage. "If you'll excuse us, Mr. Sutton?"

He glared at her. She steered her sister around him, twitching her skirts as they passed, for effect. The action seemed to infuriate him. "Think you're so high and mighty, don't you?" he muttered at her. "Too good for the likes of me. Well, you're not." Amelia and Julia exchanged pained glances and went to walk on. "You wait and see," he continued. "I'll be in the money soon, likely more than your family ever dreamed of. Then you won't be so eager to dismiss me, will you?" When the ladies did not answer, did not even turn to acknowledge his statement, he growled and stormed away.

"Insufferable oaf!" said Amelia. "Are you all right?"

Julia nodded. "He is naught but a braggart." She laughed. "In the money, indeed. Where is Abe Sutton going to find this fortune?"

"Mayhap the fairies will leave it in his chamber pot." They giggled.

"What kind of women does he think we are?" asked Julia, sending a frosty glance over her shoulder at his retreating form. "Do we look like a pair of fortune hunters?"

If we were, mused Amelia, I'd be preparing to go and gather dukes and nabobs, not spending my time hankering after the penniless cousin of a penniless earl.

Oh, for goodness' sake! What on earth was wrong with her? She was supposed to be persuading Papa that she was sensible and well behaved so that he would reinstate her Season, yet here she was, proving she was anything but, by yearning after a man who could never win the approval of her parents. A man, moreover, who did not return her regard, for had he not told her plainly that he would not court her? Why, he hadn't even enjoyed their tryst. A tryst that, to Amelia, had been wonderful, as spectacular as it was scandalous. It had made her lips tingle and her heart sing, and robbed her momentarily of both breath and senses. And he had apologized for it.

Lord, but she could have hit him!

She huffed and pulled Julia closer. They walked toward their parents, arms tightly entwined, shoulders pressed together, Amelia taking as much comfort and protection from her sister as she was giving.

They had almost reached Mama's side when Amelia realized why she needed Julia's comfort. She was in love with Josh—Mr. Winter! The thought hit her so hard and so unexpectedly that she stumbled, and Julia braced herself to hold Amelia upright. Amelia muttered about uneven paths and dragging hems and hoped her sister asked no questions.

Amelia loved Joshua Winter. She loved his slightly crooked smile, and the way his eyes changed from brown to green, depending on his mood. She loved his protectiveness toward her, which had been evident from their first encounter, and yet he was capable of trusting her too, as he had done in Frantham Manor's library. The way he held her, as if she were precious. She even loved his overbearing bossiness.

She loved him.

The warmth of the revelation left her chest as suddenly as it had arrived, dislodged by the chill realization that, while she may love him, he certainly did not love her. Anything but. In fact, his eagerness to return to India at the earliest opportunity spoke of his wish to put as much distance between them as he possibly could.

It was a frozen, dejected Amelia who climbed into the carriage and stared, unseeing, through the window as her family chattered their way home.

Even now, hours after the truth had hit her so forcefully, her heart hurt. Amelia wanted to throw herself onto her bed and sob until all the love and pain and desire for him was washed from her, but if she did that, her eyes would swell and redden, and Mama would demand to know why. Amelia could no more explain this to Mama than she could fly, so instead of crying into her pillow, she paced the floor, hands clasped tightly in front of her waist as she fought the painful pressure in her head and occasionally wiped tears roughly from her cheeks.

****

Josh walked his horse beside Rotherton's after church, his heart heavy. Amelia had looked delectable today in a pastel blue dress that showed her slender figure to perfection, while the darker blue spencer and matching bonnet made her hair shine and her eyes sparkle. It was all he could do throughout the service to keep his eyes front, his attention on the vicar.

Afterwards, in the churchyard, he had hoped for a few moments, time to pass pleasantries with her. He had even planned what he would say to her, words innocuous enough to satisfy her parents but in which she, and she alone, would hear a truer meaning and know how he felt. He'd mentally rehearsed them while the vicar preached.

All to no avail. Amelia had come out of the church, seen him waiting on the path, and veered away, preferring to spend time with her sister and that oaf, Sutton. Josh's heart had tumbled to his boots, blackening his mood and freezing the air around him. It had taken all his effort not to stride across to her and demand her attention. Instead, he'd turned to join the conversation Rotherton was having with a tittering lady and her blushing daughter. Josh hardly knew what they said, and answered by rote, but it seemed to be enough, for nobody noticed his distractedness.

When, after a few minutes, he chanced another look in Amelia's direction, she had gone.

He blamed himself. His words yesterday had been brutal, and he knew he had hurt her. At the time, he had honestly believed what he was saying, but even so, he could have phrased it better, been more of a gentleman about it. 'Twas no wonder she didn't wish to speak further with him now. Just one more in a long list of wrongs he needed to set right. He hoped she would forgive him and be amenable to his change of heart.

"I sent for the captain of the militia this morning," said Rotherton, drawing Josh from his thoughts. They rode slowly along the driveway to Rotherton Hall. The cold air pinched Josh's nose and slapped at his cheeks. Pigeons cooed and other birds trilled in the woods to one side of the drive, while deer grazed in the large park on the other side. An idyllic Sunday morning, despite the wintry air and gray skies. It seemed wrong, somehow, to taint the day with talk of treason and military assaults, but needs must.

"The captain says he can have his men in place by noon tomorrow. That should be early enough to be well hidden before our villains set up a perimeter watch, and ensure our force remains a surprise."

Josh prayed so. It would go a lot easier if they took their prey unawares.

"The parish constable was keen to join them, but I

pulled him back. Sutton means well, but he isn't as competent as I'd like." Rotherton shook his head and smiled, ruefully. "If only someone else had applied for the post. But he was the only candidate, and I am stuck with him, so that's that."

"Does he know of your plans?" Josh hoped the answer was no. Abe Sutton made him uneasy. A bully and a braggart, he was not the sort of man Josh would trust to have his back. Although, he was willing to allow, his judgment could be colored by the way the man had treated Amelia in the stables, and the way she had preferred his company today.

"Not the finer detail, no," answered Rotherton. "I don't trust him not to speak of it in his cups." The earl grinned. "Being a diplomat at heart, I softened the blow, though. Told him I needed to keep him in reserve, in case the militia wasn't enough. He went away quite puffed up." Josh chuckled. Rotherton sobered. "I impressed upon the captain the need to take Sykes alive. I need information. His men are unlikely to know it, and Harcourt cannot speak, so I need Sykes."

"Information?"

Rotherton nodded, his face grim. "Sykes is not the ringleader of this plot, of that I am certain. I hope he can tell us who he works for. Otherwise, the danger will not go away completely, and we'll be fighting another attempt in a few months' time." When Josh did not answer, he studied him closely and asked, "Penny for them?"

I was thinking about a golden-haired beauty entering that nest of vipers the way Daniel entered the lion's den—and me not being there to rescue her.

"I was just thinking about innocent bystanders," he

said aloud. "What can we do if a neighbor pays Summersby a call on the morrow?"

"We let them."

No. No, no, no. We cannot let her walk into such danger. I cannot risk her being hurt.

"People call during the daytime," reasoned Rotherton. "The nefarious activities are scheduled to begin after dark." His tone was light, as if he discussed plans for a ball, not the proposed assassination of two politicians. He watched Josh carefully before adding, "If you're thinking we could dissuade Mrs. Bell from making her calls, you're on a lashing to nothing. Prinny himself couldn't stop her from her decided course."

Josh sighed, knowing Rotherton spoke the truth.

They rode up to the house in silence, and dismounted. A groom came and led the horses away. The two gentlemen climbed the steps to the front door, and Rotherton asked, "What is between you and Amelia Bell, my friend?"

Josh turned to face the earl, startled. "Nothing." The lie came before he could stop it, and he cursed himself for it. Of all people, it did not pay to try to mislead Rotherton. He had always had an uncanny knack for knowing truth from fiction, and Josh had no appetite for an argument.

Rotherton didn't give him one. He simply said, "Do not break her heart, Josh, or you will answer to me. She's a dear girl, and she doesn't deserve it."

"You need not worry on that score," Josh told him, the bitterness plain in his voice. "The lady's heart is not engaged. She is far too eager to have her Season and marry a title. The last person she would break her heart over is me."

"Hmm." Rotherton smiled. "That's not what her eyes say when she looks at you."

His words caught Josh unprepared, and he couldn't stop the tiny spark of hope catching inside him. "How so?" he asked, warily. "How does she look at me?"

Rotherton gave him a speaking look, grinned and said nothing.

Chapter Eighteen

The fitting for Amelia's dress seemed to take all day. Under normal circumstances, she would not have minded in the least, and would have taken the opportunity to look at new patterns and discuss future orders with Madame Henri, but today she needed to visit Viscount Frantham. With every alteration Mama insisted upon, every suggestion she discussed at length with Madame, the time moved inexorably on. If they did not return home soon, Amelia would have to abandon her plans and run the risk that Josh would discover his evidence before she could be of help to him.

That mattered to her far more than it should. She bit her lip against the uneasiness she felt at the realization, and told herself she simply did not wish to be denied her part in the adventure. She even almost believed it.

At long last, Mama was satisfied, and they returned home to a late nuncheon, after which Mama went to her rooms to rest. Julia had promised to help Louisa with a difficult piece of sewing, and Papa was, as usual, ensconced in his study. There would never be a more opportune moment to leave the house.

Amelia changed into a round gown of brown wool and a pair of sensible shoes. If she was going to be where she shouldn't be, she did not want to stand out in fine clothes and bright colors. She donned her warmest coat and set out for the manor house. As she had done before, she took the shortest route across the fields and through the woods, pondering while she walked.

There had to be a way into the house that didn't involve announcing one's presence at the front door. Perhaps, she mused, a secret way in, for the house was centuries old. Could there be a way through which the Cavalier owners of the house had escaped their Roundhead pursuers? Or had a Jesuit priest used it to escape with his life?

She sighed and shook her head at her own absurdity. Even if such an entrance had ever existed, Amelia would be unable to find it, for if it was easily discovered it would not have served its purpose, would it?

Still, she was intrigued to know how Josh had gained access. "I will ask him when next I see him," she murmured and decided, though it made her feel less than intrepid, she would go into the house by the front door, as she always did.

Lost in thought, she stumbled upon the soldier before she realized he was there. He sat propped against a tree, his head hanging forward so his chin almost touched his chest, his hands held loosely at his sides. She started at the sight of him, but he didn't move, which made her frown.

"Sir?" she asked, softly. "Are you all right?" He did not respond. The only movement came from the breeze playing through the ivy leaves entwined around the old tree trunk. "Sir?" she asked, a little louder. "Are you awake?" He stayed absolutely still. "Are you in need of assistance?" No response.

A little frightened now, Amelia looked around her. Surely, this man would not be here alone? Soldiers usually travelled in groups, did they not? She prayed she could find his companions and they could help him, for it shamed her to admit, even to herself, that she knew nothing.

Peering into the trees, she saw something glint. She took a step nearer, then moved backward, hand over her mouth, heart pounding in horror when she found the second man. He lay face down, completely motionless, and there was no mistaking the large, dark puddle beneath his head.

She turned slowly and saw the others. Seven men all together, all lying still, some in unnatural poses, some covered in blood. The last man was face up, eyes staring glassily at the sky, his expression one of surprise and the gaping wound across his throat a testament to how he had died.

Bile burned the back of Amelia's throat. She swallowed, furiously. Her heart thrashed against her ribs so hard and fast it hurt. Every muscle trembled with terror, every nerve stood on end. She took a deep breath, trying to calm herself, then retched as she inhaled the coppery scent of blood, mixed with sweat and the smells of the outhouse.

Amelia stood there for well over a minute, pushing down panic and trying to make her thoughts coherent. In the end, only one thought would come: Josh. Josh would know what to do. He would come to her aid, take care of her, take care of these poor men. There was nobody else. She needed Josh.

She turned to go and squealed when she collided with a brawny man in coarse, homespun clothes. His coat was worn and tight across his chest, and his stockings were spattered with the mud he'd kicked up as he walked. His hat, however, was prim, and a size too small for him. It sat incongruously on his head, as if daring Amelia to laugh at it. Suddenly, she had the almost overwhelming urge to do just that: laugh hysterically at the hat, the man, the entire situation.

"What've you got, Matt?" asked a rough voice, and the feeling of hysteria disappeared, swallowed by her terror. She whirled to see two more men, dressed like the first. However, these two had something he didn't—guns. Long, gleaming, dangerous-looking muskets, held close across their bodies, ready to swing round and fire at a moment's notice.

They looked Amelia up and down as if she was a horse they were purchasing, and they grinned lasciviously. She swallowed and looked around for the best escape route, then froze in shock as Abe Sutton stepped from behind a tree and walked forward.

"You always turn up where you're not wanted, don't you, Millie Bell?"

"Abe, I—" She what? Amelia couldn't think of a single thing to say that would help her.

"Not so high in the instep now, are you, Lady Millie?" he taunted. He grinned as he rubbed at the faintly discolored skin around his eye. "There's no one here to help you this time, neither."

Amelia took a step backward. Perhaps if she moved very slowly and carefully she could lull them into a false sense of security until she was near enough to the trees. She could lose them in the trees.

"Going somewhere, precious?" The man was so close behind her she felt his hot breath on her neck. She turned to find him leering at her, his teeth black and misshapen. He smelled of sweat and leather. Amelia backed away from him, straight into Abe's arms.

"Now," he said, his voice husky, "about that kiss you owe me." He untied her ribbons and tossed her bonnet aside, then ran his tongue up the side of her face. She shuddered and squirmed, but he held her fast.

"Leave it out, Sutton," growled the man called Matt. "There's no time for that."

"There's always time for that," argued Abe. The other two men guffawed.

"Not today there's not."

One of the other men drew a knife from his belt and held it so it caught the weak sunlight. Amelia couldn't help it. She whimpered.

"Put it away," said Matt. "Nobody does nothing to her unless Mr. Sykes says so. Bring her to the manor." Reluctantly, the man put his knife away.

Matt set off through the trees. Abe pulled Amelia behind him, and the other two men brought up the rear. Amelia dragged her feet, trying to slow Abe down, but it did no good—he was just too strong.

"You shouldn't have been so quick to refuse me," he told her. "I can give you just as much as what that ponce Summersby can."

Amelia didn't answer. Instead, she tried to look around, hoping for that split second when she could escape.

"You don't want to be dismissing me. After tonight, I'm going to be rich, too." Abe grinned. "There's this big meeting, see, and when it's over, everyone who helped is getting a hundred pounds."

"Shut up," growled Matt. "Idiot."

"I'll give you two hundred if you let me go," whispered Amelia.

He frowned, unsure. "You haven't got two hundred

pounds."

"I have," she lied. She tried to look and sound sincere. "It's my quarterly allowance. It's yours, if you get me away from here."

"Show me."

"I don't carry it around with me. It's at home."

"What, like your sister's handkerchief you swiped from me? You're a tricky minx, Millie Bell. If you think I'm falling for your wiles again, you've got another think coming."

He pulled her along the path. She tugged back, to no avail. He chuckled. "Don't worry. You'll be fine."

"Like those soldiers were fine?"

"That's different. They were traitors, come to try and stop the deal."

Amelia made a conscious effort to seem relaxed. Could she be about to discover what this was all about? "What deal?" she asked.

"Big deal," he said.

"What sort of deal?"

He sniffed. "Big one."

Amelia gave him a sidelong glance. "You don't know, do you?"

Abe puffed out his chest like a strutting pigeon. "I do," he argued. "I'm the constable. I have to know these things. But I can't tell you. It's a matter of—erm—national incurity."

"Security," she corrected him, almost automatically.

"That's what I said."

"Will you shut up?" hissed Matt. "Your mouth flaps more than all the women in an old maid's tea party. Put together."

"Don't talk to me like that," answered Abe. He

stepped forward, his attention on the other man, and Amelia took her chance. She stuck out her foot and tripped him, just as she'd done so many times when they were children. Abe went sprawling, grabbing Matt in a vain effort to save himself, and both fell to the ground, cursing. Amelia picked up her skirts and ran, weaving between tree trunks, jumping over long roots and tangles of brown bracken. She didn't know which direction she faced, or where she was going, but that wasn't important at this moment. All that mattered now was getting away from these men. She could regroup and change course after that.

Years of hoydenism came into their own as she sped through the woods. Small branches slapped her and brambles snagged at her stockings, tearing them to shreds around her ankles. Her hair fell in hanks around her face. She ran on and on, jumping puddles and fallen logs, until the sounds of her pursuers grew fainter. She was going to do this. She would get away. Then she'd get her bearings and make for Rotherton Hall, and Josh.

The thought of him gave her comfort. He would hold her close and make sure she was safe, while Lord Rotherton rounded up those murderous villains. No doubt he'd scold her, but then he'd smile at her, pride shining in his eyes as he told her...

She cried out as her feet slipped on thick, wet mud, sending her tumbling down a steep incline. She grabbed at bushes, trying to slow her descent, wrenching her shoulders and sending spasms through her back. Her gloves ripped and the rough wood stung her hands and pulled at her hair, making her eyes burn with the pain at her scalp. She landed at the bottom, on the bank of a narrow stream, the wind completely knocked out of her.

For a moment she lay there, unable to move, to feel, even to breathe. Then she began to shiver, her heart pounding and her stomach churning with the shock. Her coat was ripped, hair across her eyes. She could feel the twigs and dead leaves tangled in the tresses. Her shoulders ached and her ankle throbbed.

It took her three attempts to stand, and then she began to limp along the bank, her vision blurred by tears. She could hear the men thrashing through the woods, but she couldn't see them.

And then one of them was standing on the bank in front of her, grinning malevolently. He beckoned at her. Amelia turned, although she knew she had no hope of outrunning him. A second man stood on the bank behind her. He was panting heavily from the run and sweat sheened his face. His fisted hands were on his waist, pressing in to him as if to take away the pain of a stitch.

"Bring her," barked Matt. The men grabbed Amelia and began to drag her up the slope. She pulled back, but it did no good. They were far too strong. At the top, Abe scowled at her. Matt shook his head. "Don't let go of her," he commanded, and he marched away. The men followed, pulling Amelia along with them.

Not a word was spoken as they made their way to the manor house. They bypassed the front door and took Amelia in by a side door which led past the kitchens and along several corridors before they went down steep stone steps to the cellars. Matt produced a key, opened an old wooden door, and the men pushed Amelia inside. She righted herself and turned, in time to see the door slam shut. She heard the scrape of the key in the lock, and she pounded on the door. "Let me out!" she yelled. From the other side of the door she heard them laughing, and their muffled voices, then boots on concrete as they moved away. She gave a half scream, half growl of frustration, kicked the door, then turned and looked around.

By the light of narrow windows just below the ceiling, she could see she was in a well-stocked wine cellar. Racks and racks of bottles lay on their sides, some covered in dust and cobwebs, others gleaming as if they had only recently been laid down. Along one wall were small casks marked Brandy, Whisky, and Madeira. And lined up between the wine racks, the all-too-familiar larger barrels she had first seen in the cave at Marshy Meadow. Long coils of what looked like wire protruded from each one.

"Oh, no," she whispered as realization swept through her. The barrels were not being stored here for safekeeping. They'd been primed, fuses added, ready to light. Sykes was going to blow up Frantham Manor.

Amelia had to stop them. But how? She picked up the fuse jutting out of the first barrel. If she could separate them, perhaps that would render the powder inside the barrels harmless? She tugged, but the fuse did not come free. She wrapped it around her hand and pulled again, put one foot against the barrel and tried once more. The barrel wobbled under the force of her weight, hitting the rack and making the bottles rattle. The fuse stayed in place, and hurt her hand.

Hands on hips, jaw clenched determinedly, she looked around for a knife to cut the fuse. There was nothing. All she found was a mallet and a piece of wood about a foot long and just over an inch in diameter. It was tapered at one end, but it wasn't sharp enough to cut through the fuses.

Defeated, Amelia leaned back against the rack. The bottles rattled in their beds and the nearest one dislodged. She reached out and grabbed it before it could fall and spill everywhere.

Holding it in her hand gave her an idea. She knew, from listening to the boys talk, that gunpowder had to be kept dry or it wouldn't work. If she soaked this gunpowder in wine, perhaps she could thwart the plan to blow the manor up. On the other hand, she knew from watching the Christmas pudding burn that alcohol was flammable. What if pouring it onto gunpowder merely added fuel to the fire, so to speak?

One thing she did know. If she did nothing, the gunpowder would remain usable for certain. The house, Amelia, and possibly the viscount would be blown up.

She took a deep breath. "Please be on my side, Lord," she prayed, and counted the barrels. There were eleven, giving her more than enough wine to completely flood all of them.

Confidence restored, Amelia picked up the mallet and the tapered wood and used them to prise off the lids of the barrels. It took several attempts to lift the first lid, and she hit her hand twice, starting a dull ache in her wrist that made her feel nauseous, but she persevered and, eventually, all eleven barrels were opened. She looked around but could find nothing with which to open the wine, so she did the only other thing she could think of—she smashed the neck of the bottle. Wine slopped, splashing the hem of her dress and sending its musty-sweet perfume into the air. With some trepidation, she poured it over the powder in the first barrel.

****

The daylight was gone, and Rotherton's study was

lit by several candles, which gave the room a warm glow. A fire crackled in the hearth, the merry sounds at odds with the serious mood of Josh and Rotherton. They had discussed the plans to a standstill, trying to make preparations for any and every eventuality, allowing for anything that could go wrong.

There was a light scratching at the door, and Rotherton's man appeared, carrying two matching boxes made of rosewood, elaborately inlaid with satinwood. He laid them on the desk and left the room as Rotherton opened the boxes to reveal two pairs of dueling pistols.

"Hopefully, we won't need them," he said, his face grim. He picked up one gun and proceeded to load it. Josh followed suit.

They had just loaded the second pair when a commotion in the hall had them both straightening, guns in hands. Seconds later, the butler came into the room.

"I'm sorry, my lord, but Mr. Bell has arrived and insists he must speak to you. He says it is important."

Josh sighed and relaxed, lowering his pistol, then tensed again as Bell pushed past the butler and approached Rotherton. "My lord, I need you to raise the hue and cry," he said. "One of my daughters has not returned home, and nobody has any intimation of where she might have gone."

Before the man said her name, Josh knew the missing daughter was Amelia. The headstrong minx would be the death of them all! He prayed she hadn't carried out her threat to visit Frantham Manor today, even as he knew that was her most likely destination.

An image came to him of Amelia discovered in her search of the Frantham library. If Sykes thought for one moment that she suspected him of anything... The thought made Josh feel sick. He exchanged glances with Rotherton, as Bell paced back and forth in front of the hearth, wringing his hands and recounting Amelia's actions that day up until the moment she had last been seen.

Josh could not, would not alert the man to his own suspicions. Bell was ill-equipped to rush to his daughter's rescue, but that was exactly what he would do, likely getting himself and others killed in the process. Rotherton clearly thought the same, because he smiled at Bell and gave him a reassuring pat on the back.

"I am sure it will turn out to be nothing," he said. "She has overstayed in the dress shop—"

"She returned from the modiste several hours ago, my lord." Bell bristled, plainly unhappy at Rotherton's patronization. Josh could not blame him. "Apparently," Bell continued, "she went for a walk, and nobody has seen her since. I have men scouring the area around my own property, but they have found no sign of her. Her sisters do not know where she went, nor do her particular friends. Worse," he struggled to keep his emotions in check, wringing his hands so tightly now his knuckles showed white and his fingers took on unnatural shapes, "the parish constable is not to be found either."

Rotherton shook his head. "If he is not at his post, you should search the alehouses. They are his natural habitat."

"Not this night."

Josh frowned. Sutton should be at his post. He knew what was happening tonight, knew he might be called upon. Incompetent fool!

Bell swallowed. His eyes filled and his chin quivered. "You are not in full possession of the facts, my lord," he said. "I need your word this will go no further."

Oh Lord! What else had Amelia done?

"You have it," Rotherton promised.

Bell looked pointedly at Josh. He probably expected him to leave the room, but that would not happen. If there was the slightest chance she was in trouble, he wanted to hear of it. Instead of excusing himself, therefore, he held her father's eye steadily. "Not a word of it will pass my lips," he vowed, then braced himself to learn of some scandal in which she had become embroiled. When this was over, he was going to have to marry her, if for no other reason than to save her from herself. Although, the prospect of wedding her was not an altogether unpleasant one...

He was getting ahead of himself. First, they must find her and see her safely back home.

Bell stood at the hearth and stared glumly at the burning logs. The red glow of the fire painted his face. After a few moments, he turned back to the other men. "I think," he said, his words catching on the jagged edge of his heartbreak, "I think my daughter has a *tendresse* for Mr. Sutton." He gulped down his emotions. Shame drained his cheeks of color. "She met him in the stables at the Golden Goose. I—I don't believe anything—untoward happened between them, but they were both there."

The idea was absurd. Josh could certainly disabuse her father of that notion. Except—he could not. Not without revealing that he himself had been with her, unchaperoned. Besides, he had the feeling that if he explained what he had interrupted in the stables that day, it would make things much, much worse.

"Then, after church on Sunday," continued Bell,

"she made a deliberate effort to speak with him. I—" his voice cracked, "I believe they may have eloped."

Rotherton and Josh exchanged glances before Rotherton said, "I think not, sir. You may be easy on that. Sutton has a mission for me this evening." Bell frowned, confused, and Rotherton added, quickly, "'Tis why I thought he was in the alehouses. I sent him to discover what he could about—a gang of smugglers."

"Smugglers?" Bell's eyebrows rose to his hairline.

"We need to stamp it out." Rotherton looked grave and his voice was steady. Had Josh not known better, he would have believed him. Bell, however, looked less sure.

"I am sure Miss Bell has arrived safely home, ready to face a scolding for making you anxious," continued Rotherton. "But just to be safe, I will have my men look for her. Do you go home, Mr. Bell, and send word if she is found." He ushered the man from the room, returning moments later, alone.

"I'll have to send my stable lads," he told Josh, "for I have nobody else, not if Abe has deserted his post. Why can't the man do as he is told for once?" He rang the bell.

"I think I know where she may be," Josh said, quietly.

Rotherton studied him for a moment, then grimaced. "No."

Josh nodded.

The earl closed his eyes, then opened them again as the butler entered. Rotherton apologized for having sent for him in error, and the man went away again. Rotherton glared at Josh. "If she is at Frantham Manor, it's your fault."

Josh sighed and ran his hand through his hair.

Rotherton was right; it was his fault. He should have worked harder to dissuade her, impressed upon her the dangers. Hell and damnation! It was his fault she even knew there was anything amiss at all. Had he been more alert, he would have hidden before she found him in the library, and Amelia would have remained in blissful ignorance.

A small part of him did not feel guilty, though—the part of his soul that knew if she had not caught him that day, their paths would likely never have crossed again. He'd never have gazed into those bright blue eyes, or touched that silky blonde hair, tasted the warmth of her creamy skin, felt the soft curve of her breast. No, he could not regret meeting her in his father's library. But if she was there now…

"If she went to Frantham," he reasoned, "one of our men will have seen her. I'll leave now, and ask them before I go in. I'll send you word." He stood and picked up two of the pistols. "I'll take these."

"Be careful," said Rotherton, his mouth a thin slash and his eyes hard.

"You too," and Josh left the room.

Chapter Nineteen

Josh made his way through the woods using a smuggler's lantern that Rotherton had confiscated from some miscreant in the past. The lantern's glass was almost completely blacked out, leaving only a thin sliver through which the light could escape. It was enough to see his way, if he was careful, but would likely be missed by all but the most determined of observers, allowing him to move without detection.

He walked in a wide circle around the perimeter of Frantham Manor, looking for the militia, but there was no sign of any of them. At first, Josh was impressed that the soldiers had hidden themselves so well, and not responded to his presence, but after a while, he began to feel uneasy, certain he should have detected at least one of them by now. The feeling grew as he approached the clearing where he expected to find the sergeant-at-arms. The sergeant knew Josh, had met him when Rotherton briefed him, so he had no reason to hide. Josh's chest ached with a strange queasiness, a foreboding as he turned in a slow circle, then stopped, his eye catching something small and dark lying, inert, on the ground.

At first, he thought it was a dead animal, a squirrel or a rat. He took two steps forward, until he could make it out in the meagre light of his lantern. A bonnet, crushed out of shape, its ribbons lying forlornly in the mud.

The queasy feeling turned into a sharp pain that pulled him up short and made him catch his breath. He had no doubt whatsoever but that this bonnet belonged to Amelia Bell. That it lay there, abandoned, could only mean she was in terrible danger.

Fear for her bubbled up through him, threatening to make him vomit. He took several deep breaths in the effort to keep his stomach down, and massaged his side, willing the pain in his heart to dissipate, while he pondered his next move.

He could do one of two things, he reasoned. He could return to warn Rotherton that, somehow, their plans had gone awry, or he could press on and hope to find Amelia and get her out of the manor at the same time as his father. It depended very much on how much time he had.

That question was answered when, through the trees, he heard the sound of coach wheels, rattling over the uneven road that led to the manor. It had to be Liverpool's coach. Things were coming to a head. There was no time to warn Rotherton, who could take care of himself in any case. Josh needed to be in place to rescue the Prime Minister and save his country. At the same time, he determined, he would find and save the two people who meant more to him than his own life, and who were now trapped in a house packed with gunpowder.

And, he vowed, when this was finished and the villains arrested or dead, he would find that naughty minx and make her pay for taking years from his life. Whether he would shake her or kiss her senseless, he hadn't quite decided.

"I might do both," he mused as he made his way

back through the woods toward the family chapel and the secret tunnel.

Hicks was waiting in his father's bedroom, along with Mrs. Hargreaves and two of her sons, strapping lads made strong from years of physical labor. Mrs. Hargreaves wept when she saw Josh.

"Oh, Mr. Summersby," she said, "Hicks said as how it was you, but I daren't believe till I saw you with my own eyes. And a welcome sight you are. Praise the Lord that you've come home."

He nodded, slightly embarrassed at her effusive welcome.

"My boys came in through the secret way," she told him. "You could have blown me over with a feather when Hicks told me of it. I never guessed it was there."

"Are you ready to leave?" he asked. The boys nodded and picked up Josh's father between them. "Make your way to Rotherton Hall. You are expected, and they will make you comfortable."

Josh saw them safely into the tunnel, Hicks leading and Mrs. Hargreaves bringing up the rear. They rounded a bend in the walkway and disappeared from sight.

Satisfied they were as safe as he could make them, Josh made his way to the library, hoping against hope that Amelia was in there, safe. The moment he entered the room, he knew she wasn't. The room was in darkness, with only the wintry moon providing any light at all, and there was an air about the place, the kind of emptiness that comes only when there is no living creature within. To be sure, Josh checked the window seat in the alcove, lifting the seat and peering into the darkness below. It was empty.

Where was she? He had no way of knowing. She

might be in any room in the house. And wherever she was, Josh could not say whether she had managed to sneak there to search for whatever she thought she sought, or had been dragged there as a prisoner.

Josh wanted to tear the place apart to look for her. It took every ounce of will power not to race down the corridor, flinging open every door in his quest to find her. All that would do was get both of them killed. Much better to thwart Sykes' scheme completely, saving not only Amelia but Lord Liverpool, Richelieu, and the peace between England and France as well.

With the disappearance of the militia, it was clear their original plan was shot to hell, so Josh would have to go with his instincts and hope Rotherton arrived in time to back his actions. If not—he refused to contemplate what would happen if not.

He slipped out of the library, giving a cursory glance up and down the corridor before making his way toward the sitting room at the front of the house, the most likely place to find Sykes and his victims. Sure enough, as he approached the door he heard laughter and muffled conversation. He put his ear to the panels, but the wood was too thick and he could distinguish none of the words. Loathe to burst in without knowing what he faced, he made his way to the anteroom next door, where he knew there was a connecting door. It was a smaller door, and in a part of the room that would be deeply shadowed at this time of the evening. If he opened it very slowly, he probably would not be observed.

Josh opened the door just enough to see inside the room. What he saw did not please him: Summersby and another man, whom Josh assumed was Lord Liverpool, were seated side by side on a sofa, their backs stiff with the tension that radiated from them. Harcourt stood a little way from them, a pistol in each hand trained in their direction. Sykes stood near the tantalus, a whisky in his hand. He sipped it, then took out his fob watch and checked it, before shaking his head and making a tutting sound. "Richelieu is late," he said.

Liverpool scowled contemptuously at him. "You're English," he said. "Why would you wish to help Bonaparte?"

Sykes' smile was cold and did not reach his eyes. "Being English does not mean I cannot recognize genius. He is going to rule the world."

"Hah! You say so, even after all his defeats?"

"I say so after all his victories."

Liverpool snorted. "He won't care about you. He abandoned his own army in Egypt, and again in Russia. The only man Bonaparte cares for is himself."

Sykes scowled. "You don't have to be alive when Richelieu gets here," he said, his voice low and menacing.

Josh pulled back, intending to close the door quietly and make his way back to the tunnel, but he froze when he felt something hard and cold press against his neck. The click of the gun's hammer being cocked was deafening. The gun barrel did not waver as the man reached forward and divested Josh of the dueling pistols. He let them drop to the floor.

"Open the door again," he whispered. Clenching his jaw against the bitterness of defeat, Josh did so. The man prodded him with the gun barrel, forcing him into the sitting room.

"Mr. Winter," Sykes sneered. "We weren't expecting you until a little later. I suppose that means the viscount has left us. Pity."

Josh glanced at Summersby, who gave a small, almost imperceptible shake of his head. He didn't look like a man who had betrayed them, and yet, how else would Sykes have known?

"I wonder if we can still expect your exalted cousin this evening? Or will he cancel his visit when he realizes his militia is no longer in place?"

Summersby had not known those details. Which meant someone involved in the attack had been a spy. The thought sickened him, and made him more determined that these people would not win. He had to get free, try to warn Rotherton, stop Richelieu's approach if he could. And he had to find Amelia. That she was somewhere in this house, he made no doubt, although whether she was locked away as a prisoner or sneaking around the place, looking for an opportunity to cause chaos, Josh could not say. Part of him wanted to demand that she be brought to him, so he could see that she was unharmed. But then, if Sykes did not know she was there... All he could do at present was fight his own battle. Then he could find her.

Mind focused completely on his task, he took another step forward, and was relieved when the man behind him stayed where he was, the gun barrel no longer pressed against Josh's neck. Another step, then he ducked to the side and swung round, delivering a sharp blow to the gunman's chin. The man staggered back but did not fall. Josh followed through with two more punches, which finally downed the man. Behind him there was a crash and the sounds of a scuffle.

Josh grabbed the man's gun and rolled, all the while expecting a ball from one of Harcourt's guns to find him.

Coming to his feet, gun ready, he saw Harcourt no longer held his weapons, and was fighting, fist to fist, with Summersby. Both men used street tactics that betrayed humble beginnings, but they seemed evenly matched.

Content that Summersby could handle his man, Josh looked around to see Liverpool perched on the edge of his seat glaring at Sykes, who held a gun on him.

"Give it up, Sykes," coaxed Josh. "You've failed."

Sykes grinned and cocked the hammer. Josh dove at him, pushing his gun arm as he pulled the trigger. The report blasted through him, filling his ears with the same thick deafness he had experienced when swimming under water. From the corner of his eye, he saw Liverpool dive for the floor, covering his head, and the ball hit the wall behind the Prime Minister's chair.

A draught of air warned him as Sykes aimed a punch. He ducked away, not managing to avoid the blow completely but lessening its impact so it was no more than a sting. Then all thought was lost as he and Sykes wrestled, knocking over tables and chairs. Josh's ears popped, the deafness replaced by loud ringing.

Hands grabbed his arms, pulling him away from Sykes. He struggled but could not break the hold of the two men who hauled him to his feet. He could see another two men held Summersby, while a fifth man aimed a gun at Lord Liverpool's head. Josh stopped struggling.

Sykes got to his feet, adjusted his jacket, straightened his cravat, and ran a hand through his disheveled hair. Then he gave an icy smile and punched Josh hard in the stomach. The breath whooshed from Josh and his knees buckled. Had the two men not been holding him, he would have fallen. He tried to catch his breath, but ended in a coughing fit. On the other side of the room, Harcourt stood over Summersby, his fists clenched. Summersby was on the floor, wheezing and clutching his own midriff. Harcourt's lip was split and red with blood, and there was a cut on his cheek just below his swelling eye. He looked as if he wanted to hit Summersby again, but stepped back when Sykes gestured that he should.

"Sit them down," ordered Sykes, "and don't let them move again." The prisoners were dragged to their seats and thrown into them. Sykes addressed them as if they were naughty children. "I don't really want to put bullet holes in you," he said, "but if I have to, I will." He turned to Harcourt. "Richelieu will be here any moment. Go and prime the barrels."

Harcourt wiped his mouth, smearing blood over the back of his hand and lower cheek. He stared at his hand for a moment, then narrowed his eyes at Summersby.

"Now." Sykes' tone brooked no opposition. Harcourt gave a grunt and left the room. Sykes turned back to his prisoners, his eyes filled with glee. "Don't worry, my lord," he told Liverpool in a friendly tone, "not long to wait now."

****

Amelia emptied the latest bottle of wine into the eleventh barrel and stood back, broken glass from the bottle necks crunching beneath her feet. Her coat was dark from splashes of wine, and splatters covered the floor. She'd pulled her gloves off when they'd grown stiff and wet with spilt wine, and now her fingers were sticky and stained, the tips wrinkled, and the air was so heavy with the sickly sweet smells of fermented fruits that she could taste it. Her lower back protested the unaccustomed movements, and the alcoholic atmosphere had given her a headache.

She leaned back against the now-empty wine rack and wondered if she'd done enough. There were other racks, stacked with more bottles, but since she'd poured about ten bottles into each barrel already, she could not see how any more would make much difference. Now all she could do was wait, and hope the fumes didn't render her insensible before she could escape.

As she replaced the lid on the last barrel, she heard the door lock rattle. Amelia snatched up both the tapper and the mallet and stood by the door where, she hoped, she would not be seen until it was too late.

"Please let this work," she prayed under her breath, then she bit her lip, fists tight around her weapons, breath caught, heart pounding.

Mr. Harcourt pushed open the door, flooding the cellar with the light from his lantern and making her squint. He focused his gaze on the barrels ahead of him and made no effort to look for Amelia at all, almost as if he didn't know she was there. Which could not be: the men must have reported her capture, surely?

She took full advantage of his seeming ignorance of her presence and swung the mallet at him with all her might. It connected with the back of his skull with a sickening thwack. Vibrations travelled up her arms and jarred her shoulders, and it was all she could do to keep hold of the heavy mallet.

For a moment, she thought it wasn't enough. Harcourt just stood there, his back to her while he swayed. Then he crumpled, falling in a heap and hitting the first barrel, which toppled. The lid flew off and wine-soaked powder spilled onto the floor.

Then he lay still, and the only noise was the soft rocking of the downed barrel against the stone floor.

Amelia took a deep breath, trying to calm herself. She had to get out of here before anyone else came. She needed to find Josh as quickly as she could and tell him all that had happened, but more than that, she needed to see him, to feel his arms around her, comforting her, her head resting on his chest, his heartbeat steady and soothing in her ear. Mayhap he would kiss her, his lips firm against hers, the taste of him pushing away the taste of the wine and the fear while she told him...

The sound of footsteps running along the corridors overhead pulled her back to the present. She clicked her tongue, impatient with herself. This was hardly the place or the time for senseless wool gathering. First, she must find a way to leave the house unseen, then raise the alarm. There would be time enough for dreams of Josh Winter after that.

She looked both ways along the corridor to make sure it was clear, then shut the cellar door and turned the key Harcourt had left in the lock. She took two steps, then turned back. It might be prudent to have a weapon.

Back in the cellar, she picked up the mallet, then dropped it as impractical and put the tapper in her pocket instead. Then she locked the door again and made her way upstairs as quietly and as quickly as she could.

The cellar steps led to a tiny corridor between the butler's pantry and the door that led to the main part of the house. The butler's door was open, his cup of tea cooling on a small table beside an armchair, his newspaper folded carelessly, waiting for him to return from whatever duty he'd been asked to perform. Amelia needed to be gone before he returned, and she turned left, making her way along the dimly lit hallway toward the kitchen and the door to the gardens beyond.

She stopped and silently mouthed something very unladylike to see that the kitchen door was wide open, light spilling onto the bare corridor. Pans clattered and Cook shouted insults at a scullery maid. Other voices murmured conversations, punctuated by laughter.

Amelia did not think she could get past the kitchen unseen. Which meant she would have to go through the door to the main house, make her way to the hall, and try to open the front door, all without alerting anyone to her presence.

"You can do it," she whispered. "You got past Miss Snettisham." Her governess had been a termagant who declared herself wise to all Amelia's antics. The woman had seemed to have eyes and ears everywhere, which the thirteen-year-old Amelia took as a challenge, one she had risen to. "If I could get past her, I can get past anybody," she assured herself now, and cautiously pushed the door so it opened just enough for her to slip through.

The hall seemed deserted. Candles burned near the front door, giving a welcome light, but back here, the shadows were long and disguising. Which was all to the good. Shadows would aid Amelia's quest to reach the front door unseen.

Staying close to the wall, tiptoeing so her heels did not clack against the tiled floor, she made her way forward and reached the door without incident. She took a quick and furtive glance over her shoulder before she turned the key in the lock, slowly so it would make no noise. There was a soft click, and she reached for the handle, then gave an involuntary squeal as strong arms enveloped her.

"And where do you think you're going, Millie girl?" Abe Sutton murmured, nuzzling her ear.

"Get off me." She squirmed, kicking back at him. He stepped back, holding himself at an awkward angle so he could maintain his grip on her, yet stay out of her reach at the same time.

He chuckled. "You should be nice to me, Miss High-and-Mighty. Unless you want to share the fate of your friends, Summersby and Winter. Hey, how about that? They go together, in more ways than one. Summer and Winter. Get it?" He laughed again, but it was what he'd said before his joke that had snagged Amelia's interest.

"What do you mean, their fate?"

"Going to hang, aren't they? No more than they deserve, either. Treasonous nobs."

"Treason?" The word came out on a squeak as panic rose within her. This could not be true! They could not accuse Josh—and Summersby—of treason. She struggled to look at Abe. He grinned and turned her to face him. As she swung round, the tapper in her pocket hit her leg.

"Aye, treason," he said, smugly. "They're being arrested in the sitting room as we speak. Lord Liverpool himself come to take charge of it. It's the gallows for them, and that's for sure."

Keeping her movements slow, trying not to alert him, Amelia reached into her pocket. "What did they do?" she asked, widening her eyes and hoping she looked intrigued.

Abe frowned, then shrugged. "Can't tell you that," he said, at last. "Government secrets." He grinned. "But I can keep your pretty neck out of the noose, if you want me to."

Amelia nodded. He bent his head forward, his lips puckering, ready for a kiss, and Amelia took her chance. She drew her hand up quickly and hit him between the shoulder blades with the tapper. He shouted with the pain and arched his back, and she punched his chest with it. He staggered back from her. She swung with all her might and caught his chin, knocking him completely off balance. His arms flailed, and he knocked against the planter which stood beside the banister at the foot of the stairs. The heavy pot wobbled in a strange slow motion, then crashed to the floor, shattering. Pottery shards and soil and plant scattered across the hall. Abe stepped back, trod on a piece of broken pottery, and lost his footing, ending flat on his back.

For a moment, Amelia stood there, staring stupidly at the mess. Then, as her senses returned, she pulled open the door and ran down the steps as a carriage pulled up on the drive below. Unsure if the newcomer would be friend or foe, she jumped the last two steps and ran as fast as she could along the drive.

Chapter Twenty

Something crashed in the hall, loud and destructive, and close to the sitting room door. Hoping it was Rotherton, come to the rescue, Josh tensed, ready.

"What the devil—" Sykes turned to the door as if he could see through it to the commotion beyond. His men looked bemused, glancing from the door to each other. It was all the opportunity Josh needed.

He powered up from the sofa and tackled the man nearest to him, taking him by surprise and easily knocking him down. The man's grip on his pistol eased and Josh snatched it from him, using it to club the man, who lay still.

Immediately, Josh attacked a second man. The element of surprise had faded, and this one was not such easy prey. They wrestled for control of the man's weapon. From the corner of his eye, Josh saw Summersby, fighting two of the villains, ducking and weaving like the street fighter he undoubtedly had been, while Lord Liverpool, older and less agile, fought with the last of Sykes' men.

Sykes stood back from the melee, holding his gun, finger on the trigger and watching, ready should he get a good shot. His snarl of frustration was lost in the cacophony coming from the hall. There was banging and crashing, the sound of pottery breaking and heavy metal hitting the floor, mingled with shouts and cries.

The noise seemed to spur Sykes on. Unable to draw a bead on Josh or Summersby, he turned to Liverpool, whose back presented a fine target. He cocked the pistol and steadied it.

Josh broke free of his own opponent and dove at the Prime Minister, knocking him to the ground an instant before the loud report sounded. Josh rolled in a strange slow motion, all sound banished, sight clearer than it had ever been. He saw the speck of dust on Lord Liverpool's waistcoat, the individual tufts of wool in the rug, the wisp of smoke rising from the barrel of Sykes' pistol. His shoulder connected with the floor, jarring him, though there was no pain, no feeling at all. Everything spun, slower and slower, to a standstill.

A heartbeat of time passed. Another. A third.

Then the world came rushing back in like a river breaching a dam. His shoulder hurt. His ears popped and filled with the sounds of fighting and cursing. The smell of burnt powder hung in the air, mixing with the metallic odor of fresh blood.

Josh glanced down. He wasn't bleeding that he could see. Neither was Liverpool. Josh looked up and met the surprised expression on Liverpool's opponent. The man stared down at his chest where a darkening patch grew. He raised his eyes and stared at Sykes, then fell backward, hitting the floor with a thud. He lay still, eyes open and unseeing as they stared at the ceiling.

For a moment, all within the room was still. Then Rotherton burst in, almost taking the door from its hinges. He looked like an avenging angel, hat gone, hair wild, and a pistol in each hand. Behind him were three other men, all armed. More were in the hall, fighting with Sykes' men.

Within moments, the fight was at an end. Sykes and his followers were herded at gunpoint through the door of the sitting room and outside where, Rotherton told them, there was a prison box waiting to take them to Horsham, where there was a sizeable jail. "Although," said the earl, "it'll be a tight fit. The box was only designed to hold half a dozen prisoners, and there are at least double that number. Serves you right."

Sykes glowered at him. A guard grabbed his arm, turned him, and shoved him. Muttering under his breath, Sykes followed his men out.

Another guard grabbed Abe Sutton, who howled, "You can't arrest me! I'm the constable."

The guard hesitated and looked to Rotherton for confirmation. "Some constable. Not only were you not there to aid us, you told the enemy where and when to find us. Take him away."

"Not true!" yelled Abe. "Summersby's a traitor. I helped bring him down. You can't arrest me!"

Rotherton swiped his hand through the air, gesturing that they should take Abe away. He was still shouting as they loaded him into the prison box.

"Where's the Duc de Richelieu?" demanded Liverpool, peering into the darkness at the carriage which had been abandoned on the drive. "That is his carriage, I'll warrant?"

"Yes, my lord," said Rotherton. "The Duc is safe. He's at my home, where he is undoubtedly enjoying a fine meal and a bottle of my best wine. We thought using his conveyance would get us through the gates more easily. We were right—Josh? Where the devil are you going now?"

Josh looked back over his shoulder from the

doorway. "Amelia's here. I have to find her." Rotherton shook his head, but Josh would brook no argument. The woman he loved was somewhere in this house, frightened, perhaps hurt. He would overturn every stone, if that's what it took to free her.

"We have need of you here," argued Rotherton. "There are questions still unanswered." Josh felt his temper rise. What was Rotherton thinking? Did he seriously think a post mortem on the arrest was more important than Amelia? If so, he could take his blasted questions and...

"Josh?" The quiet voice penetrated his thoughts, stopping them dead. He turned his head, hardly daring to look, then breathed a loud sigh of relief to see Amelia standing in the hallway, gazing at him with suspiciously shiny eyes. Her hair was tousled, half hanging down her back, and there was dirt on her face. The skin on her hands was a dark purple, and there were purple splotches on her coat. She smelled of fruit and yeast and alcohol. He thought she had never been lovelier.

He reached out and grabbed her shoulders, pulled her in close, and hugged her before he held her at arm's length and glared at her. "What the hel—deuce do you think you are doing, woman?"

Amelia opened her mouth to speak, but clearly thought better of it. Instead, she shrugged.

"You could have been killed," Josh went on, through gritted teeth. "Of all the addle-pated, hobnail-brained things you have done, this is, by far, the worst! You, madam, are a danger to yourself and others. If you had even a smidgen more wit than hair, you'd be at home now, where your parents are worrying themselves sick about you. Have you no shame?"

As soon as the words left his mouth, he regretted them, but it was too late. Her eyes clouded with hurt and her bottom lip trembled before she firmed her jaw to stop it. She raised her chin, defiantly, pulled out of his grasp, and strode from the room. One of Rotherton's men nodded at Josh. "I'll see she gets home safely, sir," he said, and he followed Amelia through the front door.

Rotherton approached Josh and leaned close, so nobody else could hear. "Ill done, my friend. I see both grovel broth and humble pie in your future."

"She should not have been here," Josh insisted, though in truth, he agreed with every word.

"Had she not been, it might have ended differently. 'Twas her that opened the door for us. I believe she gave you the distraction you needed, as well?"

Josh closed his eyes and nodded, acknowledging his friend's statement. While he truly believed Amelia should not have been at the manor, he could not doubt her presence had proved useful. If he was honest, he was not angry with her. His harsh words were born of the anxiety he felt when he imagined all that might have befallen her.

"I am a fool," he muttered.

"If you expect me to argue with that, you will be sorely disappointed."

Josh opened his mouth to say something more but changed his mind when he saw two of Rotherton's men grab Summersby. The man didn't protest. Josh, however, did. "Leave him." The men looked from Josh to Rotherton, unsure. Summersby watched them, the resignation on his face warring with the hope in his eyes. "Rotherton," whispered Josh. "Please. We could not have done it without his aid. He was naught but a dupe."

The two men stared at one another for a long moment. Then Rotherton nodded. "On your head be it," he murmured. Louder, he told his men, "Release him. He was working for me." With mumbled apologies, the men left the room. Summersby sagged with relief.

Liverpool approached him. "I don't yet know what is happening here," he said, "but I trust Rotherton's judgment. However, I suggest that, in future, you take more care with the company you keep. Next time, it may not go so well for you."

Summersby swallowed, hard, then nodded. "Thank you, my lord."

"Get out of here," Rotherton told him, "before I change my mind."

Summersby bowed, and left the house with alacrity.

"I hope you know what you are doing, Rotherton," said Liverpool, after Summersby had gone. "If we have released a traitor, plotting the return of that tyrant, Bonaparte—"

"We haven't, my lord. I told the truth. He worked with us to foil their plot."

"Hmm." Liverpool flicked an imaginary speck of lint from his coat. "Well, then, if the Duc is at your home, might I suggest we repair to there? Seems a shame to have come so far and not to meet," and he led the way outside to the Duc's coach.

Chapter Twenty-One

Amelia spent the next few days in her bedchamber, pleading a heavy cold. At first, her parents allowed it, partly because they were terrified that news of her escapades would reach the ears of all and sundry, ruining not just her reputation but putting the entire family beyond the pale.

"If we can say she has been unwell these past few days," said Mama as she sat in the armchair in Amelia's room on Tuesday, "we can laugh off any suggestion she was out of the house."

"Except," Papa pointed out, glumly, "I raised the hue and cry for her." He stood by the window, looking out over the gardens, his hands clasped behind his back.

"A misunderstanding," retorted Mama. Papa stared at her over his shoulder. Mama raised her chin, defiantly. "It's hardly surprising she has been suffering, is it? Out there, lost in the woods after she fell and turned her ankle, waiting for hours in the cold and dark for rescue to come. 'Tis a wonder she didn't take an inflammation of the lungs."

Papa clearly realized he would not win this particular battle. Instead, he turned to Amelia, his face stern. "Inflammation of the lungs, eh? Well, we can rest easy, assured that is not a danger to her in the future, because you, miss," he pointed one angry finger at Amelia, "will not be going into the woods or anywhere else unaccompanied, from now on."

"No, Papa." Amelia's voice was flat, devoid of spirit. It reflected how she felt.

"Henceforth, whenever you leave this house," continued Papa, "you will be accompanied by a maid, at the very least. You will also tell your mother or me—or preferably, both of us—where you are going, who you expect to meet, and what time we should expect you home. Do I make myself perfectly clear?"

"Yes, Papa."

Papa harrumphed and made a show of looking at his timepiece, although he had no appointment. He turned his attention back to the view through the window. Mama sighed and wrung her hands together tightly.

Seeing them both, Josh's words echoed through Amelia's head. "Your parents are worrying themselves sick about you." He was right; she should be ashamed. Mama and Papa were good parents. They had given her and her sisters all that was in their power to give, and Amelia had never once had occasion to doubt their love for her. In return, she had treated them abominably.

"I am truly sorry for worrying you, Papa," she said. Her eyes stung and her vision blurred. "And for distressing you, Mama." A tear escaped and tickled its way down her cheek. "I was selfish and thoughtless, I know."

Instead of agreeing, Mama came and sat on the bed beside Amelia. She put her arm around her daughter's shoulders and pulled her close into her chest, then made soothing noises and rubbed Amelia's back. It was too much. The dam broke and Amelia sobbed.

Two days later, Mama burst into Amelia's chamber, clearly flustered. Amelia's heart sank. Had word of her behavior finally reached the gossips? But Mama did not seem distressed, or even angry. Instead, she was excited, and eager to share news.

"Can you guess what I learned this morning?" she asked, sitting heavily into Amelia's armchair. "No, you never will, so I shall tell you. Mr. Winter—oh, it is too much! I was never so shocked in all my born days. Mr. Winter has not been entirely honest with us."

Amelia had guessed as much. From the moment she found him prying into the viscount's papers, she had known him for an investigator. With what she now knew, she surmised he worked for the Crown. Which was just as well, she decided, for now that the investigation was finished and the villains apprehended, he would leave the area, sparing her the agony of having to endure meeting with him again. She did not wish to see him view her with disgust. The thought brought fresh tears.

Now, she watched her agitated Mama, who stood up, paced the floor from the hearth to the window and back, and sat down again. "You could have blown me sideways with a dove's feather when I heard," she said. "It's not the done thing, of course, but I suppose he had good reason, for he could not let the blackguards who had overrun Frantham know the truth, could he? Although, I do feel he might have taken us into his confidence. It's plain to everyone that we are not traitors."

She sat forward in the chair and studied Amelia through narrowed eyes. "As for you, my girl, you should consider this a second chance. I know you did not care for Summersby, and why should you? A Crown agent he may have been, but he was hardly from the top echelons of society. I always suspected he wasn't quite the thing, you know. Some things cannot be pretended." She stood and paced to the window again. "But never mind him. He has gone, and the real Mr. Summersby is here. And, they say, as rich as Croesus into the bargain!" She turned and watched Amelia, as if searching for her reaction.

Amelia frowned. The movement, combined with the copious tears she'd cried and the sleep she'd lost, served to make her head ache badly. She rubbed at her forehead, hoping to ease it enough to make sense of Mama's words. "The real Mr. Summersby?" she asked.

Mama clicked her tongue, impatiently. "Mr. Winter as was. Honestly, Amelia Jane, I declare you have not listened to a word I've said."

Amelia blinked. "Mr. Winter is…"

"Mr. Summersby. The real Mr. Summersby. Come to take his place beside his father." She grinned. "Of course, that means he will be needing a wife." At Amelia's groan she turned and wagged her finger. "You will not be telling me you don't care for this gentleman, for I know you do."

Care for him? Amelia did not care for him. Unless to care for him was to think about him in every waking moment, and to dream of him every night. Longing to be with him, to talk to him, share with him. To kiss him.

All of which made no matter. "He does not care for me," she told Mama. Her voice caught on the heavy stone in her throat.

"Pish-posh! I've seen the way he looks at you. He cares for you, my girl, you mark my words."

Amelia blinked rapidly, trying to keep the tears back. "He thinks me addle-pated," she said, her words breaking over the jagged edges of her broken heart. "H-hobnail-b-brained."

Mama shrugged. "On occasion, I would agree with him. As a gentleman, he should not say so, I suppose, but then, you probably provoked him beyond endurance. Lord knows, but you certainly do that to your father and me."

"But you and P-papa forgive m-me. I don't th-think Mr. Summersby will."

"Fiddle-faddle. Of course he will. Already has, unless I miss my guess. Why, has he not called these last three days? That is not the behavior of a man who does not care for you."

Amelia stared at her mother as if she had just spoken fluent Chinese. "He has?"

"Of course he has. Your father had given orders that you were not at home, but now you are feeling better, I'm sure all will be well."

Josh had called on her. Three times. Hope fluttered within her like butterflies, then took a dive. "He is returning to India," she said. The words tasted bitter. "He said so."

"His father needs him here." Mama's tone was final. Despite herself, hope fluttered in Amelia's chest as Mama continued. "It stands to reason that he will stay. He is the heir and must learn all he needs to know. And with his father so sick, why, surely the man would not be so heartless as to leave again. No, that man will stay, or I am a fish."

Could it be? Would Josh stay? Her heart fluttered, sending a shiver along her spine. She suppressed it. It would crush her to build her hopes, only to be disappointed if Mama was wrong.

Mama had no such doubts. "Your father and I have been remiss in our duties as a neighbor and friend," she said. "We really should visit Viscount Frantham and enquire after his health following his recent ordeal. It would be a good thing for you to come with us. You know how your presence always cheers his lordship." Amelia opened her mouth to disagree, and Mama held up her hand. "I will brook no opposition, Amelia. You are coming with us. And wear your jonquil dress. It looks so well on you. Be quick, now. We will leave in half an hour."

****

"I wish I had never come home." Josh stared into the fireplace, where flames danced cheerfully, in direct opposition to his own miserable mood.

"Had you not, your father would likely be dead now, and this house reduced to rubble. Is that truly what you want?" Rotherton sat back in his chair, crossed his legs and watched Josh closely.

"No, of course not. But—" Josh sighed and ran a hand over his face. He had shaved this morning, but even so, his cheeks were already rough with new growth. "Now I am here, I must stay."

"Would that be so terrible?"

Yes, thought Josh. It would. Staying would mean seeing her every time he went into the village, meeting her at every Assembly, watching her smile at other men while reserving nothing but contempt for him. "I cannot stand it," he whispered.

There was a long moment of silence while Rotherton stared at Josh. Uncomfortable, Josh cast around for something to do. He picked up the poker and jabbed it into the fireplace. The half-burned log split with a pop, sending sparks dancing up into the chimney.

"I never took you for a coward," said Rotherton,

quietly.

"Damn it, man, what would you have me do? She will not see me."

"You seem very sure of that."

"I am. Three times I have tried. Three times I have been turned away. There comes a point when a hint is less than subtle."

Before he could say more, there was a knock and the door opened to the new butler, hired just two days ago to replace the man who now languished in prison, awaiting his trial. "Your pardon, sir," he said with an officious bow, "you have callers. Are you at home?"

"Yes, he's at home," said Rotherton before Josh could answer. The butler retreated. Josh glared at Rotherton, who shrugged, nonchalantly. "You're too young to become a recluse."

The retort died on Josh's lips as the door opened and Mr. and Mrs. Bell came in, followed by Amelia. She wore a bright yellow dress under a dark green spencer. Her hair curled around her face and seemed brighter because of the pallor of her skin. There were smudges under her eyes, which suggested she had truly been unwell these last few days. Perhaps she had not been rejecting him after all. Hope stirred within him.

"We simply had to know how Lord Frantham fares after his recent ordeal," said Mrs. Bell, arranging herself decorously on one of the sofas.

"He is much improved," said Josh.

How Mrs. Bell reacted to that news, he had no idea. He could not shift his gaze from Amelia, who sat on the sofa next to her mother, hands demurely in her lap. She looked up at him, and their eyes caught for a moment before she colored and lowered her lashes. Josh's heart beat faster until he could feel the pulse at his neck. Every nerve within him seemed to buzz. It was all he could do to sit still and not jump up like a jack-in-the-box.

The conversation carried on around him while tea was drunk and delicate cakes eaten. Then, suddenly, Rotherton stood. "Mrs. Bell, perhaps you would permit me to accompany you and your husband to see Lord Frantham? He would be glad to see you." Amelia started to rise but Rotherton held up his hand. "We do not want to tax him with too many visitors at once, Miss Bell. I am sure Mr. Summersby will be glad to keep you company while we are with his lordship."

The Bells looked extremely pleased as they accompanied Rotherton from the room, carefully leaving the door ajar. He heard their conversation fading away as they climbed the stairs.

There was an awkward silence. Then they both spoke at once.

"I was sorry to hear you were unwell," he said at the same instant she told him, "I was unaware you had called."

They smiled, then Josh gestured that Amelia should speak first. She cleared her throat and looked into the fire. Her color was high and her voice trembled. "I wished to apologize to you. My behavior on Monday was unforgiveable."

"No," he argued. "It was not. But mine was. I should not have spoken to you as I did."

"You said nothing but the truth."

"Don't think that!" He shook his head, shame at Monday's outburst rushing through him. "My words were unreasonable and unfair, and I have wanted to beg your pardon for them since the moment they were uttered." He sat on the sofa beside her. Her scent filled him, fresh and summery. "Can we cry friends?"

Her smile was sad. "Friends. Yes," she said. Her disappointment made his heart skip a beat. Could it be...?

He took a deep breath and dived over the edge. "Perhaps more than friends?"

She looked up at him, and the hope in her eyes made his spirit soar. "I would like that." Her smile faded and her eyes clouded. "When do you return to India?"

"I'm not returning to India. I'm staying here, with my father."

"You are?" She brightened, then looked down at her lap. "He will be pleased to know it."

"And you? Are you pleased?"

Her eyebrows rose. "Me?"

"To know that I will stay here?"

"Why—I—" She gave a tiny shrug. "That is to say..."

Josh slid off the sofa, landing on one knee on the floor. Her eyes widened, and her shock made his heart rise to his throat. For an instant he thought he might not be able to speak. He swallowed, hard. "I love you, Amelia Bell," he said, amazed at the steadiness of his voice.

Her smile was dazzling now. It lit her whole face, pushing the last vestiges of her sadness away. "I love you, too, Josh Win—Summersby."

He felt like crowing. She loved him! In which case, there would never be a better moment. "Amelia Bell," he said, taking her hand in both of his, "would you please, please, do me the honor of marrying me?"

Amelia didn't hesitate. "Yes," she said. She fell to

her knees beside him, her arms going around his neck, pulling him close to her.

He wasn't sure if she kissed him or he kissed her. In truth, it didn't matter. All that mattered was that it continued for the rest of their lives.

A word about the author…

Caitlyn Callery lives in Sussex, southern England, near the Regency towns of Brighton and Tunbridge Wells. She is passionate about writing and suffers withdrawal symptoms when she takes a few days away from her work.

Before becoming a full-time writer, she worked in banking, as a waitress, in the motor repair industry, in a call centre, and for a charity. As part of this last job, she helped build a school in Kenya and also drove a vanload of wheelchairs from the UK to Morocco.

She loves reading, knitting, walking by the sea, the theatre, and spending time with her family.

Visit her at:

CaitlynCallery.com

Thank you for purchasing
this publication of The Wild Rose Press, Inc.

For questions or more information
contact us at
info@thewildrosepress.com.

The Wild Rose Press, Inc.

Milton Keynes UK
Ingram Content Group UK Ltd.
UKHW020736161023
430697UK00016B/655